NPC

They're just
non-player
characters,
aren't they?

The game is *The Village of Fate.*

Even if it's just because of some characters in a game, I want to change.

Returned hits for "monster" (179)

0: Anonymous player 0:00:00 ID: aWs7JlEsei

1. Do not post real names or addresses.
2. Do not post any personally identifiable information.
3. Feel free to leave abusive messages about the corrupted gods.
4. Do not post any false information in this thread.
5. Other players will not be able to read any information they are not allowed to know.
6. This forum is for players on the side of the major gods only. Players of corrupted gods are unable to see this forum.

1: Anonymous player 0:05:29 ID: 8D6gf0fpJz

Green goblins have gotta be the poster monsters of this game.

2: Anonymous player 0:10:16 ID: eV5QQpXH2u

Yeah, they're kinda smart so actually annoying to deal with.

3: Anonymous player 0:14:52 ID: z043040nnT

Smart in the same way as monkeys, yeah.

4: Anonymous player 0:19:28 ID: r4rQWWFril

Hey, that makes them as smart as some humans.

5: Anonymous player 0:23:33 ID: G2DtJUMffc

That's it! Who's making fun of me?!

TITLE ∨ SEARCH 🔍

The villagers didn't need me cheering them on from the sidelines. They needed the power of a god!

THE NPCs IN THIS VILLAGE SIM GAME MUST BE REAL! ↵

NOVEL

03

WRITTEN BY

Hirukuma

ILLUSTRATED BY

Namako

Airship

Seven Seas Entertainment

▣ ▸**NPC** Short for non-player character.
[NOUN] A character which the player cannot control.

CONTENTS

MURAZUKURI GAME NO NPC GA NAMAMI
NO NINGEN TOSHIKA OMOENAI Vol. 3
©Hirukuma 2020
First published in Japan in 2020 by
KADOKAWA CORPORATION, Tokyo.
English translation rights arranged with
KADOKAWA CORPORATION, Tokyo.

Seven Seas press and purchase enquiries can be sent to
Marketing Manager Lianne Sentar at press@gomanga.com.
Information regarding the distribution and purchase of
digital editions is available from Digital Manager CK Russell
at digital@gomanga.com.

Seven Seas and the Seven Seas logo are trademarks of
Seven Seas Entertainment. All rights reserved.

Follow Seven Seas Entertainment online at
sevenseasentertainment.com.

TRANSLATION: Alexandra Owen-Burns
ADAPTATION: Aysha U. Farah
COVER DESIGN: H. Qi
LOGO DESIGN: George Panella
INTERIOR LAYOUT & DESIGN: Clay Gardner
COPY EDITOR: Jade Gardner
LIGHT NOVEL EDITOR: Rebecca Scoble
PREPRESS TECHNICIAN: Melanie Ujimori
PRINT MANAGER: Rhiannon Rasmussen-Silverstein
PRODUCTION MANAGER: Lissa Pattillo
EDITOR-IN-CHIEF: Julie Davis
ASSOCIATE PUBLISHER: Adam Arnold
PUBLISHER: Jason DeAngelis

ISBN: 978-1-64827-628-6
Printed in Canada
First Printing: April 2022
10 9 8 7 6 5 4 3 2 1

Prologue

"**T**HIS ISN'T GOOD... This isn't good at all!" I grimaced at the PC screen.

Today was the Day of Corruption. Some of us had stayed behind after work, worried about the outcome, but this late at night there were very few of us left. From what I could tell, all the players assigned to my neighboring coworkers got through the day safely. We lost players every month, so I was glad to see my colleagues had cause to celebrate over the new year. I glanced from side to side, staring across the empty room. It was way too big to have to myself.

The tendons crackled in my neck. "I'm so stiff. I've been sitting here for ages."

All I wanted was to go home and take a long, hot bath, but I couldn't. Not yet. I had to know what he was doing. What he was thinking. Why else would I stay in an empty office long after everyone else had left?

I leaned back in my chair and stretched, catching sight of the clock on the wall. It was past midnight. Just a few minutes into the new year, and everything was already falling apart.

"So he really was a corrupted god. I never thought he'd go this far."

I'd had my eye on the player in question for a while, but his day-to-day behavior held no suggestion that he was capable of such extreme measures. I knew he had a mire of dark emotions brewing under the surface, but I always figured his rationality would hold him back.

I wanted to believe I'd just been wrong about him, but I couldn't shake the feeling that someone had put him up to this. Though I had no idea why anyone would.

"Maybe it was the other side."

This had been a bad situation from the start, but it was only getting worse.

Should I tell someone? I should at least inform the top six minor gods, right? But what if...

No, I can't risk this information leaking.

I could only talk to those I knew I could trust. Keeping it totally to myself would just cause problems down the line. Still, trying to come up with a way to explain all of it made my head hurt. I'd inevitably get blamed for this, especially by some of the more stubborn members of the team.

"Whatcha doin', Senpai?" a casual voice called out from behind me.

I turned to find a woman watching me, drinking a bubble tea. That stuff used to be super popular, but at this point it was pretty passé.

I let out a small sigh. She was always like this. Never bothering with professionalism. Her blonde hair was gathered up high on her head, and her skin was tanned a dark brown. Her ears were pierced in several places, and her top bared her arms and stomach, her cleavage so apparent it was obvious she wanted to show it off. She wore low-rise shorts, which suited her long legs, even if they were a little too revealing for work.

"Speak properly. You're always dressed so casually. Don't take things too far."

"I like dressin' like this. I'm laid back."

I hated the way she drawled out her words, but I knew she didn't do it to be annoying. I'd grown so used to her that I barely even bothered to correct her anymore. She'd always been out there, but I never thought her fashion sense would get this... niche. It suited her, though.

"Anyway, Senpai, what's up?"

"An unexpected development. It's not something I've ever dealt with before, so I'm not really sure what to do."

"Oh. Want me to help?" She grinned and leaned forward to peer at my screen.

Her manner and presentation might suggest otherwise, but deep down she was very kindhearted. She always had been, though occasionally her awkwardness shone through. For better or worse, she was always herself. Accepting that made her easier to be around.

Under better circumstances, I'd deal with my problems on my own, but this was an emergency, and time was running out. I trusted this woman. Besides...

I glanced over at a nearby desk with the nameplate "Kusuri." The owner had already left for the evening. If I wanted anybody else's help, I'd have to call them back to the office. My subordinates would come immediately if I asked them to, but there just wasn't enough time.

"Yeah, I could use your help. Thanks."

"No worries!" She gave her chest a hearty thump, making her breasts wobble and almost spill over her top. Lucky for her there weren't any men around; no way they wouldn't notice something like that.

"Could you help me with the programming first? Let's make sure he has the same version as us."

"Sure thing."

She sat down in the seat next to mine and booted up the computer without a word of complaint. In fact, she seemed happy to help me out. I'd have to thank her properly once we dealt with this. I quickly explained the situation, and a rare expression of worry crossed her face.

"This sounds like some real crazy shit, Senpai." Even she could tell how bad this was. "The portal's unstable. I don't think this has ever happened before."

"It hasn't. I know we're still in the testing period, but this is a bug we can't ignore. We need to fix this as soon as possible."

The game often acted independently from the will of the developers, but we couldn't allow the players to exploit any dangerous loopholes in the rules. On the off chance they *did*, we had to clean up after them. Usually, these incidents were the fault of other departments, but this time it was us. This couldn't happen again. I needed to deal with it *now*.

"Senpai, if we need more people, we could ask Un-chan. She really likes you, right? I just passed her on the stairs. She's probably still on the second floor."

Un, huh? She was serious and very stubborn, but a smart kid. She'd be a great help at a time like this. There was just one problem.

"No, we can't ask her. She transferred to another department; we can't just haul her back in. Besides, people working on the second floor aren't allowed up on the third."

"Man, everyone's so strict around here! You guys need to take a chill pill. Take a leaf outta my book. It's 'cause you're so obsessed with following their rules that this happened in the first place."

"And you never pay attention to the rules at all!" I quickly closed my mouth, hoping she wouldn't take offense.

I glanced at her, but her smile didn't change.

"I'm laid back." She continued to type away at the keyboard in front of her.

Once this is over, I'll treat her to her favorite sweets or something.

If only Un were this relaxed. Maybe then things would be different. Not that I had a right to say anything when I hadn't even noticed what was happening under my nose.

Wait, this isn't the time to relive the pain of memory lane! I've got work to do!

"Hang in there, Yoshio-kun."

part 9

THEY PROTECTED ME,

NOW I'LL PROTECT THEM ↵

THE NPCs IN THIS VILLAGE SIM GAME MUST BE REAL! ↵

chapter 01
The End of the Year and New Beginnings

I BROUGHT CAROL TO MY BEDROOM and laid her down on the futon. I patted her innocent head gently, careful not to wake her. I'd calmed down a bit, but when I thought of what was coming next, I couldn't help but let out a heavy sigh.

"Talk about a dark future..."

My senior from work, Yamamoto-san, had showed up at my place on New Year's Eve. He'd told me he played a corrupted god in the game and then attacked me with a crowbar. The wounds I received were severe, but they'd healed completely when I took the medicine sent by *The Village of Fate*. My golden lizard, Destiny, managed to put an end to Yamamoto-san's attack. I knew Destiny was smart, but I had no idea it could breathe out a toxic gas or petrify people. Despite its appearance, I could no longer kid myself that it was just an ordinary, spiky-skinned lizard. Witnessing its abilities led me to a single conclusion.

Destiny sat next to Carol's futon and stared up at me evenly.

"I want you to answer me honestly. Are you a basilisk?"

Destiny nodded once.

I thought so.

Destiny had a habit of playing dumb when I spoke to it, but this time it answered immediately. It must've known I had it dead to rights.

Basilisks were common in fantasy settings. They had a lizard-like appearance, could breathe noxious gases, and could petrify people with a glare. On the Internet, they were often depicted with six legs, but Destiny only had four. Would it grow an extra two at some point? I sort of hoped so.

The basilisk used to be synonymous with the cockatrice, but a cockatrice had a chicken's body and a snake's tail, while the basilisk was way more lizard-like.

"Y'know, I thought I was just imagining things."

But there was just no escaping the truth anymore. And it wasn't just Destiny's identity that dealt a heavy blow to my sense of reality. There was Carol, the kid sleeping on my futon.

A young girl of seven, her curly blonde hair made quite the impression. I was so used to seeing her face from the other side of the screen, and I'd tried so hard to convince myself she was nothing more than a character in a video game. Yet she had shown up to my house in a cardboard box, along with that holy book.

As far as I could tell, I hadn't gone insane. But what if everything up until this point was just a dream or a delusion? It would explain everything.

Everything except the reality staring me in the face at this very moment.

"She's Carol, no matter how I look at her."

No Japanese girl would have hair that color. No one from this country would wear clothes like that. I'd seen that sleeping face of hers almost every night for two months now.

"What d'you think I should do, Destiny?"

Destiny ignored me and continued to nibble at a piece of fruit. Message received.

"Figure it out yourself."

Harsh, but fair. I needed to solve my problems without relying on other people all the time. And I'd start by setting everything straight in my head.

The Village of Fate wasn't just a game. It was a real, parallel world. A world where my villagers lived and went about their daily lives. A world I watched over through my PC. That was how they sent me all those offerings. Yamamoto-san, a corrupted god, attacked my village and destroyed it. Chem did something, the screen went black, and Carol was sent to my house.

"And I think I know what she did."

At the last moment, Chem said something about how one of them could be saved. The villagers must have sent Carol to me as an offering, through the altar. That made sense. As long as you ignored everything else weird about this situation.

"That's really the only explanation, though."

So much impossible stuff had happened that my brain felt overloaded. I wanted to crawl into my futon, go to sleep, and hope this was all a bad dream. But Carol was in the way.

The game world, the safety of my villagers, and the existence of the gods. There were still so many questions that remained unanswered, although "questions" really seemed like too trivial a word.

"All the thinking in the world won't help me figure this out. I gotta stick to the stuff I *can* do."

I'd already decided I wasn't going to run away from reality anymore. I was prepared to accept anything—even the stuff that should be impossible.

I would make a list and tackle each problem in order of urgency.

"Number one. Carol."

I was a single man in his thirties with a small girl in his room. Anyone who walked in on this would go straight to the police and I wouldn't stand a chance, even though I hadn't done anything wrong. I watched Carol's peaceful face as I tried to come up with a solution.

"Mmmngh…" she mumbled sweetly.

She blinked, sitting up to rub her eyes and stretch. She looked around the room for a moment, but it didn't take her long to realize something was off. Her eyes widened as she caught sight of me.

"H-huh?! Where am I?! Who are you, Mister?!" Carol leapt off the futon and scrambled back, her shoulders hitting the wall. She stared at me with huge, frightened eyes.

She'd awoken to an unfamiliar room and an unfamiliar man. No wonder she was panicking. I had to keep calm, for her sake.

I need to reassure her.

I took a deep breath, swallowing down my own fear.

"My name is Yoshio. I am the God of Fate—" I paused. "The God of Fate's disciple. It's a pleasure to meet you."

Calling myself a disciple seemed like a much safer option than outright claiming I was the god myself. Gods needed to be majestic. Which I wasn't.

I spoke confidently and gently, trying to put her at ease.

"You're a disciple of the God of Fate?" Carol straightened up and then lowered her head as deeply as she could. A perfect textbook bow.

"You don't need to be so humble. I am just a disciple. Please raise your head, Carol. Deep down, I'm just a human being like you and your family. You may address me without any honorific."

Ugh. I sounded so creepy.

Well, as long as it put her at ease, I guess it didn't matter. I gave her my kindest, most reassuring smile.

"You know my name?"

"Of course."

The game wasn't voiced; this was the first time I'd ever heard her speak. She sounded adorable, and it made me wonder what the other villagers' voices were like. I was willing to bet Gams's was deep and masculine. Chem's was probably soft and gentle, and Rodice's might have been a little timid. Lyra's was definitely on the deeper, dependable end, and Lan and Kan...well, they didn't talk much, but...

"What's wrong, Mr. Yoshio? Are you crying?" Carol walked up to me, peering at my downcast face.

To think she could show concern for me in a situation like

this. What the hell was I doing? I needed to be the one comforting her!

"Thank you. I'm all right."

I reached out a hand towards her. For a split second, she froze, and a flash of fear appeared in her eyes. But then she allowed me to place my hand gently on her head. I patted it, and she sighed quietly and closed her eyes.

"Your hand is like Gams's!"

I chuckled quietly. "It's an honor to be compared to a fine man like Gams. Carol, there is no need to call me 'Mr.' I want to be your friend."

I suppressed the shudder that raced down my spine as I forced myself to talk like a creep. I couldn't afford to be shy here.

"So, um, Yoshio," Carol began. "Where am I? Where's Mommy and Daddy and everyone else?"

I knew she'd ask me that sooner or later, but it still tripped me up. I needed to get my answer right, down to the last word.

"This is a different world from the one you come from. This is where gods live."

"A world of gods?" Carol's eyebrows knitted together thoughtfully.

"I understand that you might find it hard to believe at first. Could you look at this for me?" I took one of the wooden statues from my shelf and held it out to her.

"Hey! I carved this!"

"That's right. You then sent it to the God of Fate as an offering. He was very happy, and then he gave it to me to take care of."

"Really?! Awesome!" Carol's face lit up with a smile.

I was glad I'd taken good care of all the offerings they sent. I couldn't have known something like this would happen.

Carol seemed to be relaxing a bit. Maybe it was time to explain the crux of the matter to her—but vaguely. I didn't want to upset her.

"Please listen carefully, Carol. I'm going to explain why you're here. Do you remember your village being attacked by monsters?"

"Yeah. There were lots of them, so Mommy and Daddy took me way inside the cave. Then Mommy gave me some tea, and then it's all black..."

I was relieved she didn't remember anything else.

"After that, the monsters broke down the fence. The other villagers sent you to this world on the altar to keep you safe."

I didn't have proof of that, but it was the only explanation that made sense.

"But what happened to everyone, Yoshio?" Carol's eyes were overflowing with tears.

I put my hand back on her head and smiled gently. "They ran away. They sent the holy book along with you, so we can't see what happened, but I'm sure they're safe. I asked the God of Fate to save and protect them."

I puffed out my chest and put a fist to it, injecting as much confidence into my voice as possible. I couldn't let her sense a hint of anxiety or how much I doubted my own words. I had to remember that she was way more scared than I was.

"The Lord saved them?!"

"That's right! He wouldn't let anything happen to them. Now, anybody sent to this world cannot go back to their home world straight away, so please try to enjoy your stay. We have everything you need right here, so you don't have to worry about a thing."

"Oh, okay. Um, thank you!" Carol smiled.

That was Carol dealt with. So one problem down, a million to go, but I did feel calmer. Thinking about the future made my head hurt, but right now Carol's peace of mind was my top priority.

Do I have anything for her to play with or...wait. How am I supposed to explain this to my family?

I was so preoccupied with everything else I didn't even think about that.

"So anyway, turns out that village I was helping was actually in another world! They sent me a little girl, so I was wondering if she could live with us?"

There was no way that would fly.

My family was visiting my dad's parents right now, but here was my next problem, staring me right in the face. It was only a few minutes until the new year. My family was due back on the fourth of January. I had four days to sort things out. Four days to come up with an explanation.

"Yoshio! Yoshio, this shiny lizard is really cute!" Carol cradled Destiny in her arms without a hint of fear.

Destiny *was* cute, though its size could be frightening at first glance. Carol didn't seem scared at all, though. On the contrary, her eyes shone. I guess that's what you got when you grew up in a world swarming with monsters.

"That creature hatched from the egg you sent as an offering to the God of Fate. He gave it the name 'Destiny.' Please treat it with love and kindness."

"It's from the egg? Wow! Hi, Dessie!" Carol stroked Destiny, who took it all without even squirming. It could be pretty patient when it wanted to be.

I sighed and checked the time. Almost midnight.

What a crazy year it's been. Hopefully next year's a little more normal.

I wasn't holding out much hope.

The little blonde girl from another world was now playing with the golden lizard, also from another world. Yeah, my future wasn't getting any less weird any time soon. I smiled wryly as the clock struck midnight.

"It's the new year. Happy New Year, Carol."

"Oh! Happy New Year!" Carol put Destiny down before turning to me and bowing politely. I'd thought the whole New Year's celebration thing might be unique to our world, but that didn't seem to be the case.

Speaking of New Year's, I needed to come up with a resolution. Hmm. Maybe, "No regrets." Yup. That'd do.

Doubtless there was trouble ahead, but I would keep on moving forward, no matter how slowly. I needed to take care of Carol, and I was intensely worried about my villagers' fate. I just couldn't show my anxiety in front of her; she was already frightened enough. Even if it was just an act, I had to leave behind the man I used to be and become an adult she could depend on.

I straightened my back and gritted my teeth, facing the girl and the lizard. Just then, the door behind me opened.

"Hey, Yoshi, when did I fall asleep? I had a super weird dream..."

I turned around. It was Seika. Her half-lidded eyes were heavy with sleep, but they grew wider and wider as she looked into the room. At Carol.

All emotion left her face, and she turned her icy gaze on me. A cold sweat sprang up all over my back. This was bad. Really bad.

"S-Seika-san. There's a *huge* explanation for this. Would you hear me out?"

"Please. Tell me everything, Yoshio-san."

I'd never heard her sound so cold.

chapter 02 — Me and My Flustered Innocence

I LEFT CAROL TO PLAY QUIETLY with Destiny in my room and took Seika with me. We didn't say a word as we walked down the stairs, but I felt her eyes boring into my back. Somehow managing to keep my cool, I led her to the living room. Turning to face her, I fell to my knees. Seika towered above me without a hint of emotion on her face. I already knew what she was thinking.

Hastily, I sorted through what I could tell her and what I needed to hide. Careful to avoid the latter, I began to speak.

"Before I explain the girl, do you remember how I was helping out with that village development project?"

That was the cover for *The Village of Fate* I used with my family.

"I remember. The village sent you meat and fruit as a thank you gift, and you shared some with me, right?"

"Yes, that's right. And, uh..." I couldn't help being overly stiff with her when she was looking down, judging me silently. "An overseas family relocated to that village. The girl upstairs is their daughter. I used to speak with her a lot over the computer and stuff, and said she'd be welcome to come see me, but I didn't think they'd take me seriously."

That was all nonsense, of course, but I surprised myself with how easily I was lying. I glanced up at Seika. She had her arms folded thoughtfully.

"Where are her parents?"

This was an important question. If I got it wrong, it would all be over.

"They had to go back to their home country to deal with an emergency. But Carol—uh, that's her name—threw a tantrum and said she wanted to stay in Japan. I offered to let her stay here without really thinking about it, since my parents and sister could help take care of her, but then I forgot all about it because of the stuff with Sayuki's stalker, and before I knew it, she showed up at my door." I gave my whole story in one breath so Seika wouldn't have the chance to comment until she heard it all.

Sayuki warned me that I had a habit of looking away when I lied, so I did my best to keep my eyes on Seika as I spoke. Hopefully I was convincing.

"Okay. Well, it's not really my place to judge what you do with your life, but since your mom asked me to take care of you over New Year's, I felt like I had a responsibility to find out what was going on."

I knew her well enough to recognize she was mad. She had a tendency to use long words, sounding like the straightlaced leader of a committee. She was feigning calmness well, but that twitch in her cheek told me she was only just holding back her anger. Playing innocent in front of an angry woman made me feel so much worse. I hadn't learned much during my ten years as a NEET, but I *had* learned not to piss women off.

"You didn't just make that up on the spot, right?" Seika asked hesitantly, her voice cracking. "You don't have an illegitimate child or a secret wife or something, do you?"

Don't look at me like that! Wait, does that mean she'd be sad if I was secretly married? Does that mean... No way. I shouldn't get my hopes up.

"You know there's no way I could be married, right, Seika? I was a NEET for years. I barely left the house. How could I have met someone?"

"I guess..."

Seemed like she believed me. I wished it made me happier.

Her expression was still wary, but she just sighed, unfolded her arms, and sat down in front of me. Sometimes my history as a shut-in came in handy.

Although I shouldn't consider it a net positive.

I'd managed to convince her for now, but I needed to figure out my next step. Was I really equipped to care for a girl from another world?

Ideally, I needed to send Carol back to where she came from, but I had no idea how to do that. Besides, the village was destroyed, and I didn't know if the villagers had survived. Assuming everyone was dead, it might be best to keep Carol here. I wished I lived alone or was self-sufficient. As it was, I couldn't do anything on my own. I couldn't even afford to take care of myself.

I'm so useless I can't even take care of a kid who's lost everything...

A thousand regrets floated through my head.

"Why d'you look so worried? Oh, wait, I wanted to ask—why was I sleeping in the other room? I think I had a really weird dream, but I can't remember a thing. You were cool in it, though, Yoshi. You got hurt, but you risked your life to protect me, and—hey, Yoshi, are you listening?"

"Huh? Oh, uh, sorry. I was just thinking about something."

She caught me right when I was worrying about what to do with Carol.

Seika's memories seemed to be in a muddle, which was fine with me. Better that she believed everything that happened was a dream. In fact, it was almost *too* convenient. Thinking back, Sayuki's stalkers said something similar to the police. They remembered threatening me but not much after that. At the time, I figured they were lying to protect themselves, but the situations had a common factor. Could Destiny's poison breath have some sort of amnesiac effect? It had only licked Seika, but maybe the memory-loss compound was on its tongue or in its saliva. I could always test it out by asking Destiny to lick me or breathe on me, but that sounded a little nasty. Plus, I was happier with my memories where they were—in my head.

"C'mon, Yoshi, you've been spacing out this whole time. Are you really that worried about this kid?"

"Oh. Sorry."

"Look, I don't think there's much you can do but take care of her till her parents come back. If that worries you, then..." Seika paused, "I can help you out?"

"Yes, pl—"

I cut myself off. Was accepting her help a good idea? This situation was precarious, totally detached from reality. I shouldn't involve her any more deeply; she'd already gotten wrapped up in the whole thing with Yamamoto-san. She could have been killed if Destiny hadn't stepped in, and that had just been a lucky coincidence. What if something like that happened again?

I couldn't risk it.

"I-I can take care of her by myself. I've spent too much of my life relying on other people. I'll tackle my problems alone for once. I'll come to you for help in an emergency, though. Is that okay?"

"Sure it's okay. And I get what you're saying."

"Thanks."

This is for the best.

"Are you guys done talking?"

I turned around to find Carol behind us, holding Destiny in her arms like a teddy bear.

"L-l-lizard!" Seika screeched, backing herself up against the wall. She trembled, her face pale.

"Don't bring Destiny near the young lady, okay, Carol? She's scared of lizards."

"Okay!" Carol replied brightly.

She took the long way around the room to me, avoiding Seika. Seika put a relieved hand to her chest once the distance between her and Destiny widened. "I-I'm sorry. It's gotta be upsetting that I'm scared of your pet."

"Don't worry about it. I already knew you weren't great with reptiles."

"Th-thanks. Anyway, I don't have a clue what language you guys are speaking, but it's impressive."

I basked in the admiration in her eyes, before realizing what she'd said.

What "language"? Wasn't Carol just speaking Japanese? Seika wasn't the type to joke around, though, especially not in a situation like this. That could only mean that *I* was hearing Japanese, but she was hearing something totally different.

"Carol, that lady is my friend. Could you greet her for me?"

"Oh, okay!" Carol turned to Seika and bowed her head enthusiastically. "Nice to meet you! My name's Carol!"

Seika smiled politely but said nothing. She slid over to me and whispered in my ear. "Yoshi! What did she say?"

Just as I thought, she didn't understand her. "She said: 'Nice to meet you! My name's Carol!'"

"Her name's Carol-chan, huh? That wasn't English, Spanish, or French, though. It didn't sound like any Asian language either."

Seika was familiar with several languages—at least, she could greet people and exchange pleasantries. They dealt with a lot of foreign companies at work, so she'd picked up a few simple phrases.

This wasn't something I could just wave aside. I had to come up with a convincing explanation.

"Her family comes from deep in the European mountains, and they speak with a really strong dialect. It's like how we have trouble with dialects from Tohoku or Kyushu. They even find it difficult to communicate with other native speakers sometimes."

Pretty good for something I came up with on the spot. Even Japanese natives struggled with Japanese spoken in a strong regional dialect. I could barely understand my grandparents when they spoke quickly. I had to ask Dad to translate.

"No wonder I can't understand her. Y'know, I didn't really believe you before, but your story must be true if you're fluent in her language and everything."

"I wouldn't say fluent. I only know some basic conversational stuff. We spoke on voice chat a lot, and I'm honestly kinda surprised how quickly I picked it up."

Seika believed me for sure now. *The Village of Fate* had turned me into a practiced liar.

But with this problem solved, I had to move on to the next one.

I figured I could only understand Carol because of my involvement with the game—some weird power was translating for me. What about *my* speech, then? Carol could understand me. I was definitely speaking Japanese—I wasn't a master of other-worldly languages.

Maybe I should do some testing.

"You understand me, don't you, Carol? Can you understand this lady?"

"I can understand you, but I can't understand her!"

Right...

"Did you understand what I said to Carol just now, Seika?"

"No. You were speaking a totally different language."

In my mind, I was speaking Japanese, but when I spoke to Carol, my speech seemed automatically translated into the language of her world. If a third party listened in, they heard our conversation in that unfamiliar language.

Pretty useful, but I couldn't let myself get comfortable. The mysteries were still piling up one after another.

Just then, I heard a strange, low rumbling. I turned to find Carol clutching at her stomach, her face bright red. The villagers probably hadn't had time to eat during the Day of Corruption.

"You hungry?" I asked.

"I know it's already past midnight, but let's have some soba. I'll make enough for Carol-chan, too." Seika headed for the kitchen and started her preparations with the ease of long practice. She was clearly as comfortable cooking here as she was in her own house.

"Can I help?" I asked.

"Thanks, but you'd just be in the way. Focus on Carol-chan. She's probably nervous being in a new environment."

I glanced at Carol. She was still holding on to Destiny and looking at me like she wasn't sure what she should be doing.

"Okay. I'll let you do the cooking."

Seika grinned and winked. "Leave it to me, kid!"

I was grateful she felt comfortable enough to goof around with me like that. I wanted to ask her whether she was seeing anyone right now, but I was scared she might say yes. Terrified. I wasn't a NEET anymore, but I still had plenty of worries.

"Yoshio, what's this table with the cloth here?" Carol tugged on my sleeve and pointed at the *kotatsu*.

She was her usual cheerful self, but I had to remember that she'd just woken up in a strange place surrounded by unfamiliar people. Her anxiety must be in there somewhere. I had to be as friendly as I could to put her at ease. I couldn't let my despair over my village's fate overcome me.

"This is a heater called a *kotatsu*. Try putting your feet under it. It's lovely and warm."

"Wow! It really is! That's amazing!"

Just watching Carol enjoy herself made my worries seem less pressing. I'd protect her at all costs. Even if I had to beg my parents to let her stay here. I was supposed to be the God of Fate, yet I let my village be destroyed. Protecting Carol was the least I could do.

"The soba's done, Yoshi. Could you take it to the table?"

"Sure." I stood up.

Carol followed me. Was she scared to be on her own?

"What's wrong?" I asked her.

"I wanna help."

Even in another world, her manners were flawless. I looked back toward the table where Destiny lay half under the *kotatsu*. It didn't seem inclined to help, but after what happened with Yamamoto-san, I couldn't see it as a normal lizard anymore.

That year was over, and a new one had just begun. If last year had been heavy, well...this one seemed ready to crush me completely.

THE NPCs IN THIS VILLAGE SIM GAME MUST BE REAL! ↵

chapter 03 A New Year and a New Start

CAROL ENJOYED her first taste of soba. She cleared her plate, and then began to look tired. I put her in the spare room to get some rest.

"Do you think you can sleep on this futon—um, bed?"

"Yeah! It's so fluffy! And so white and pretty! Can I really lie on it?"

Carol poked at the sheets and blanket nervously. Compared to the coarse beds they had in the cave, these must seem almost too clean and fresh. They did laundry in the village of course, but their sheets were made of different materials and far more worn. It was the difference between your sheets at home and sheets at a five-star hotel.

"Of course you can sleep on it. Make yourself at home."

"Okay. I'm so glad you're nice, Yoshio. Um...Mommy and Daddy and Gams are all okay, aren't they?"

Carol looked up at me as she lay down timidly on the futon. She seemed frightened, like the smile she'd worn all day was only a brave face. She was just a kid, but she still did her best to act cheerful out of politeness.

"Don't worry about them now. Just get some rest." I held her tiny hand in mine.

"Okay." She closed her eyes, relaxing a bit.

I waited until her breathing evened out before letting go of her hand and stepping silently out of the room. I turned to make sure she was really asleep and then slid the door shut behind me.

"Is Carol-chan sleeping?"

"Out like a light."

Seika beckoned me over to the *kotatsu*. I sat down across from her, accepting a mug of tea. I took a grateful sip. "Sorry. I didn't mean to make you cook for her, too."

"Don't worry about it. I like kids. Even if I can't understand her, I can tell she's sweet and friendly." Seika paused. "I think she might be forcing it a bit, though. She probably misses her parents."

Seika realized it too, huh?

I took another sip of tea and sighed. "She's smart. She doesn't want to let it show. I just hope she can have some fun while she's here."

I tried to inject some levity into my voice, but I couldn't escape the knowledge that I had no way to send her home. But as long as she was in Japan, I could take her places to take her mind off things.

"I was thinking of bringing Carol to the shrine tomorrow. For the new year. It'll probably be interesting for someone from a different wo—a different country."

Dammit. I almost slipped up there.

"Yeah. We used to go together every year, didn't we?"

We did, before I became a shut-in. Every year, like clockwork. We'd go round the stalls and sample whatever we wanted. Back then it seemed so simple, but I hadn't been to a shrine in a decade.

"Maybe I'll ask the gods for something this year," I said. "I mean, if there *are* gods. There might be."

There's even a god sitting by you right now, though he's kinda pathetic.

"I thought you were an atheist, Yoshi. Wait, don't tell me you've gone and joined a cult or something."

Wow, no! Completely wrong, Seika! Ever since I started playing *The Village of Fate*, I just felt more in tune with gods and stuff like that. Couldn't be helped, since I was pretending to be one myself.

"Nothin' like that. I'm way too busy to join a cult."

"You've changed, Yoshi. Wait, no, that's not it. It's more like you're back to your old self." My childhood friend smiled at me.

"I've changed? I guess I have. I made a real mess of the last ten years. I can't look back on any of it without feeling incredible regret. I'm sorry for hurting you, Seika." I straightened my posture and bowed my head to her with everything I had.

"Quit it. You never used to be so uptight. You were...selfish, prideful, arrogant, and mischievous." Seika counted off my bad attributes on her fingers.

There was nothing I could say. She was right. "You don't have to point that out..."

"But not just that. You had a strong sense of justice. You were kind, and you put others before yourself. I know what you were like these past ten years, but I also know what you were like before." Seika sounded so serious that I didn't know how to react. "The Yoshi I knew and loved is here again, and it's great. Welcome back, Yoshi."

"Thanks..." I was blushing hard, my face so hot I thought it would burst into flames.

How could she say all that cringey stuff with a straight face? I guess you learn to be less self-conscious when you spend enough time interacting as a full member of society. Oh, wait. Now that I looked closely, her cheeks were red, too.

"So I guess we can just keep hanging out like we used to?"

"Yeah. I'm looking forward to it."

I automatically took the hand she held out to me. We were thirty-year-olds acting like teenagers, two adults of the opposite sex spending time together at night. Dramas and manga had taught me that things were about to get serious.

I walked Seika home and returned to my living room, slightly damp from the rain. I dried myself off with a towel and sat down with my legs under the *kotatsu*.

So, nothing happened with Seika.

"I guess reality can be disappointing," I muttered, flopping myself down on the top of the *kotatsu*.

I was too worried about my village and Carol at the moment to try to take things any further, I reasoned with myself. I considered inviting Seika to come with us to the shrine but decided against it. I already said I wasn't going to get her any more involved.

I couldn't invite her anywhere until I knew exactly what was going on and I could guarantee her safety. I was still uneasy about Yamamoto-san. At first, I figured he'd flipped out due to stress, but the more I thought about it, the less sense it made. When he collapsed, I'd seen that weird dark mist come out of him. I'd convinced myself I was just seeing things, but what if I wasn't?

"Thinkin' about it won't get me any answers. I hope it stops raining before the morning so we can go to the shrine."

I finished the tea Seika had made for me, letting it rejuvenate my body and help me think a little more calmly.

"Is the village actually gone?"

I'd told Carol it was fine, but I'd last seen it on the brink of destruction. Carol only survived because they sent her to me through the altar. Her, and the holy book. That was all I knew for sure.

What happened to the other villagers? After sending Carol to me, it seemed like they were about to blow the monsters up, along with themselves. That was probably what happened.

But I hadn't given up on them. I *couldn't* give up on them, or let go of the hope that they were alive. I never saw them die. What if they threw the bomb out through a crack in the door and blew up the monsters without being harmed themselves? A slim hope, but it was the only one I had.

"I didn't see them die. They're alive." I had to make myself believe it. "I just need a way to find out for sure. I can't see anything through the game anymore."

I took out my phone and checked anyway. Apart from the *Village of Fate* app, everything was working as normal. The malfunction wasn't the phone itself. I opened the app, but the screen was totally black, just like before. I tapped it, expecting to see the same message again: that the holy book no longer existed on the map.

Except the message didn't show up.

"Huh?"

I hit the back button, and it brought me to the miracles menu. I looked closer. The book symbol and my Fate Points balance were still at the top right of the screen.

What's going on?

After sending Yamamoto-san away, I hadn't been able to do anything in the app at all. It just blinked a warning message in red. But now I had access to miracles.

"But I can't perform any of them, right?"

Most of the items on the list were struck through with a thick black line. I gave them an experimental tap and got a pop-up: "You can't use these right now." The only available miracle was the one that changed the weather.

"I guess that's because it's the only miracle that doesn't affect my village directly?"

Confusion filled me, but it was better just to act. I activated the miracle and set the weather to "blue skies." My FP went down, but the screen stayed black. It used points up, though, so I guess the miracle activated? That meant the game was still working, right?

The game still ran, and my villagers were still alive. I couldn't lose hope just yet.

"I need a break from all this thinking. I should go take a bath, and—crap. I probably should've offered Carol one."

The thought never even crossed my mind. I'd feel bad waking her up now, so I decided to go take one myself and then sleep on the living room couch. I opened the sliding door to the other room just a crack so that she'd be able to see me if she woke up. That way she'd know I was here.

"Man, I haven't used my brain like this in ages. I forgot how exhausting thinking can be."

I went up to my room to grab a blanket and check on Destiny, who was sleeping curled up in its tank. It must have gone back upstairs when I was walking Seika home.

I turned out the light. "Thanks for everything, Destiny. Have a nice, long rest."

I was overcome with drowsiness the moment I lay down on the living room couch. "Hopefully, I'll wake up and realize this was all a bad dream..."

I'd wake up to find my villagers safe and sound, and Carol running around beside them.

My heart wishing for nothing else, I slipped into unconsciousness.

THE NPCs IN THIS VILLAGE SIM GAME MUST BE REAL! ↵

chapter 04 My Prayer and My Determination

I WOKE UP to an unfamiliar scene.

"This isn't my room... Oh, right."

I'd slept in the living room last night. I stood up and peered into the next room to find Carol still asleep, clinging tightly to Destiny. It must've come back downstairs at some point during the night. It was awake but still lying patiently in Carol's arms. Destiny noticed me and gave me a small wave of its tail. What a thoughtful creature. Way more thoughtful than me.

"I guess I don't need to worry about it staying in its tank anymore."

Destiny wasn't just a regular lizard; I didn't need to baby it so much. I would still have to treat it like a pet in front of my family, though.

I opened the living room curtains, letting sunlight pour into the room.

"This is great weather, especially after the rain we had last night."

I opened the window to let some fresh air in, then regretted it immediately at the rush of cold wind. I hastily closed it again and dove under the *kotatsu*. I almost forgot it was New Year's Day. Of course it was cold.

At least that woke me up. I'll grab some breakfast.

Breakfast used to be toast or something similar, but lately Mom had been teaching me how to cook some simple dishes. I made a meal with ingredients I found in the fridge.

"Good morning. Ooh, that smells good!" Carol's sleepy eyes flew wide open, and she raced up to the *kotatsu* to admire the food on top of it.

She was still holding Destiny like a stuffed animal. I inclined my head to it in apology, but it held up its right claw as if to say it didn't mind. This lizard was so smooth.

"Morning. Why don't you wash your face before eating? I'll teach you to use the sink."

I'd stopped trying to be overly formal with her. It just made her nervous.

I took her to the washbasin and showed her how to turn the faucet on and off.

Carol's face lit up. "Wow! I bet Mommy would love something like this!"

She was so impressed by a simple faucet. Adorable.

We washed our faces together and then returned to the *kotatsu* to have breakfast. I'd watched the villagers eat; they weren't fussy about food. Today I was serving bread, fried meat, fruit, and soup, making the meal primarily out of the ingredients sent by the village. That might have been why Carol ate it all up happily. When we were done, we took our dishes over to the sink.

"I thought we might go to a little festival today. It's something we do in this world at the start of every year. Whaddya think?"

"A festival in the World of Gods? I wanna go! Everyone's gonna be so jealous!" Carol jumped up and down excitedly. Just seeing her so delighted was enough to cheer me up.

If we were going to the shrine, we had some preparations to do. I checked Carol over and nodded to myself.

"You should have a bath and get changed first."

"You have a bath?!"

Right. The villagers love taking baths.

I'd gleaned that their original village had a big bathing culture, but the cave they'd moved to had no traditional bath. They had to make do with dousing cloths in warm water and wiping themselves down, only ever getting clean on the very surface level. I remembered how happy they'd been—especially the women—when Kan and Lan had built them a bathtub that they could use every couple of days.

I took Carol to the bathroom and tried to explain the shower, but it seemed to frighten her. I just filled the bath up for her. As she washed, I went to the spare room and rummaged through the closet. I was pretty sure Mom kept our old clothes there.

I found a bunch of old stuff that I hadn't seen in years, tucked away in a case at the back of the closet.

"Thank God she never threw these out."

I wouldn't mind letting Carol wear some of my old stuff, but Sayuki was always better dressed than me, so I pulled out a bunch of her clothes instead. They were folded and vacuum-packed;

Carol could wear them right away. I'd let her pick her own clothes, since my fashion sense wasn't one of my strong points. I pulled out a few items that looked like they'd fit and laid them out.

I came back to the living room to find Carol wearing a towel, the steam still evaporating from her skin.

"Your hair's wet. Come here. I'll dry it for you."

I dried her hair carefully, using a hairdryer and towel.

"You're really good at this, Yoshio! It feels nice and warm!"

"Well, I've done it a lot." Sayuki always had long hair, and I used to dry it exactly like this.

When I was finished, I took Carol to pick out some clothes. She grew incredibly excited (more than she'd been since she first got here) and launched into a fashion show. She was having trouble picking out what to wear, and she kept diving back into the room to try on something else.

"How's this, Yoshio?" Carol leapt out of the room in a light-colored dress and did a twirl.

"It's cute, and a nice color. It might be a little cold for this kinda weather, though."

"Oh, yeah. Okay, I'm gonna try on something else!"

That was three outfits already.

How long is she going to do this?

I was tempted to just lie and say everything looked great, but I had enough experience with Sayuki to know that was a terrible idea. No being vague, either.

I stayed positive and honest about what I liked, and at last Carol cheerfully decided on a sweater, knitted by Mom, and a long, sturdy skirt. On top of that she layered a warm, fluffy coat. She liked the look of a backpack shaped like a bear's face, so I let her take that, too.

I wasn't exaggerating when I said she looked like a child model. Absolutely adorable. If Seika or Sayuki were here, they'd be squealing for sure. Chem better watch out.

"How do I look, Yoshio?"

"Cuter than anything I've ever seen."

"Yay! But I think that's too much praise!"

Despite her words, she grinned bashfully as I snapped a couple photos of her with my phone.

When we were both ready, I took her hand and led her out of the house. The rain had poured down last night, but the ground was completely dry.

On closer inspection, I realized that it was only the area around my house that showed no traces of last night's weather. Maybe we just happened to sit in the gap between two rain clouds.

The weather was perfectly clear now, the sky showing no threats to our outing. The shrine was about a ten-minute walk from the house and quite large. We walked up the familiar stone steps and stepped under the large archway. White gravel crunched beneath our feet. Normally, we'd be able to see the shrine by now, but today it was blocked by a huge crowd.

"I've never seen so many people, Yoshio!" Carol gasped, her gaze darting back and forth.

Crowds this thick were nonexistent in her world. Carol pointed at the stalls and the shrine maidens, pelting me with questions.

"That's a stall. You can buy food there. Let's have a look after we've been up to the shrine. That girl is a shrine maiden. She works for the gods."

"So she's just like you?"

"Yeah." I looked nothing like a shrine maiden, but I supposed we had similar duties. That didn't mean I could relate to them, though.

"Let's line up here with everyone else."

"Okay! Hey, Yoshio! What do they sell at that store over there?"

"Yakisoba. They're fried noodles."

"What's that stuff that looks like clouds?"

"Cotton candy. It's really sweet!"

I answered every one of her endless questions. Other visitors were looking at us and smiling warmly. To them, Carol must have seemed like a curious foreign girl. I felt like a proud father with an extremely cute daughter. This must be how parents felt when their relatives praised their kids.

I took more photos, hoping I could show them to Rodice and Lyra later. I was sure they'd love them. In fact, I wanted all my villagers to come to this world and spend time with me. That sounded great.

"What's all that clinking? Why is everyone clapping?" Carol asked, pulling at my sleeve and interrupting my thoughts. She pointed at the visitors in front of the offerings box, who were clapping and praying.

"That's how we pray in this world."

I taught Carol the custom of bowing twice, clapping twice, and then bowing again in front of the shrine. We practiced it over and over in line. The sight made the people around us smile again, and I couldn't help but smile with them. I'd lost the right to make fun of my relatives for showing off their kids ever again.

When it was our turn, I stepped up to the offertory box with Carol. I already knew how important microtransactions were to a god's work, so I splurged a little and pulled out two 500-yen coins, one for each of us. I glanced at Carol to see how she was doing. She had her eyes closed, deep in prayer.

"Please let Mommy and Daddy and Gams and Murus and Kan and Lan and...Chem be safe. Please let me see them again," Carol prayed desperately.

She'd been acting so cheerful, but on the inside she was fervently missing her family and the other villagers. I decided to pray for the same thing: for the villagers' safety, and for Carol to reunite with them.

"I gave you a little extra," I whispered to the gods. "Please give us a miracle."

Deep down, I wouldn't mind keeping Carol with me from now on. If I convinced my parents, I could continue to take care of her. I knew that was wrong of me. It was selfish. I should wish for her happiness, and that meant sending her home.

"What do we do now?"

"Now we go look at the stalls. Lemme know if you want anything, and I'll buy it for you."

"Really?! Won't Mommy and Daddy get mad?"

"Don't worry about that. This stuff is nothing compared to all the wonderful offerings you've made to the God of Fate. Don't hold back. Just think of this as gratitude to you and everyone in the village."

"I'll say thank you to them when I get back!"

"Good idea."

I saw countless times how well behaved she was through my PC screen, and now that she was here with me, I could feel how much love and discipline her parents had put into her upbringing.

"Where do you wanna start?" I asked.

"Um, I wanna get a fluffy cloud thingy, and one of those round things, and, um...and..."

"There's no rush." I chuckled. "The stalls aren't going anywhere. Let's get some cotton candy first, then."

Carol grabbed my hand and pulled me along. Did we look like father and daughter to everyone around us? It fit our ages. Although there was Carol's golden hair and western features... On second thought, we probably didn't look related after all. Kind of a shame.

"What's that drink those people in the pretty clothes are handing out?" Carol pointed to the priests and shrine maidens giving out sacred sake.

"That's an alcoholic drink you're supposed to offer to the gods. Today's a special day, so you're allowed to drink it."

"I'm a kid, so I'm not allowed."

"That's right. But you can eat whatever you want instead."

I never drank the sacred sake myself; I was a lightweight.

Seika loved drinking, but her tolerance was even worse than mine. I bet she'd love to be here right now.

Carol and I took our cotton candy, takoyaki, and yakisoba to a nearby bench. She was ecstatic. We chose a spot looking out over a pond, a little ways away from the shrine. Only the locals knew about this place; it was completely deserted. The low murmur of the crowd was just audible in the distance.

It was unusually warm for January, and the sky was clear, but it was still chilly in the shadows. I worried that Carol might be cold, but she was munching on her takoyaki with a huge smile on her face.

"The festival was a lot of fun! There were lots of people, and they all seemed so happy!"

I'm glad she enjoyed herself.

Carol was eating away in silence, so I reached into my coat's inside pocket and pulled out a book—the holy book that came to this world with Carol. The cover felt just like any other hardback. It was larger than an ordinary mass-market but smaller than a manga. I flipped through it. It was filled with the prophecies I sent my villagers.

For a moment I lost myself in the pages, the memories of each message coming back. I had to force myself back to reality. This book's presence in my world was the reason I couldn't see anything in *The Village of Fate* anymore.

I came up with all sorts of theories in the bath yesterday, trying to find a way out of this situation. If this book was the object that gave the God of Fate his power, then maybe its existence in this world was a problem for the game developers, too. And who *were* the developers anyway? That was the biggest mystery of all. All my supernatural experiences made me lean toward the conclusion that they were gods themselves. Not that they were, you know, *godlike* to make a game like *The Village of Fate*. Just that they were literal gods. That was the only feasible explanation.

"Why do you have a spiky head? Don't your mouth and ears hurt?"

I looked up to find Carol no longer beside me. She was standing a few feet away eating a candy apple and talking to a man wearing a super weird outfit. His face looked Japanese, but his hair was blond and gelled up into several spikes like a rooster, and his lips and ears were covered in piercings. He wore a western rock band T-shirt under a leather jacket, and his jeans were torn in several places. He was the type of person I never thought I'd meet in my entire life.

"Come on, Carol. Sorry about her." I stood up from the bench and bowed my head at the man.

"No worries. Get it all the time, lookin' this awesome."

He seemed friendly, despite how he looked. He smiled at Carol.

"You look cold!"

"Nah, my soul's always burnin' hot. I'm actually overheatin' right now."

Friendly or not, I wasn't sure about his language. I continued to bow my head and slid in behind Carol. I put a hand on her shoulder to lead her away—but my hand closed around thin air.

"Huh?"

I looked up. The man had grabbed Carol's arm, holding on to her. Did she make him mad after all?

"I'm sorry if we annoyed you. I'll apologize properly. Could you give her back to me first?"

"Afraid not...God of Fate."

part 10

THE TRUTH LIES
TO THE NORTH ↵

THE NPCs IN THIS VILLAGE SIM GAME MUST BE REAL! ↵

chapter 01 The Fire and the Frying Pan

THE PUNKY MAN smirked at me as he held on to Carol from behind.

He really did just call me the God of Fate, right? I didn't mishear him? Dammit, I'm such an idiot! He approached Carol, not the other way around! Why didn't I notice sooner?

One thing was for sure. This guy played the same game I did.

"Tell me who you are," I said.

"I'm guessing you ain't asking for my name. Listen, you don't gotta know who I am. I just wanna have a look at that book you got there, and a little chat with this rug rat."

The more he spoke, the more confused I got. What would a corrupted god want with Carol and the holy book?

"Do you even know what this book is?"

"'Course I do. It's the God of Fate's holy book. Dunno how you managed to get it to the real world, though. Check out what I got here." The man pulled out his phone and shoved it in my face.

A book that looked a lot like mine dominated the screen. Now I knew for sure he was another player.

Stay calm. Carol's counting on you!

"You a corrupted god?" I asked.

"Hey, you're sharp. Don't be a hero, though, unless you want the kid to go the rest of her life with an ugly scar on her face." He pulled a penknife from his pocket. "Wow, that was kinda corny, huh? Too basic villain, if you know what I mean. Mind if I try again?"

Was this a joke to him? Studying him closer, he was lean and scrawny. I should have an advantage with my physique, but he had that knife.

"Try it. Then see what I do to *your* face," I shot back.

"You talk tough for someone without any weapons."

I wasn't about to let him intimidate me in front of Carol. I was one of the God of Fate's disciples.

Speaking of Carol, she looked completely calm. I was worried she'd be scared, but maybe she just didn't understand what was happening. That was probably a good thing; it was safer if she didn't struggle.

As we spoke, I closed the gap between us slowly, hoping he wouldn't notice. I needed to be close enough to snatch the knife and pull Carol away from him.

"What do you need Carol and the book for?" I asked.

"Oh, y'know. This and that. Ooh, don't get too close! I don't like daredevils. That's why I brought some friends with me." The man held the knife in his mouth and snapped his fingers. Several figures appeared from behind the trees and vending machines around us.

I gritted my teeth. "These your friends?"

There was a plump guy in his twenties, a woman in a brightly colored kimono, and an old man with a slightly bent back and a cane. Nothing visibly connected them. They just looked like ordinary visitors to the shrine. Then I realized their faces were empty of emotion, their bodies gently swaying. It was like looking at a bunch of zombies. A shiver ran up my spine.

"What did you do to them?"

"You really are sharp. Stay there, guys." The three of them froze immediately at his command, so still it was like he'd stopped time. "Whaddya think? They're my puppets, and they do whatever I say. That's why you should consider things before you play the hero."

Was he serious? Whether he could control them or not, none of these three looked like they were in their right minds—so how did they understand his orders?

"What did you do? Hypnotism? Drugs?"

"Dude, you sound like you've been reading way too much manga. You really think shit like that'd give me this much control over them? I'd laugh, but the truth is even crazier. It's a miracle. I can control these guys with the power I get from being a corrupted god."

"Miracles don't work in the real world, dumbass!" I yelled.

The man looked taken aback for a split second before doubling over in laughter.

"Don't tell me you're still at level 1! Guess you don't know much about the game at all, huh?"

Levels? What?

"Didn't expect you to be this funny. Well, I'll gladly explain. I've always wanted to do a villain monologue." He wiped away his tears of laughter and turned to me with a smirk.

I hated him mocking me, but I *was* curious about his explanation. Carol was still quiet. I hoped she could hold out for a bit longer.

"So there are a ton of corrupted god players just like there are you regular gods. Now me, I'm the God of Temptation."

If there were different corrupted gods, the miracles they could perform were probably different, too.

"I can control people by amplifyin' their greed and tempting them. It's easier if they're mentally weak, or if they're drunk or kinda out of it, or something. Now these guys were gettin' drunk off the ceremonial sake, which is why I picked them out."

So these *were* just visitors to the shrine who had nothing to do with the game. My original plan of just punching everyone in sight and taking Carol back shriveled up to nothing. I couldn't risk getting these innocent people involved.

Could we really use miracles in the real world? It sounded too good to be true, but I couldn't deny the possibility after everything that happened to me yesterday. I still had a ton of stuff to learn about *The Village of Fate*.

So this guy uses people's greed to tempt and control them? Wait. Does that mean... No, that's stupid.

Before I knew it, I was voicing the question out loud.

"Are you behind what happened with Yamamoto-san?"

"Huh, never expected a NEET to be able to figure that one out. Great job. I just fixed that bum's brain up a little before he went over to your place." He stuck his tongue out at me and poked at my forehead.

Rage burned inside me. "So it was all your fault."

"Wait, back up a sec. Don't look at me like that. All I did was make him a tiny bit greedier, yeah? Just gave him a little push. I can't do anything with people who don't have those desires in the first place. You understand me, yeah?"

Each word was just ticking me off more and more.

I need to calm down. He's got Carol. He's waiting for me to give him a reason.

If I lost my cool, he could take control of me. I was at a total disadvantage. He had Carol, a knife, and three strangers under his command.

I took a deep breath and let it out slowly, cooling the fire in my mind. At least he was really willing to talk. He took this whole villain thing seriously.

"What do you need with Carol and the book?"

"I know some folks who'll pay good money for them. The book and the kid."

So his motive was money. Then what about the people he'd be selling to?

"I'm the only one who can use this book. Also, kidnapping and trafficking are illegal."

"Don't care, so long as it makes me money. This kid don't belong to this world anyway. Nothin' I do to her counts as a crime. She could die and no one would ever know, 'cause she never technically existed in the first place."

Fear flashed across Carol's face. She could understand what he was saying, because he played the game, too.

"Don't talk about her like that. Carol's my guest here!"

"Gettin' mad, are we? Man, I hate stubborn guys like you. Anyway, I'm done talkin'. Just hand over that book. You wouldn't want this cutie getting hurt, would you?" He smirked and flashed the knife at me.

"If I give you the book, will you let her go?"

"I'd rather have both, but if I had to pick one, it'd be the book. 'Sides, people'd get suspicious seeing a guy like me carting a kid around."

I wouldn't hesitate to swap the book for Carol, assuming I could trust him. The book and its role in the game was important to me, but Carol was irreplaceable.

"All right."

"You know how to play ball, huh? Good. Hey, you! Take the book off him and bring it to me," the man ordered the woman in the kimono. She walked up to me, her eyes unfocused. She was innocent in all of this; she was brainwashed.

"Can you hear me?" I whispered, but there was no response. This guy's control seemed to be absolute. I passed her the book, and she took it to the man.

"Thanks, doll. So this is a real, live holy book, huh?" The man studied it with interest, flicking through the pages. His guard was totally down, but I was too far away to do anything about it. He could reach Carol with the knife sooner than I could reach him.

"You have the book. Give Carol to me."

I knew the chances of him living up to that were low. Most kidnappers would have a second demand at this point, if they didn't just refuse to cooperate outright.

"Sure. I don't have anythin' against kids; there's no need to upset her." The man gave Carol a soft shove toward me.

I was wrong, huh? I guess I lost the book, but at least Carol's safe.

"This way, Carol. Don't rush. Everything's all right now," I called out to her gently as she hesitated.

She didn't move, instead looking between the man and me. "This is a bad guy right, Yoshio? And the book is really important. It's important to Mommy and Daddy and everyone."

"That's right, Carol, but you're more important. Don't worry about it, okay? Come here." I beckoned to her, but she still didn't move. I was terrified the guy might suddenly change his mind.

Please just listen to me, Carol.

Without the book, I wouldn't be able to send any prophecies or perform miracles ever again, even if my villagers were still alive, but I was making the right choice here. None of the villagers would thank me for picking the book over Carol's life.

"Get outta here. I'm lettin' you go."

"Over here, Carol. Quickly!"

Despite our encouragement, Carol stood her ground. She crouched down and began rummaging through her bear backpack, her back still turned to the man.

"Carol—"

"Hold on." Carol took something from her backpack and spun around.

"What's that? Some kinda crummy doll? Man, that's—gah! Ah! My eyes! My throat!" The man started to violently cough. He fell to the ground and writhed, clutching at his throat and scrabbling at his eyes. I was too shocked to say anything. Gradually, his movements slowed before stopping all together. I looked carefully at his face. Tears and snot and drool streamed from every orifice.

It was a familiar scene. The same thing happened a few months ago to Sayuki's stalker, Yoshinaga, and his men.

"Yay!" Carol spun around, clutching Destiny in her arms. It looked like it was smirking at me, but that had to be my imagination, right?

"You brought Destiny here in your bag?"

"Um, I'm sorry. I felt bad leaving it at home, and I think it wanted to come with us, so I took it." Carol stuck her tongue out bashfully. I'd be mad at her, but she'd saved us.

"Okay. Well, if you take it out again, make sure you tell me. And thanks. Both of you." I ran up and gave them both a hug.

I wanted to be relieved it was all over, but I knew it wasn't. The three people the man was controlling had also collapsed and lost consciousness. If I left them here, I'd be in trouble when the man came to. I moved the three innocents to the bench and then slung the man over my back.

chapter 02 — My Questioning, the Shocking Truth, and My Lack of Understanding

I TOOK THE MAN to a large nature park next door to the shrine and set him down on a worn-out bench. This place had a beautiful reservoir, stunning in the early spring when all the cherry blossoms were out. In midwinter it was practically deserted. The flowers were just buds right now, but they still did a good job of hiding us from view.

We were far enough from where I left the three other people that, even if he *could* control them from a distance, it would take them some time to get here. I didn't want Carol seeing what I was about to do, so I told her to go play in a spot where I could still keep an eye on her.

"Here goes!" she announced. "Aw, it didn't work."

She was busy entertaining herself with some crappy yo-yo she'd won at one of the stalls; hopefully she wouldn't get bored.

I glanced around to confirm there were no witnesses before shaking the man's shoulder. Seated beside him, Destiny swayed its body in time with his blond spikes, as though entranced by their movement.

"Whazzat? What's going on?" The man yawned, his words a slur of confusion, but when he caught sight of me, his eyes flew wide open. "H-hey, you—ngh! I can't move!"

He wanted to run, but he couldn't move any part of his body below the neck. He was stuck on the bench

"You're not going anywhere. Take a look." I tried to smirk threateningly. I had no idea if it was convincing or not. Destiny hunched its shoulders up and shot me an exasperated look.

I guess it's not convincing, then. You're pretty expressive for a lizard.

The man didn't have time to evaluate my acting skills. Now that he realized he couldn't move, his face turned pale, and his mouth clamped shut. A perfectly natural reaction for someone in his situation.

"Wh-what did you do to me?!"

I moved close, getting in his face. "Shut up. Cause a fuss, and I'll paralyze your head, too." I picked up Destiny and made sure he got a good look.

"What, the lizard did somethin' to me? C'mon, man! Look, if you lemme go now, I'll forget this ever—no, keep that gross lizard away from me! And say something, dammit! Just keep that thing back!"

He was terrified of Destiny. I got the feeling he was trying to run, but of course his body didn't even twitch.

"I told you not to make a fuss. Hey, Destiny. If he shouts again, could you paralyze his lips for me?"

Destiny nodded, its tongue slipping in and out of its mouth. The man shook his head from side to side in a panic.

I grinned. "Do it."

With every muscle below his nose frozen, the punky man was immobilized. His eyes were stretched so wide in shock that it was a wonder they didn't fall from his skull. He wasn't going to give me any more trouble.

"I'll unpetrify your mouth now, but if you shout again, it's gonna be your nose *and* mouth. If you understand what I just said, blink twice." I smiled, trying to keep the threat in my voice. He blinked several times, not just twice. I had him completely at my mercy. "Destiny."

Destiny padded toward the man. It placed one foot on his body and blinked once. The color immediately returned to the man's lips.

"I can talk..."

"Right. I have some questions for you. Don't you dare lie to me. Okay?"

"G-go ahead. Just don't kill me!"

"I won't have to if you're good." He was more frightened than I expected. Maybe I went too far. "First question. How exactly do you control people?"

"Duh—Uh, I mean, with the power I got from the game."

He'd been on the verge of taunting me again before I held Destiny up to his face.

"So you can use the miracles in the real world, too?"

"That's right, yeah. When you destroy villages and kill people and stuff, you level up. At some point you get the ability to use the miracles in real life. You sure are d—uninformed, sir. So you're still at level 1? That means your lizard isn't using a miracle or anythin'?"

The last part of what he said was too quiet for me to make out, but the rest had me blinking at him in surprise.

There were levels in the game? And they gave you the ability to use miracles in real life? That was crazy!

Wait, I remembered something about this. I cast my mind back to a certain message I saw when I played the game for the first time.

"This is a list of miracles you can perform. As your village improves and your population increases, you will unlock more powerful miracles."

By "more powerful miracles," I assumed it just meant that I would unlock different kinds of miracles, not that my current miracles would level up. I had to meet conditions to level up as well. Corrupted gods needed to destroy villages, and major gods needed to improve their own settlements. By fulfilling these conditions, players could level up to use their miracles in the real world. I already knew this was no ordinary game, but how many times was it going to blow my expectations apart?

"Question number two. Who asked you to get them Carol and the holy book? What do they want them for?"

"I dunno that much. I swear I don't know! I just got an email with your address tellin' me they'd pay me. I'm being serious. I mean, I thought it was real suspicious at first, but then I thought that there are hardly any people who know about this game, right? And money's all y'need to buy more points, and more points meant more miracles. I thought it was worth a try, even if it turned out to be a grift."

He really *was* in it for the money and nothing else. I needed to learn more about the person who sent him the email, but he didn't seem to know much.

"Next question. Why didn't you just get me drunk or something and then use your temptation miracle on me?"

All it took was a weakened mental state to control someone, right? It would've been quicker for him to pick me as his miracle's target.

"Um, well. It's against the rules to use miracles directly on an enemy player. If you do, and that player comes to harm, it's an instant game over. So I needed to be smarter than that."

Did this rule apply to major god players, too, or was it only for the corrupted gods?

"Wait, where did you hear about this rule? I've never seen anything like that in my version of the game. Have you been talking to other players?"

"Huh? Whaddya—What do you mean? Oh, wait. Right, if you're still level 1, you probably don't have access to the forums yet." Though he muttered the words to himself, they didn't escape my notice. He said "forums," right? As in, *online* forums? Places for players to discuss strategies and information about the game?

"Online forums? I thought you weren't allowed to leak information about the game to other people?"

"Kinda, but not quite. You're not supposed to talk about the game, you're right, but there's an exception. You can talk about it with other players. What, didn't ya even—ahem."

Every time he was on the brink of insulting me, Destiny shot him a hard stare, and he backed off. It was amusing, but I didn't have time to laugh.

We're allowed to talk about the game to other players, huh?

I was getting a lot from this guy. But the more I learned, the more questions I had.

"You knew about me from the email, right? Did you tell any other players about Carol or the holy book?" If he did, I might have more creeps coming after me.

"I didn't tell anyone. I think the email got sent to all the corrupted gods, though, 'cause everyone was talkin' about it on the forums. You can tell I'm in a band, right? Bands cost a ton to run. We gotta rent our studio, buy the instruments, distribute tickets. The expenses never stop, I swear."

I thought his outfit might just be a fashion thing, but I figured that made sense.

"Anyway, so I got that email with your photo and address on it, and it said I could get, like, ten million yen just for snatchin' your book. Impossible to resist, right?"

Ten million yen?!

Was he serious? My book was worth ten million yen? Wait. Thinking back, Yamamoto-san mentioned he got five million for destroying a big village, so maybe it wasn't that crazy.

The money wasn't the only issue, though.

"Are you telling me that every single corrupted god got sent a photo of my face and address?!" I was so horrified I reached out to grab the neck of his shirt, but since he was paralyzed, I couldn't get a good grip.

"I reckon so. When you're done with me, you'll probably get them all comin' at you. I mean, it's ten million yen, right? And you get a bonus if you bring the kid."

What should I do? What *could* I do? They knew my face. My address. Destiny saved us this time, but I couldn't rely on that in the future.

"Think you could unfreeze me now? I told you everything already, and I promise I'll leave you alone from now on!"

I couldn't trust him. Not with that stupid grin on his face. My book was worth ten million yen, and this guy was broke. Would he really let a chance like this pass him by?

"You should just lemme go and get outta here. You never know, there might be some more guys watchin' and waitin' in the shadows right now, trying to get their hands on the book and that girl."

I looked around reflexively but only saw Carol struggling with her yo-yo. The park was empty.

But that didn't mean we were safe. Someone might be along any minute. We needed to be sensible and leave, but what about him? What if he used his miracle? What if he controlled a whole crowd to come after me? He was way too overpowered. I couldn't just let him go. That left me a single option.

"Okay. I'll unfreeze you. Destiny, can you unfreeze him in just this spot?" I pointed at the man's pocket, which clearly had something inside it.

"W-wait, whaddya doin'?! Hold it! Stop! Stop right there, lizard! Dammit! If I don't have my phone, I can't use any miracles!" The man protested loudly, at which point Destiny very kindly petrified his mouth again. At the same time, it unfroze his thigh, allowing me to take out the guy's phone and check the screen.

There—the other world. Not even a day had passed since I'd last seen it, but a lump formed in my throat all the same. I watched a huge, one-eyed monster stomp through the wilderness, apparently out on reconnaissance. I would've loved to do a bit more poking around to see what the game was like from the other side, but I had no time. I ignored the monster, checking his miracles instead. He had "charm," "tempt," and "control." I suppressed the urge to try them out.

"The main option screen is the same as in *The Village of Fate*." I opened it and searched until I found "Abandon Game."

"Here it is!"

That button was in *The Village of Fate*, too. I glanced up at the guy. He was staring at me, his face pale with horror. I could almost hear him screaming at me to stop. I pressed the button without hesitation.

Are you sure?

Yes No

A confirmation message flashed on the screen. I tapped "yes." The same game over message that Yamamoto-san got appeared on the screen, and the next second the game disappeared from the phone. The guy's eyes rolled back into his head. His memories were most likely being deleted along with the game. He was no longer a threat to me, but that didn't mean I could relax yet. More like him would be coming, and I needed to be ready. If they went after just me, that was fine, but I didn't want my family or Seika to get wrapped up in this.

I gritted my teeth. I knew what to do. I just needed to gather the determination.

"There's only one way out of this mess. Carol?"

"Yeah?" Carol scampered up to me, her yo-yo tangled around itself.

I knelt down, looking her in the eye. I took a deep breath. "We're gonna go see God."

THE NPCs IN THIS VILLAGE SIM GAME MUST BE REAL! ↵

chapter 03
The Waves of Information and My Drowning

"**G**OD?" Carol asked. "You mean the God of Fate?"

"That's right. This man with the spiky hair was a servant of a corrupted god. That god told him to come and take the holy book." I didn't mention that he was after Carol, too. It would only scare her. "We're gonna go ask the God of Fate for help. He might even help us get you home quicker."

"Really?! Yay! Let's go!" Carol's face lit up, and she jumped up and down. She seemed to be having fun in this world, but I couldn't blame her for wanting to go home.

My idea sounded crazy, but I knew I was right. There was a high risk of other players showing up to take the book and Carol. I couldn't just hang out at home and ignore the threat.

I had two options.

The first was to hand over the book without complaint. After that, I should be left alone...except for the problem of Carol. A greedy opponent would go after her, too. On top of that, the book was my connection to the village. Without it, I couldn't perform miracles or send prophecies. I wouldn't be able to play *The Village of Fate* at all.

My second option was to keep the book and Carol to myself. That meant I would, for all intents and purposes, be at war with the corrupted gods. I didn't know how many there were or what sort of miracles they could use. And my team was just a small girl, a former NEET, and a yellow lizard.

Destiny was my strongest fighter. Its petrifying gaze and poison breath were invaluable, but not invincible. Its breath could blow back in my face if the wind was coming from the wrong direction or if we were in an enclosed space. The petrifying gaze required the target to be in Destiny's line of sight. If the opponent attacked from afar, or snuck up from behind, we were dead. And I still didn't know everything about Destiny's powers. I needed to experiment with them.

"Where is the Lord, Yoshio?"

I'd been waiting for her to ask that.

"He lives in a cold place to the north."

I didn't make that up. I didn't know if this game was created by actual gods, but I had a general idea of where they were based. They sent packages to my house, and the return address was always right there on the label: Hokkaido. It might be a fake address, but right now it was my only lead. If I wanted to find out more about the game and get Carol home, I had to speak to the developers. I also wanted to thank them for sending me the game...and make a few complaints.

"Shall we head home, Carol?"

It was too dangerous to stay here. Leaving the unconscious punk behind, I took Carol by the hand, and we started home.

I carefully scoped out the area around my house, but there was nothing unusual. I ushered Carol in first before hastening after her, making sure to lock the door behind us. I'd spent the walk home on high alert, peering back and forth. I probably looked super suspicious, but that didn't matter to me right now. Thanks to the past ten years, my reputation in the neighborhood was already at rock bottom.

Carol immediately fell into a doze under the *kotatsu* in the living room. I wasn't surprised she was tired after all that. I thought about putting her to bed in the spare room, but it would be safer to have her nearby. I scooped her up and took her to my bedroom, offering her Destiny to cuddle to help her fall asleep. It wasn't long until she was out cold. All the food she'd had at the festival probably helped.

"I gotta be careful not to wake her."

I sat down at my desk, taking the holy book from my pocket and setting it aside. I switched on my PC monitor. This computer (which I used exclusively for *The Village of Fate*) had been on since the Day of Corruption. I'd just kept the monitor off. Seeing the blank screen constantly drained me of hope. As expected, the screen was...

"Completely different?!"

On my computer screen was an overhead view of a world. My heart jumped, thinking *The Village of Fate* was back, but this view was of something else entirely. It was familiar, but it wasn't my village.

"This is...my house? This roof is Seika's. And the rest is the neighborhood..."

Why was my PC showing a map of my house and its surroundings? A realistic, detailed map, too, like a satellite image you could find online, but with one major difference. The second floor of my house was displayed with a cross-section view. The roof was cut away and you could see my room, Sayuki's room, my parents' room, and even the bathroom.

"That's Carol...and this is me?" I looked up instinctively, but the ceiling was there as always. Well, I would've noticed if it disappeared. I looked back at the screen and raised my hand. The me onscreen raised his hand, too. I tried scrolling to zoom in, just like you could on *The Village of Fate*. It worked. You could see Carol's sleeping face and Destiny, who looked a little uncomfortable in her arms. "What's going on?"

Think. There's gotta be a reason for this. Until now, this computer only ran The Village of Fate. *So why is it showing me my house now?*

The screen was centered around my room. "Wait..." I looked at the holy book on my desk. That had to be it.

That book played an important role in the game. Was its existence in this world the reason I was seeing my own house on the screen now?

"I can worry about the whys later. I just gotta figure out what to do now."

At this point, I was used to the game doing impossible things. I was developing a tolerance to insanity. If I thought about it too much, I'd freeze up and possibly just lose my mind.

I tried moving around the map on screen. My FP was displayed in the corner, and I had access to the options screen and miracles menu, just like on my phone.

"Which means..."

I pulled out my phone and opened the app. Sure enough, the same image from my PC appeared on the smaller screen. So I could play on my phone, too. Except this wasn't the same parallel world I was used to playing with. It was Japan.

"I can see why someone might want the book if it meant they could see their surroundings from above like this. It's like an instant, personal satellite. And it can see through walls. That's even more valuable."

I'd balked when that guy said the book was worth ten million yen, but if this was what you could do with it, I understood why it was so valuable. Big companies, or even nations, would shell out billions for a tool like this.

"I wonder what made it suddenly start working."

My PC screen had been dark for a while, even after Carol brought the book to this world. I racked my brain as I tried out the "game," but nothing I could think of made sense.

"Guess I'll start with what I do know instead of trying to

answer impossible questions." I purposely spoke out loud to myself to help collect my thoughts.

First, I checked the backlog. It contained every conversation I'd had with Carol since her arrival.

"There's nothing from my villagers. Not that I'm surprised."

Still, it was too soon to conclude that they were dead. The book only picked up on conversations close to it; I knew that from when Gams and everyone fought the one-eyed red goblin. I scrolled through the backlog, hoping to find a hint. Then I noticed a message in red.

"Congratulations. You have reached level 2."

I leveled up?! When?

Apparently, it happened around the time when Yamamoto-san left and I discovered the package with Carol inside. But I hadn't noticed a notification or anything.

The guy in the park said that corrupted god players leveled up by killing people and destroying villages, but I didn't know how players on my side did it. Most likely it had to do with the growth of your village, but that was just a guess. Part of me wished I'd asked him more, but sticking around much longer would have been dangerous.

"If I know video games, you probably level up when your village reaches a certain size. Either that, or there's some hidden condition to fulfill. Or maybe it's based on experience gained from a bunch of different factors?"

The most common way of gaining experience in games was completing assigned missions. Do enough quests and gain enough experience, and your level would go up. In *The Village of Fate's* case, maybe you gained a load of experience points every time you overcame a Day of Corruption. Or maybe defeating monsters? That was another common way to level up.

"Maybe my villagers survived, defeated the monsters, and made it through the Day of Corruption after sending Carol to my place, and that's how I leveled up. That might be it, right?"

It was plausible. Maybe it was my optimism talking, but this could be evidence that my villagers were still alive.

"I gotta hold on to hope. My villagers survived. Every one of them is safe!"

That was better than believing they were dead, and it helped me work out what to do next.

"Mm... Mommy... Daddy..."

I spun around, worried I'd woken Carol up. She was just mumbling in her sleep with a heavy frown. I sat down next to her and gently stroked her pretty blonde curls.

"Don't worry, Carol. I'll take you home to the village."

Her expression seemed to soften a little. I gave Destiny a pat, too, as it slept next to her. It glanced at me and flicked its tongue out a few times, as if to say it would take care of Carol for me. I couldn't repress a smile. Leaving Destiny to babysit, I moved back to my computer.

"If I leveled up, that means I have more options."

The punk in the park said something about unlocking forums. *I should be able to access them now, right?*

I scrolled through the options menu and found a new button

labeled "Discussion Forums." Was this what he was talking about? Would I find other players discussing the game here? I was curious but also slightly anxious.

There were still way too many mysteries surrounding this game, and I was scared to delve too deep. What if the truth just complicated and confused my everyday life even further? Just thinking about stuff getting even crazier made me hesitate.

"I always did try to stay out of anything that seemed like a hassle."

But things were different now. I had people I wanted to protect. I had things I needed to do. I had favors to repay.

I grabbed the mouse and clicked firmly on the forums button.

"These look just like any other forums."

Their layout and design were reminiscent of the most famous discussion boards in Japan. The "discussion forums" header was at the top in big letters, and underneath was a list of threads. I let my eyes wander down.

Monster Identification Thread (179)

Corrupted God Positivity Thread (Anti-Corrupted God
　　Discussion Strictly Forbidden) (234)

Who's the Cutest Minor God? (66)

How to Save up Fate Points Effectively (16)

Do you guys not know how to read the rules? (7)

Elite Players Thread (Level 3 and Over) (18)

Level 2 Noobs Complaints Thread (7)

I'll rate your village! (32)

Something cool I did with miracles... (14)

I think there's something wrong with my villagers? (3)
Need advice for my village! (22)
Just learned female dwarves can grow beards too (5)
Let's see who's got the strongest villager! (33)
My villager asked me about his divorce, but I'm a single
  guy... (4)
The religious stuff in this game is kinda weird (5)
Cat- and Dogmen suddenly showed up at my village! (23)

"This is totally not what I was expecting," I muttered to myself.

There had to be at least a hundred threads here. Some of them seemed serious, others less so. This was almost weirdly casual. I clicked on the first thread curiously. A warning popped up.

Do not post real names or addresses.

Do not post any personally identifiable information.

Feel free to leave abusive messages about the corrupted gods.

Do not post any false information in this thread.

Other players will not be able to read any information they are not allowed to know.

This forum is for players on the side of the major gods only. Players of corrupted gods are unable to see this forum.

A hundred thoughts rushed into my head all at once, and not all of them were great. Players weren't allowed to post any personally identifiable information according to points 1 and 2, but I already knew that rule had been broken. That guy in the park said everyone was talking about me. The discrepancy likely had something to do with rule number 6. Players who controlled corrupted gods used a different forum from us, meaning we couldn't communicate with them here. 4 and 5 gave me pause, too, but I could deal with that later. I just wanted to read the thread itself for now.

> 1: Green goblins have gotta be the poster monsters of this game.
> 2: Yeah, they're kinda smart so actually annoying to deal with.
> 3: Smart in the same way as monkeys, yeah.
> 4: Hey, that makes them as smart as some humans.
> 5: That's it! Who's making fun of me?!
> 6: Let's talk about sharks instead of monkeys!

It was just like any other Internet forum: twenty percent serious discussion, eighty percent off-topic nonsense. There was some useful stuff on monsters in there, though, and I made a note to come back to it later. I scrolled through until I came across thread 27: Newbie FAQ Thread.

"Now *this* looks helpful."

"Your points are named after your god."

I was the God of Fate, so my points were called Fate Points. Made sense.

"The number of gods in the game is currently undetermined. However, each god has only one human player. No gods are controlled by more than one player."

In other words, I had sole control of the God of Fate.

"Players are separated into those allied with the corrupted gods and those allied with the major gods. Players allied with the major gods are generally discouraged from fighting with each other, though there may not be any punishment for doing so."

That meant there *could* be a punishment, which was probably enough to dissuade people from turning on each other, though I wondered about the use of the word "generally."

"It is thought there are up to five levels, but only four have been confirmed."

I still had a long way to go, huh?

"Using miracles for criminal purposes will get you an immediate game over."

That looked like a rule for players on the major gods' side only. Controlling people to steal a book had to count as a crime, right?

"Some thread content will be invisible to players beneath a certain level. Visible text is color-coded. Black means that the text can be seen by all players. Yellow is for level 3 and above. Red is for level 4 and above."

That explained the different colors. I tried clicking on the thread for level 3 and above players. Most of the text in there was red or yellow and had a message saying, "You cannot read this message." over it. I still had tons of questions, but a few unlocked threads looked promising. I'd check those out later. First, though, I had to make a post of my own.

"How should I write this?"

I was used to making threads on regular forums, but this was a completely new experience.

"*'A corrupted god player came and harassed me in real life. Is that not against the rules?'* That should do it."

I had my first responses in seconds.

543 Sure they did lol
545 Nope
546 Sure this "player" wasn't just in your imagination?

"Bastards..."

Those sorts of responses were common on regular boards. I figured I didn't need to be so formal after all. I didn't feel nervous anymore, either. But it really did seem like what happened to me was rare.

547 Wait, why do you guys think he's lying? These boards
    don't let you post any false information, right?
548 Oh yeah. Wait, you mean he's telling the truth?
549 Ok, now I need to know! Tell us everything, 542!

They were starting to believe me. 542 was my post number.

"How am I supposed to explain? *The corrupted god found out my address and came to steal my holy book. He said there was a group of people who would pay ten million yen for it.'* That was okay, right?"

552 He came to steal your ***? For *** yen?! Kinky.
553 You must've written something against the rules,
    because some of that got censored.

554 He came to steal his ass lol
555 Did someone say yaoi?
556 No. Get outta here.

What were they talking about? The thread was going way off topic.

Oh, wait. There was that rule about players not being able to read information they weren't allowed to know, right? So I wasn't allowed to talk about the situation with my holy book to them? I guess this was an unprecedented situation.

Thinking back, it was strange how honest that punk was with me. I let the other forum users know there was some information I couldn't tell them before trying to explain in as much detail as I could. I told them I was targeted by two separate corrupted god players in the two months since I started playing the game. I told them what had happened since New Year's Eve while trying not to trigger the censor again.

560 This sounds serious. There's a thread where you can talk to the devs directly, so why not ask there?
561 This is crazy. But if it's true, it sounds like you're in deep trouble.
562 Let us know what the devs say.
563 I wanna know too.
564 I'm sitting here naked, and I'm not gonna move till you're back.
565 Put some clothes on.

566 And if I'm a girl with E-cup tits?
567 Send nudes.

And we were off topic again. Regardless, the advice was reassuring, even if the interaction was all via text. I'd always thought I was in this alone, so it was nice to know there were so many other god players out there willing to help. Just knowing that filled me with determination.

I found the thread to contact the developers and told them everything that happened over these past two days without sparing the slightest detail.

Nothing'll get censored from them, right?

I wasn't expecting an answer right away, so I went to browse other threads in the meantime. Then my phone rang. The name on the screen said "Developers."

chapter 04 — A Call from the Developers and My Nervousness

WERE THE ACTUAL DEVELOPERS calling me?!

"Their timing's way too perfect!"

I never put the developers' number into my phone, though. I didn't even know their number. But there was no mistaking the text on my phone screen. The phone kept ringing, but I couldn't pluck up the courage to answer. I was clearly naive to think that nothing could surprise me anymore after what had happened over the past couple of days. I took a deep breath and picked up the phone.

"H-hello?"

"Hello! I'm a developer from *The Village of Fate*!" A cheerful voice battered against my eardrum.

It was a woman, her casual tone giving the impression she was calling to chat with an old friend. She sounded young, but I didn't have enough experience with women to judge by her voice.

"Oh, um, hi. You're a developer?"

"That's right! I was going to email you, but I thought it might get intercepted, you know? Leaving textual evidence only leads to trouble! So I thought a phone call would be safer!"

"R-right."

How did she get my number in the first place? Why did my phone know the call was from the "Developers"? I had a ton of questions for her, but I held them in.

"I'll keep things brief, in case we're being watched. If you come here, I think we can get Carol and the book sent back to the other world. We'd come to you if we could, but that's not possible, I'm afraid!"

"You can send her home?! Really?! Thank you so much!" I couldn't help but cry out in joy.

"No worries. It was kinda our fault in the first place. I guess you'd call it a bug. We never thought something like this would happen, see. We're trying to patch it out right now. Stuff is crazy over here! We were super busy trying to finagle things so you can use the book in this world, too."

That explained why the game had been out of commission for a while.

"Welp, I guess discovering these bugs and stuff is what you play testers are for, huh?"

Right, the game's still in alpha. I totally forgot!

"Where are you based?" I asked.

"You should already know. Listen, I'm gonna hang up before things get dicey, but I'm looking forward to meeting you, Yoshio-kun! Oh, and make sure you don't tell anyone about our conversation! If you post about it on the forums, no one will be able to read it."

"Okay. And—oh, she hung up..."

I had more questions, but at least I had a starting point. Still, she said a lot of weird stuff... Her super-familiar way of speaking threw me for a loop. I'd been nursing this image of the developers as gods—I was expecting something a little more majestic.

"Will I really be meeting with gods when I get there?" I pulled out a small slip of paper from my desk drawer. The return address from one of the parcels. "This is where I need to go."

I felt overwhelmed with how fast events were transpiring, but I finally had a clear goal. I checked the balance in my bank account and looked up routes and prices for travel to Hokkaido.

"Looks like the choices are train or plane. Oh, or we could take the ferry."

I'd been on planes and the bullet train before, but only with my family or school. I'd never gone through the process of buying a ticket and planning a journey by myself. I was anxious, but adults did this every day. I repeated that to myself again and again.

I continued my research, feeling the old familiar sting of my own uselessness

The next morning, I was surprised to remember it was only January 2nd.

"Only three days since all that crazy stuff happened."

I'd gone through enough in the last couple of days to last me an entire month, not to mention how much had happened since I began playing *The Village of Fate*. My whole life had changed;

it wasn't an exaggeration to say I was an entirely different person. Between my sister's stalker and Yamamoto-san, I'd been through two life-threatening events, plus a whole bunch of unexplainable ones.

They say adversity is supposed to make you stronger, but it didn't feel like it. Instead, it made me realize how inexperienced I was—*that* was what made me want to change. I wanted to become an adult worthy of my physical age. The fact that I was struggling to organize a trip to Hokkaido showed how far I still had to go.

"There are plane tickets cheaper than the bullet train. Huh."

The price for flying varied significantly depending on the company. I always thought flying was a classy way to travel, but I guess things changed. The new year was a popular time to fly, however, and the upcoming days were more expensive than those further off. Still cheaper than I expected.

"Looks like all the plane tickets are sold out or close to it. Flying might be difficult."

Even if I managed to get tickets, there was still the problem of Destiny. I doubted reptiles were allowed on planes. Even if I stowed it away in my bag, they checked your luggage at airports. I couldn't get it past security.

Maybe I could get Carol to hold it and pretend it's just a stuffed animal?

I studied Destiny, who was sitting on the corner of my desk watching me carefully. It had tough, spiky skin and huge eyes.

"Yeah, you don't look stuffed at all."

Flying would be the quickest, but yeah, it was firmly out of the question. The next contender was the train, preferably the bullet train. I checked whether there were any reserved seats available, but they were all taken. Going on the day to try and get an unreserved seat was an option, but they were currently expecting a passenger rate of fifty percent above capacity. Getting a seat now was easier than on New Year's Day, but then it got worse again around January 4th; I guessed people restarted work on the fifth. They'd want time to get home and prepare. That was common sense for most people, but for me, who'd spent the last ten years shut away from society, it never even crossed my mind.

We needed to leave for Hokkaido as soon as possible. It wasn't just the corrupted gods I was worried about—there was my family, too. They were coming back on the fourth. If we weren't gone by then, I'd have to explain Carol. I wanted to introduce them, of course, but realistically that would just be more trouble.

Dad would frown at me. Mom would be suspicious. Sayuki would outright hate me without waiting for an explanation.

I decided that Carol and I would leave tomorrow, on the third. We'd prepare for it to be busy but still try to get seats. That meant this was Carol's last day here. I wanted her to have fun. I wanted her to love my world.

It was January 3rd, the day of our departure. I only managed to take Carol around to some shops and the mall yesterday, but she got so excited at all the sights and sounds that just looking at her put a smile on my face.

"Did you have fun yesterday?"

Carol nodded enthusiastically. We were done with breakfast, and she was all dressed and ready to go. She climbed out from under the *kotatsu*, put on her favorite bear-shaped backpack, and gave me a little twirl.

"It was really, *really* fun! The world of the gods is amazing! Everything's so big, and there are tons of people, and everything's so shiny! It's like a story world!"

Despite the early hour, she was full of energy. The clothes we bought at the mall yesterday suited her perfectly. A pastel sweater and a long skirt with a pink pattern. She really did look like a child model, but that would be true in any outfit. It took her an entire hour to pick these out. I had to remind myself how long women could take at a shop—even children. I chose the mall because it would be crowded, which would discourage any corrupted gods from targeting me. More witnesses.

I didn't come up with that myself, though. I spent a lot of time on the forums after my initial post and picked up a bunch of valuable information. For instance: miracles in the real world were less effective than in the game world. Using them on multiple people or over a wide area was also very expensive, and was difficult for level 2 and level 3 players. That was why the other users suggested I stay in crowded areas. If an enemy accidentally caught me in a miracle, it would count as using it against another player, and they'd get an instant game over.

I used all that advice to give Carol a fun day out, ensuring she didn't need to think about her parents or the village. That was all I wanted for her.

"I already told Seika and my parents that I was going to Hokkaido."

I'd phoned Dad last night and told him I was going up to the village that was always sending me stuff.

"I see. Make sure you keep yourself out of trouble."

That was all he said, no follow-up questions. Despite his usual brevity, he sounded happy for me. But maybe that was just wishful thinking.

Seika already knew about Carol, so the trip was easy to explain. She even managed to get us two reserved seats on the bullet train. I could hardly believe it and thanked her profusely.

"There's an art to ticket-buying, plus I know someone," she explained. "Make sure you wrap up warm, okay? And bring me back something nice. Have a great trip!"

I spent all day with Carol yesterday, but she was an early sleeper. By eight o'clock she was cuddling Destiny and settling down. That was when I had the opportunity to gather information. The forums were hopping at night.

Turned out I wasn't the only one who had doubts about the game. The majority of players seemed to have figured out the game was set in a parallel world and wasn't just a computer program. All the gods had access to different miracles. For example, the God of Clear Streams, who was under the God of Water, had the power to control and purify water. That player was very excited; they were level 3 and an outdoorsy type. They liked using their purification miracles to promote the health of the natural world.

I discovered that no other players had access to a golem or a miracle to control the weather. Those seemed to be exclusive to the God of Fate, although I wasn't sure what those things had to do with fate. I had a theory, though.

Fate was linked to luck. If you had bad luck, you could be caught in the rain. Good luck meant it would be sunny. In that sense, controlling the weather was like controlling someone's luck, or fate. And fate was linked to life itself. Being born in the first place meant you were fated to have a life. Summoning the golem was giving temporary life to a statue. That made sense to me, I guess, but I could ask the developer gods directly when I saw them.

All player gods had access to a holy book and the ability to send one prophecy a day. The more I heard about other gods and their miracles, the more pleased I was with my own element. Other gods had miracles that sounded useful in the real world, but mine were better equipped for developing my village. Still, I felt like I never had the chance to use my miracles to their full potential.

"How come you're staring into space, Yoshio? Aren't we going out?"

Carol's question snapped me back to reality. I was so deep in thought that I lost sight of my surroundings. She and Destiny peered at me anxiously, the lizard's head poking out of her teddy bear backpack.

Destiny was coming with us. Without its power, I wouldn't have escaped all those close calls. It was our bodyguard, as well as Carol's sleeping buddy. I patted its head gently.

"You were born in the other world, too."

It came over here in an egg, so it couldn't remember anything about where it was born, but I was sure it would love somewhere it could run around and explore. I thought of Destiny as my pet lizard, but it was a basilisk, a creature that shouldn't exist in this world. It didn't belong here. I planned to ask the developers to send it back, if they could.

"Let's go, then. Have you got everything, Carol?"

We double-checked our luggage just inside the front door, the door that used to be a heavy, overbearing gate to me. Two months later and it no longer held any threat. I grabbed the doorknob and flung it open.

"Here we go!"

chapter 05 The Journey

"**W**ow! There are even more people than at the festival!"

"That's right. So make sure you don't let go."

"Okay!"

Carol clung to the hem of my coat, looking around in wonder. I wanted to talk to her properly, but right now I was busy checking the timetable. We stood in front of the ticket machines at the train station. It was a bullet train hub, meaning it was huge and packed. There were several women dressed in kimono, likely on their way to a shrine for the new year.

Wait, stop getting distracted! Stay on task!

I approached the ticket machine to retrieve our tickets. This was my first time doing anything of the sort. The expense hurt a little, but it was necessary. Seika offered to pay for our tickets, but I politely declined. She already went through the trouble of booking them for us—I couldn't ask her to pay.

I can just press the button for online reservations, right?

I'd looked up online how to do this, but I was still nervous.

I managed it in the end and led Carol, who was still humming with excitement, toward the ticket gate. The hard part was over. I used to take the train to school—now I was on familiar ground.

"I'll show you what to do next, okay, Carol? You just copy me."

"Okay!"

This was a simple procedure, but the innocent Carol looked at me with great respect. I didn't think I deserved it, but it felt good. I put my ticket through the slot and tried to go through the gate. It closed right in front of me.

"Huh?"

I put it in properly, didn't I?

"Yoshio?" Carol looked up at me questioningly. I wished she wouldn't. My face grew hot with embarrassment and confusion. What did I do wrong?

In my panic, I noticed a station staff member approaching at a quick pace.

"You need to put the express ticket on top of the regular ticket and put them both in at once."

"Oh, right. Sorry."

Wait, then why did we have two of them? I thought one was to show the staff in the train or something, just like I'd seen in TV dramas.

"What's wrong, Yoshio?"

"Oh, uh...the man came over to apologize because the gate didn't accept my ticket."

Sorry, mysterious station staff member.

He couldn't understand us, so I pinned the blame on him. I put both tickets in this time, and Carol did the same. We checked which car we were in, then bought some lunch boxes on the platform while we waited. I'd always wanted to eat a fancy lunch box on a bullet train. Trivial to most people, maybe, but to a shut-in, it felt impossible. I loved being able to do something other people did without thinking. There was a hidden beauty to that.

"Hey, how does that big, long snake thingy go so fast? Is it magic?" Carol asked, her eyes sparkling. Trains were a staple of our society, but she'd never seen one before.

"It's not magic. It's technology we use in the god's world; a power everyone can use."

"So I can make the snake go fast, too?"

"You could if you studied and learned how to do it, sure."

"Wow! That's so amazing!"

Despite me having nothing to do with it, I enjoyed hearing her praise my country's technology.

When the train stopped and it was time to get on, Carol's face went stiff with nerves. Then she gathered her courage and launched herself inside.

"It's not gonna eat us, right?" she asked nervously.

"Don't worry. It's not really a snake." I took Carol's hand and led her to our seats. A bullet train had seating laid out in twos and threes. Carol and I had a two-seat arrangement together. "Here we are. You can have the window seat."

"Really?! Yay!"

I preferred to have the window seat because I often got motion sick, but she'd appreciate it more than me. Besides, if a corrupted god player showed up, I needed to be able to get up.

"Can I let Destiny out, Yoshio?" Carol asked, shuffling her bear backpack off and pointing at the zipper.

"Hmm. Put the bag down by your feet and unzip it. Then it can get some air."

"Okay." Carol unzipped the bag, and Destiny poked its head out. It stretched out its front legs like a cramped old man.

"Sorry. Try and relax a little, Destiny."

It lay down on the floor, curled up, and closed its eyes. I put my bag on the floor as well, blocking the view. If anyone realized we brought a huge lizard on the train, there'd be panic.

"Wow! We're moving, but we're not rocking at all! And it's so quiet!"

I realized that we'd left the station. I was so stressed, my shoulders so tensed up, that I was losing sight of my surroundings. I needed to be more careful. I couldn't let my guard down, but staying this high strung was also no good. I was about to warn Carol to keep her voice down so as not to disturb the other passengers, when I noticed something. Her voice was echoing throughout the car, but she wasn't actually that loud. The surroundings were just eerily quiet.

When we came in, the train was packed, but no one was saying anything. It didn't make sense. There were even some other children here.

"Carol, would you mind being quiet for a second?"

"Oh, sorry." She put her hands over her mouth. I had no time to feel guilty.

The silence was even more conspicuous now that she wasn't talking. Not a single voice anywhere. The only sound was the train speeding along its path. I held my breath, listening, when the door to the next car opened. I stuck my head out into the aisle to look.

"No way..."

My mind went blank at the impossibility of the scene in front of me. A horrifying, green-skinned monster was making its way into the carriage. It was a goblin. A goblin I'd seen tons of times in the game world.

"Yoshio! It's a green goblin!" Carol whimpered, clinging to my arm and trembling.

I wanted to reassure her, but although I opened my mouth, no words came out. Fear parched my throat. I never realized how terrifying a creature it was until now, when it was right in front of me. How could something like this exist in real life? It was so fantastical it felt like the space inside the car had been torn away from reality. A cold sweat sprung up over my skin, and I began to shake.

Was this how my villagers felt when they fought for their lives? For the first time, I knew what true fear felt like. I wanted desperately to run for it. If this was how the outside world could be, I was prepared to throw everything away and shut myself up again.

No...

"Yoshio..." Carol yanked at my sleeve, her voice small and weak.

Didn't I say it was time to stop running from reality?! I have to protect her!

I swallowed, curled my hands into fists, and drew in a breath. "Carol. Put your head down and stay quiet."

"O-okay."

I gave her a reassuring pat on the head, then stood up and stepped out into the aisle. The goblin halted a few feet in front of me. None of the passengers batted an eyelid at the grotesque monster standing in the middle of the train. I swept my gaze over them, wondering if a corrupted god player might be among them, but they all seemed fast asleep. How? No way every single person on this train decided to take a nap at the same time.

I looked back to the green goblin, studying it carefully. It was a little shorter than me, and aside from a sash of animal pelt around its waist, its green skin was on full display. Its arms and legs were thick with muscle, and it carried a primitive club in one hand. This one was bigger than any of the goblins I'd seen in-game, but it was smaller than me. Still, it was a *monster.* That was enough to sap me of my courage.

First things first. This thing must have a connection to a corrupted god player. I just didn't expect someone to make a move this bold with so many witnesses.

"What's a green goblin doing in Japan?" I asked, not expecting it to reply.

"Give me the book and girl."

It *did* respond! And way more fluently than I expected. Did that mean it could understand human speech? The goblins made sounds in the game, but they never conversed or anything like that. What *was* this thing?

It was most likely a monster summoned by a miracle. That would make sense for a corrupted god. Still terrifying, though.

"Give me the book and girl," the goblin repeated impatiently.

"And if I say no?"

"I will use force." The goblin stepped towards me slowly.

It had a club, and all I had were my bare hands. I was bigger, but I had no real fighting experience. I wasn't confident in my chances.

"What do you mean 'book'?" I asked, playing dumb.

"Don't be stupid. I mean the holy book. I won't hurt you if you give it to me."

It was smart and calm, easier to talk to than that punk in the park. Either way, it knew about the holy book.

"Why are you here? You're a green goblin. Is someone controlling you?"

"I don't have to answer your questions. Give me the holy book and the girl."

It clearly wasn't keen on unnecessary conversation. I calmed down a little as I realized it could understand me fully, despite its appearance.

"If I refuse, you threatened to use force. Isn't that against the rules? You're not allowed to harm other players directly."

"I heard you were only level 1. Sounds like my sources need updating."

It knew who I was, and now it knew I was level 2. I sucked

in a breath and looked to my side. I whispered to Carol, who was still clinging to my pants, and after a moment's thought she whispered back to me.

"Stop that. I have many ways to get what I want."

"Why not just go for it? Get your game over." I pulled the holy book out of my pocket and flashed it at the goblin. I noticed it twitch, but nothing more than that.

If it tried to take the book by force, all I needed to do was fight back. Assuming this creature was summoned by a miracle, it would be game over the moment it laid a finger on me. I'd let myself get hit. Of course, this was a last resort. I'd rather get this thing to leave us alone without a fuss.

"You're not a real goblin, are you? You're some kinda illusion or disguise created by a miracle." I knew that different gods had access to different miracles, and that those miracles often corresponded to the god's attributes. I'd seen similar abilities to this one in manga, anime, and games before. That was one small leg up I had from my years of self-quarantine.

"Saw right through me, huh?"

"Wait, I was right?"

"What was that?"

"Oh, nothing..."

Wow, got it in one. The goblin's figure began to blur, and the next second it was gone and replaced with a slightly plump middle-aged man. He had a threadbare suit and a receding hairline. Your average salaryman.

"I didn't expect you to see through my powers."

"You were too tall to be a real green goblin. The in-game ones are shorter."

This sort of disguise often had the drawback of being unable to account for a person's height. An illusion needed to cover you completely or parts of your real self would remain visible. In the game, green goblins were about as tall as a human child. This one was obviously taller.

And then there was the way he spoke. The people from the Village of Fate didn't speak an Earth language—I'd learned that by observing Carol. Our whispered conversation just now was to confirm that she couldn't understand what he was saying. He wasn't being automatically translated. He was speaking Japanese.

My guess could have been way off, but the guy himself admitted to it. I wasn't about to complain.

"I suppose there's no point hiding anymore." He smiled amicably at me. "Anyway, how would you like to sell that book to me?"

"I thought you were going to use force?"

"I could simply take it from you, sure. I'd make more money that way, but I thought I'd be nice and offer a negotiation. This way, we can both profit."

Assuming he was telling the truth, he wasn't planning to hurt me anymore. Talking *was* preferable to fighting, but I still had to keep my wits about me.

"So how much would you give me for the book, then?"

"Let's say five million yen? That's half its value."

So he would sell it on for ten million yen, presumably. That was the same price the punk mentioned—at least this guy was being honest about the value.

"You were a shut-in NEET for a long time, weren't you? That means you need money, right?"

"You know that much about me?"

"Of course. In my job—ah, I'm a salesman by the way. I don't just sell products; I gather information in certain circumstances as well. I never thought you'd become independent enough to take a small girl—from another world no less—all the way to Hokkaido."

So he was snooping around my neighborhood and gathering information on me? I was glad I got out of my house as soon as I could.

"I need money myself. The game and its microtransactions—and gambling—are my life now. I was buried in a mountain of debt, you see. My wife and daughter were sick of it all. They left me. I only work now to pay off my debts. I've never had any hopes or dreams."

Isn't that your own fault?

I wasn't in a position to criticize anyone, but this guy was the very definition of a waste of air.

"Then I had a turn of good luck. Not only can I make money off this amazing video game, but your book and that little girl are going to net me a hefty bonus. Enough to wipe out my debts completely. Then I can go back to gambling and spending money on the game."

He really *was* a waste of air.

Are all the corrupted god players people struggling to make ends meet? This guy, that punk, Yamamoto-san...all the corrupted gods can trade in points for money.

If this was a coincidence, it was a big one. But then again, *I* struggled with money, and I was on the side of the major gods. Maybe finances weren't the only factor.

"I understand you need cash, but I'm not going to just hand over this book or the girl. They're both irreplaceable to me."

"In the business, this is what we call a breakdown of negotiations. It's a shame, but I suppose I have no choice but to give up. Please do be sure to contact me if you change your mind. I'll put my card here." The man placed his business card down on the floor before turning to leave the carriage.

Was that really all he wanted?

The man paused just before opening the door. "I'll be going now. Contact me if you manage to survive long enough."

With those sinister words, he was gone.

I cautiously picked up the card. It was stamped with a company name and a phone number. His own name was scrawled on one side.

"Is it safe yet, Yoshio?" Carol looked up at me anxiously as she clung to my waist.

"We're done talking. I think it's probably okay now." His final words troubled me, but I was hoping the threat was empty. "Just remember, there are lots of bad people like that. Make sure you stay close, okay?"

"Okay!"

We went back to our seats. It was still quiet. The other passengers all remained asleep. A wave of drowsiness crashed over me, but I would be an idiot to give in to it. I needed to stay awake, at least until we got to Hokkaido.

"Yoshio? Yoshio, I'm hungry." Carol looked up at me, her face flushed as her stomach let out a little gurgle.

"Right, it's past lunchtime. Shall we have our lunch boxes?" I tried to sound as normal as possible.

"Yeah!"

Fighting on an empty stomach was impossible. We dug into our lunches together.

THE NPCs IN THIS VILLAGE SIM GAME MUST BE REAL! ↵

chapter 06 A Dream Come True and My Faith

"**I** THINK WE'VE DONE ENOUGH here to get by," remarked a pretty girl with long brown hair. She wore a robe reminiscent of a priestess, which at one time had been white. She'd look like she belonged in a church, were it not for her dirty clothes and the rubble in her arms.

"Yes. This area is basically clear." Next to the girl stood a young woman with her gorgeous black hair tied back. She wiped sweat from her brow. As an elf, her features were androgynous, but I knew she was female.

"Why don't we take a break?" a man called from where he was repairing the log fence around the cave. His face and arms were covered in scars, and while his behavior was aloof, he had a kind heart.

"Yes, we should. The holes in the fence have been covered. We don't need to worry about monsters from outside anymore," said the younger girl.

"I'm just glad the watchtower survived, though it's a shame we lost the horses."

The remains of several buildings surrounded the cave, their foundations all that was left. One had housed one of the cave's couples, and the other was a stable, although there was no way to tell anymore. By some miracle, the watchtower remained unscathed.

The three of them sat down on some logs they were using for repairs, where they were joined by two others.

"Hello, Kan, Lan. Are you going to take a rest with us?"

"Yes."

"We will."

As usual, they didn't say much. The two of them lay down on the bare earth. They were both beastmen with the appearance of red pandas. A couple, they were also skilled carpenters. Normally clean, bath-loving creatures, their fur was currently so filthy that it was hard to tell what color it was, a testament to how hard they were working to repair the village.

"I'll go and see if Rodice and Lyra wish to join us." The girl was about to stand up when her brother caught hold of her hand.

"No, leave them be. We shouldn't crowd them."

"Oh...you're right. Do you think I made the right choice sending Carol to the Lord?"

Her brother took her by the shoulders and pulled her into his embrace. She closed her eyes and leaned into him.

"We didn't know we'd survive back then. You did the right thing," the elf said quietly, approaching the siblings.

"Thank you, Murus."

The two beastmen nodded their agreement. The group surveyed their damaged cave, where a couple was busy working on the repairs in silence. One of them was an ex-merchant. Formerly timid and weak-willed, he now wore a stony expression as he collected tools that could no longer be used. His wife worked as close to him as she could. She was the woman who gave confidence and support to the villagers. Their faces were dull and expressionless as they toiled.

"You should rest a while, Lyra."

"So should you."

Though clearly worried about each other, their voices lacked energy. It was easy to tell that they were grieving and anxious about their daughter. They wanted her to know that they were safe, but they had no way to send that message.

"Lyra. Please believe that we'll see Carol again. The Lord is just taking care of her for a while."

"Dear...even if she's made it to where the Lord is, how would she come back? I don't think we'll ever see her again." Tears sprang to the mother's eyes, and her husband ran to hold her tightly.

"We *will* see her again. The Lord must be watching over us, even now. We must have faith. Everything's going to be okay."

It was usually his wife who comforted him, but at times like this, he was very capable of stepping up to the plate.

Wait for me. I promise I'll send Carol home to you safe and sound.

"I knew it was just a dream."

When I opened my eyes, the villagers were gone, and I was back on the bullet train. It was nothing but a vision created from my own wishful thinking. Still, the joy of seeing my villagers again after so long flooded through me.

"I don't have any time to relax." I straightened up, attempting to clear my head.

I hadn't meant to doze off, but my full stomach and mental strain won over. I checked my phone. It was just after lunch.

"I slept for twenty minutes, huh?"

Carol was leaning against me, sound asleep. The holy book was still safely in my pocket, but I still kicked myself for being stupid. Now was the time to stay on guard.

At least no one seemed to have tried anything while I was asleep, even though that guy could easily have come back and just taken the book from me. Maybe he really *was* backing off. I wanted to believe it, but he didn't seem particularly trustworthy. Maybe some other factor prevented him from coming back.

I was staring at the floor in thought when Destiny poked its head out from Carol's backpack. It met my eyes squarely.

"Were you watching over us?"

It didn't respond. Either way, I was just glad we were safe. Anxiety no longer clouding my mind, I checked the situation around us. The deathly silence from before I fell asleep was gone. The passengers were talking again.

"I guess whatever miracle he used on them wore off."

Assuming that's what it was, I had to add "surprise narcolepsy" to the businessman's powers. Although he could have an accomplice.

Now that they're awake, we should be a little safer.

I allowed a small wave of relief to wash over me, even as I resolved not to fall back asleep.

After a long, long train ride, we finally arrived. We changed to a local train at the bullet train's final stop and rode that for just over an hour. Only then did we take our first steps into Hokkaido.

"Yoshio, look! Everywhere is white! Whoa! And it's so cold!" Carol raced around in front of the station as I stood there shivering.

I guess this is why they say kids belong in the outdoors.

My face was too frozen to give her a proper smile, but I managed a stiff grin.

"It's so cold it hurts." The words left my mouth as white mist. We wandered around the station for a while before stepping outside, where I had my first experience of truly frozen temperatures.

The station itself was a new building and very clean. The surrounding area was lively and flourishing. It was a far more impressive station than the one back at home.

A large plaza and traffic circle stood just in front of the station, all of it blanketed in snow. The word "beautiful" crossed my mind for a split second, before the frigid wind blew it away. My hometown could get cold, but it was nothing compared to Hokkaido. I'd barely gone outside these past ten years, and I wasn't used to any sort of weather at all. The cold wind was relentless in its assault on me, uncaring of my sensitivities.

"Let's go back inside the station."

"What? We just got out here!"

"We've got a lot of preparations to make."

"Okay..."

Carol was very obedient and rarely threw tantrums, making this trip a whole lot easier than it might've been. I thought back to my young cousin and how badly he behaved. He'd go through people's fridges when he was visiting, eat loudly at mealtimes, and refuse to even try anything he didn't like. He was such a little monster that even Dad snapped and told his sister not to bring him around anymore. He called the kid "a little monkey". Compared to him, Carol was an angel. I was really impressed at Rodice and Lyra's parenting skills.

We went into a station café and sat down at a table in the corner. I ordered us hot drinks, cake, and fried food. The cake was for Carol, and the fried stuff was for me.

"You okay, Destiny?" I gently unzipped Carol's bear backpack on the seat next to us. Destiny was inside, curled around a disposable hand warmer. I took the breadcrumb coating off the fried food and passed it the meat. It grabbed it with both front claws and sunk its teeth in eagerly. It was keeping that hand warmer close. It must have been sensitive to the cold like normal lizards. "Use the warmer as much as you need to, okay?"

Destiny nodded tiredly. It looked a little fragile, so I took a towel out of my own bag to wrap it up in. Hopefully that would keep in some heat. It had a stack of hand warmers; it could use as many as it needed. I'd taught it how to activate them before we left, and it could use them on its own. A journey with a little girl and a lizard could have been a nightmare, but they were both smart enough to greatly simplify the process.

I pulled out my phone in case I got a call. I'd contacted my boss at the cleaning company to let him know I was in Hokkaido, and he'd told me that work shouldn't be too busy even when they opened back up again on the 5th. I could relax and enjoy myself for a bit. I'd asked about Yamamoto-san, and the boss told me they bumped into each other at the shrine. Apparently, Yamamoto-san was strangely cheerful and incredibly eager to get back to work. His enthusiasm was partly why the boss was okay with letting me kick around Hokkaido for a bit. I was both relieved and a little disheartened to hear that I wasn't needed.

"Maybe I'm turning into a corporate drone..."

Anyone who worked a full-time job would punch me if they heard that. We drank our warm tea and rested for a bit, Carol blissfully stuffing cake into her mouth and getting cream on her cheeks in the process. I wiped her face with a handkerchief as she squirmed, embarrassed. It made me chuckle. I wondered what an outsider would think if they saw us together. She was a cute, golden-haired girl, and I was just a dull thirty-year-old. Since Carol seemed happy, most people wouldn't be suspicious, but no one could deny that we were mismatched. What if the police questioned me about our relationship? It was unlikely, but what if someone thought I'd kidnapped her? I was trying to come up with a solution to the imagined situation when I noticed something in my phone's log.

"Whoa, so many missed calls. Who are they—oh."

I had missed calls from Mom, Dad, Sayuki, and Seika. Messages, too. I still wasn't used to using a smartphone, and I often forgot to check the notifications.

When I'd told my family I was going to Hokkaido yesterday, Mom and Sayuki badgered me about it. They were probably checking up on me. It would take too long to phone everyone now, so I typed up one message to send to my family and Seika together.

"I've made it to Hokkaido, and I'm heading for the village now."

They knew I was going to Hokkaido, but they didn't know it was to visit a game studio. I also asked Seika not to tell my family about Carol. She agreed, though I didn't know if that was because she believed me when I said I didn't want to put up with a lot of questions or whether she sensed that there was something more going on behind the scenes.

Destiny was my second problem. As soon as my family was home, they'd notice it wasn't in its tank. I knew they'd question me on it, so I had to come up with some excuse.

"Destiny was looking a little unwell, so the villagers asked me to bring it along so they can take a look."

That doubled as an excuse for me leaving for Hokkaido so suddenly. Dad and Seika understood immediately, being big Destiny fans themselves. I wanted to send Destiny back to the other world along with Carol, and I'm sure those two wouldn't be happy. Thinking about it made me depressed. I took a sip of my tea to redirect my thoughts.

The most pressing matter was our next move. We'd made it to Hokkaido, but the developers' building was much farther out. Hokkaido was as big as the distance between Tokyo and Osaka. We'd only made it to the right prefecture.

The most direct route would mean taking a taxi, but that would raise our transport costs even higher. We still needed a place to stay and money for the return journey, and I didn't want to spend too much more than I already had.

The studio was in a small town I'd never heard of. It would take a lot of changes on trains and buses to get there, which raised the risk of connections being canceled or thrown off schedule by heavy snowfall. The weather forecast wasn't predicting anything right now, but that could change.

I checked the bus schedule. The one we needed arrived in twenty-five minutes. Though the skies were clear, it was unbearably cold outside. We'd stay in the warmth of the station until the last moment.

"Yoshio, are we going in one of those horseless carriages again? Um, a...car?"

Her pronunciation of "car" sounded a little off. She must have attempted to say it in Japanese. We were watching TV yesterday, and I explained to her about cars, which had to have been where she learned it.

"That's right. We're going on a big car. It's called a bus. It'll be a while until it arrives, so let's wait here until then."

"Um, Yoshio, can we wait outside? I wanna see more of the snow," she asked me sweetly, tilting her head to one side.

I couldn't say no when she was looking at me like *that*.

"It's really cold outside," I warned her.

"I know, but I wanna make a snowdoll!"

A snowdoll must have been what they called snowmen in the other world.

When was the last time I made a snowman? Probably when I was in junior high. With this much snow, you could create a whole snow village.

"Okay then. Let's play in the snow until the bus comes."

"Yay! I love you, Yoshio!" Carol cheered, throwing herself at me.

Sayuki used to do that, too—clinging to me and calling "Oniichan! Oniichan!" Of course, there was no way she'd do anything like that nowadays.

I followed Carol as she dashed out of the station.

"It's *freezing*!"

I'd prepared myself, but I still wanted to turn right back around. My nose stung, and my breath came out as white smoke. I followed Carol as best I could on my shivering legs. She was running around happily on top of the snow.

"It'd be nice to be a kid again." I sounded like a middle-aged man, but I truly meant it.

"Wanna make a snowdoll together?" Carol ran up to me, grabbed my hand, and dragged me out into the plaza.

Welp, it'll be better to move around with her than to stand still and freeze to death, I thought, hyping myself up to play with her.

"Take this!" Carol giggled, throwing a snowball at me.

"Ah! Nice hit!" I tossed one back at her underhanded.

Carol jumped behind our snowdoll to dodge and restock her ammo. We still had time after making our masterpiece, so we were having a snowball fight and playing tag until the bus arrived. A year ago, I would've run out of energy after three minutes, but my physical job had built up my endurance. Carol was a kid, meaning she never got tired. I was trying to channel my inner child and keep up with her, but it wasn't long before I started to drag.

"Truce, Carol," I gasped. "The bus'll be here soon."

"Okay!"

I brushed snow off her, pausing to open up the zipper on her backpack. Destiny was wrapped in two towels and clinging to three hand warmers at once. It looked cold.

"You okay?" I asked softly.

It blinked twice in response before rummaging around deeper in the backpack, pulling out another hand warmer, deftly opening the packaging, and activating it with its hands. It curled up into a ball with its back to me, holding the hand warmer carefully to its body.

Looks like it's doing okay for now.

"Let us know if it gets too bad."

It turned its head back to me and nodded.

I looked up at the sky. It had become overcast, like it was about to snow. If it did, it would only get colder.

I checked the big clock on the station wall. The bus was due in five minutes. Time to start lining up for it. I looked over at our stop to see there was already a bus waiting. There weren't any other passengers about—they probably got on already. If we missed this bus, it would be nearly an hour until the next one, so I took Carol's hand and led her toward it at a jog. My legs seemed to get gradually heavier as we went, and soon they stopped moving all together.

"What's wrong, Yoshio? Aren't we getting on the bus?"

"Um, yeah..."

We needed to get on that bus and make it to our next destination before the weather took a turn for the worse. So why weren't my legs moving? Was it instinct? Looking at that bus was making me uneasy. Something was off.

The bus doors were closed. Why wasn't anyone waiting to get on? This was a bus stop at a big station; there should have been a lot of passengers who needed to go in this direction. Had they really all continued their journeys by car or train? Were we the only ones planning to take this bus? Maybe I was just paranoid at this point, but I couldn't shake the feeling. The bus aside, the fact that Carol and I were alone in the plaza was weird in itself.

"Yoshio? The bus."

I put a comforting hand on Carol's head and told her to wait a second. The bus was due to depart in less than three minutes. Our bodies had warmed up while we played, but I felt completely frozen now. Any longer out here and we'd risk catching a cold. I needed to make a decision.

I pulled out my phone to check alternate routes. This bus was the fastest no matter how you cut it. I put my phone away and looked back toward the station. There were several people inside, but none of them were coming out. This was the front entrance, but everyone seemed to be making use of the other exits instead, which were farther away.

"We're going back inside the station for now, Carol."

"O-okay."

Carol followed me obediently, but she was clearly confused. I couldn't blame her. The decision whether to take a bus shouldn't have been this big a deal.

Just as we were about to go into the station again, I realized the glass door was gone, replaced with a concrete wall. We'd used that door less than half an hour ago. I couldn't have forgotten its position. It *should* be here.

"Where's the door gone?"

Carol remembered it being here, too. I took her tightly by the hand, turned around, and called out the name from the business card I'd picked up on the bullet train.

"Why don't you show yourself, Habatake-san?"

THE NPCs IN THIS VILLAGE SIM GAME MUST BE REAL! ↵

chapter 07 An Unavoidable Fight and My Courage

"LOOKS LIKE YOU GOT ME again." The unremarkable salary-man from the train stepped out of the bus. Habatake. He was a sneak, but apparently he was sportsmanlike enough to admit when he was caught.

"That bus is another illusion, right? What is it underneath, a minivan or something?"

"Right again! My, nothing gets past you, does it?" He snapped his fingers, and the bus was replaced with a van.

It looked just like the white van we used at my job, with curtains drawn across its windows. If someone else was hiding in there, I couldn't tell. This was clearly the same trick he'd used to make himself look like a goblin.

"Did you use your illusions to trick the people inside the station so they wouldn't come out here?"

"Yes, that's right."

That meant he could have at least two illusions active at a time.

"You're not working alone, are you?"

"Oh? What makes you think that? I'm very interested in your reasoning."

Was that sarcasm? Despite his polite tone, he was obviously mocking me. It was beginning to grate on my nerves.

"You can't use miracles directly to harm another player, so you need a way to get around that rule. Getting me to voluntarily walk onto a disguised bus would just toe the line of acceptable. This must be the sort of twisted gambling you're so hyped about."

"I see, I see. Please, do go on." Habatake nodded mockingly.

"You planned to drop the illusion and have your accomplice grab us from inside the bus once we were close enough, weren't you?"

"Oh, I am impressed! You're smart for a shut-in. To think I thought you'd never amount to anything."

He really is trying to rile me up. Joke's on him. I never thought I'd amount to anything either.

The snow was getting heavier, but I barely felt the cold. My anger and the heat of Carol clinging to me kept me warm.

"But how did you know the bus was a fake? I thought I did a pretty good job with it."

He was right. Put it beside a real bus, and I wouldn't have been able to tell the difference. But he didn't factor in the snow. Because the bus was really a small van, the snow seemed to disappear through the roof as it fell. Without that, I would have fallen for it.

A few minutes ago, after checking our route options on my phone, I'd activated the weather miracle to make it snow. I was level 2 now—I could perform miracles in the real world as well.

"What now? You wanna negotiate again?" I smirked, trying to act tough. I couldn't afford to show any weakness and worry Carol. Besides, we had a trump card. I glanced down at Carol's backpack. A tiny hand poked out of a gap in the zipper, giving me a confident thumbs-up. Destiny really was a reliable ally.

"No. Our negotiations already broke down. Even if I offered you a better deal, you wouldn't take it, would you?"

"That's right."

"You're correct, I can't harm you directly. That was why I had no choice but to enlist some help, much as I didn't want to." Habatake sighed and raised his left hand.

Three men emerged from the minivan. They all had brown-dyed hair, flashy clothes, and grins on their faces. To sum them up in one word, they looked dim. They seemed very similar to the guys Yoshinaga sent after me. If Habatake was telling the truth, these men weren't players. That came with its own set of problems.

"You're not allowed to tell outsiders about the game."

"Correct. I just said I had a little job for them. Get me the book and the girl, and I'd reward them handsomely. That girl doesn't even have a nationality. Kidnapping her won't technically be a crime."

So they were just a group of paid toughs. And since there were no miracles involved, it wouldn't be against the rules for these men to harm me. Maybe the curtains in the van were less for hiding them from me and more so that they wouldn't witness the illusions.

"Hey, you're making it sound so bad! We're just here to take that book back, which you borrowed from a friend. And you said that girl was your daughter, right?" One of the toughs grinned, but it was obvious he didn't believe the story Habatake fed them. He knew he was abetting a crime.

"Ah yes, sorry," Habatake said. "That's right. Now, I'm going to give you one final chance to negotiate. Would you kindly pass me the book and the girl? I won't be paying you anything, of course."

This stingy bastard. Though obviously he could offer me any amount of money and I'd never give him what he wanted.

I held Carol closer to me. "No way in hell."

Habatake shrugged and smiled. "I didn't think so. Please accept my sincerest apologies. Gentlemen?"

"Yes, sir!"

The three toughs slowly approached. I knew what I had to do. I plunged my hand into Carol's backpack and pulled out the towel-wrapped Destiny. I held it out in front of me.

"Don't move," I warned. "I'm not about to pull any punches."

One of the toughs screwed up his nose. "What's that gross-looking lizard thing?"

Destiny lashed its tail threateningly. It didn't like being insulted one bit.

"What, you think we're scared of a little reptile?"

"You know they taste great if you skin and fry 'em!"

"Or we could sell it to a pet store—make some money."

The toughs didn't slow their approach or show any fear. That was fine by me, especially since they were downwind of us.

"Use your poison breath to—"

"Spread out, boys! That man has a spray that can paralyze you!" Habatake called out.

The toughs immediately kept their distance and began to surround me in a semicircle.

He knows about Destiny?! Was he watching me fight against that punk?

"You got some sort of spray? And you think we're the criminals?"

"I'm nothing like you!" I shouted.

Destiny's breath would only hit one of them if they were spread out like this, and which one depended on the wind's direction.

"You might wanna look out in front of you!" One of the toughs jumped at me from around the side, having closed the gap between us as I was thinking.

I turned my back to him quickly to protect Carol from his strike.

"Your back's wide open! Now—Hey! I can't move!"

I spun around to see the tough frozen mid-run from the neck down. Meanwhile, Destiny was clinging on to my front with its head resting on my shoulder. But its petrifying gaze only worked on one person at a time, so while one tough was dealt with, the other two were still threats.

"What the hell? I thought this guy was some good-for-nothing NEET! You lied to us, old man!"

"How the hell is he frozen like that?!"

The two other toughs backed away when they saw their friend go still as a statue. Anyone with any common sense would do the same. Maybe I was the strange one for accepting that Destiny could just do something like this.

Now's our chance. If I step up the intimidation, they should lose the will to fight.

"Come at me. Your friend seems to be having fun." I beckoned to them, and they began to back away slowly.

"Forget about the girl! I'll pay triple to whoever can get that book first!" Habatake cried.

You really didn't need to do that...

The toughs exchanged a glance and nodded before coming to surround me from either side. They just saw me use a superpower, and they were still willing to risk it for the money.

I guess money really is all-powerful!

"Gack! My eyes! My throat!" The tough to my left choked, taking a face full of Destiny's poison breath.

That left only one to deal with, but it would take too long to unparalyze the first tough and then freeze this guy. He was right on top of us.

"Take this!"

As I faltered, Carol leapt forward and clung to the man's leg.

"Get off me, kid! I don't need you anymore!" The man raised his fist to bring it down on Carol's head.

"Don't you dare touch her!" I kicked out at the man's side as hard as I could.

Carol had his full attention—he didn't see me coming. My foot collided with him, and he bent over double and went flying. I rushed over to Carol and grabbed her shoulders.

"Are you okay? You're not hurt?"

"I-I'm okay. Thanks, Yoshio."

I checked her over and let out a sigh of relief. "Thank goodness. Don't do anything like that again, okay?"

"I'm sorry."

I gave her a hug. She was trembling. That must have been terrifying—going up against a grown man—but she'd done it. For me.

Thanks, Carol.

"Oh, my! You've downed all three of them! I suppose that's what I get for hiring those sorts. This is troublesome indeed." Despite his words, Habatake looked perfectly calm.

I just defeated his men, but he didn't seem bothered at all. Did he have another trick up his sleeve?

"Would you mind helping me out now?"

"Guess I've got no choice, huh?"

Someone else stepped out of the minivan. I gasped.

His golden hair was gelled into spikes, and his jeans were full of holes.

"You again?"

"Hey. Nice to see ya." It was the punk who attacked me in the park near the shrine. "Y'look like you've seen a ghost. What, you weren't expectin' me to make it out of the mess you put me in?"

Before I could stop myself, I shook my head.

"Okay, well what if I said that phone was my spare and that the screen you saw on it was just an illusion?"

Oh.

I glanced at Habatake, who grinned and gave me an enthusiastic thumbs-up. I wasn't sure I'd ever met anyone more annoying.

"You two were working together even back then?"

"That's right," Habatake said. "You can't make a move without knowing your opponent and how big a threat they pose."

The punk laughed. "I had you fooled, right?"

His panic in the park was just an act. *This guy should quit his band and become an actor.*

"What do you mean 'fooled'?" said Habatake. "You're the one who went off alone after agreeing we'd work together, and you let a lizard turn the tables on you. You didn't even know about the illusion I placed on your phone! It was supposed to be a safety measure, just in case."

"I thought you said you wouldn't tell 'im..."

Apparently, he wasn't a very good actor after all. If Habatake was with him when he attacked me by the shrine, things could've been a lot worse.

Even with all this new information, the situation remained unchanged. This just meant I had another enemy to deal with.

"Enough chitchat for now. Are you ready to help me out?"

"Sure. C'mon, do your thing." The punk pressed some buttons on his phone. The poisoned tough and the one I kicked stood up straight. "These guys are weak, so I can control them easy. Poisoning this one with your lizard was a waste of time!"

They knew all about Destiny's powers, which put me in a tough spot. They'd probably already planned this under Habatake's direction. I could still get Destiny to use its poison breath on the punk, but he was keeping his distance. He knew I'd try it. He did his best to stay upwind.

I could tell Destiny to release its petrification on the tough and use it on the punk instead, but there was no guarantee that would interrupt his miracle. Plus, I'd have a whole other tough to deal with. The only conceivable option was to get out of here. Fast.

"Carol. When I give the signal, we're gonna run as fast as we can, okay?" I whispered in her ear.

"Okay." She gave a small nod.

"Oh, I probably should have mentioned that trying to run is a waste of time. Turn around and see for yourself." Habatake pointed behind me.

I glanced over my shoulder as quickly as I dared, scared it might be an attempt to distract me. There were two men in overalls holding signs that read "Do Not Enter."

"They were blocking the road to prevent any innocent people from wandering over, but I called them in as backup. I always do try to have all my bases covered. Did you know that phrase comes from baseball?"

I didn't care about the etymology of his idiom, but that did explain why he was so calm.

Is there nothing else I can do?

In front of me were the three toughs, one petrified and two under the punk's control. Behind and to the right of them were Habatake and the punk himself. Directly behind me were the two men in overalls. The station was to our right, but there was quite a distance between it and us. The bus lane was to our left, but that wasn't very close either. I couldn't see anyone else outside apart from us, probably because of the snow (which was no longer influenced by my miracle).

"Do be kind and give up now, please. We'll be taking the book and the girl."

"Go get 'em." At the punk's order, the two toughs began to walk towards us, their eyes void of emotion. Worse still, they were upwind.

What do I do now? Use Destiny's gaze on one and wait till the other is close enough to be affected by its poison? I'll need to hold my own breath. It's risky, but I've got no other choice!

I exchanged a glance with Destiny, whispering my instructions. It nodded. The toughs kept approaching one step after another. Two more steps, and we'd attack.

The men disappeared, suddenly knocked aside by the figure of a woman soaring past us, leg outstretched in a flying kick.

"Huh?"

I didn't know if it was me, Habatake, or the punk who said that. They were as surprised as I was, standing stock-still as though time itself had stopped. This was more than unexpected. Who was this person?

Her bangs were cut perfectly straight, and she wore a neat skirt-suit. The slender legs that stretched out from under it were clad in black tights. She looked around the same age as Sayuki: early twenties.

"Hey! You're still reeling after seeing how great my legs look, right?" She smiled at me and winked.

She must've had nerves of steel if she could say something like that at a time like this.

"Who are you?" I asked.

She was on my side, right? I mean, she did just save me.

"I'll explain later! But I'm on the side of the major gods! Now let's get out of here!"

Right. It's not important who she is right now. I can ask her more about herself once we're far away from these guys!

"You had allies working with you, too? I suppose I was foolish to assume you didn't. You just don't look like the type to have many friends."

Habatake was free to wax lyrical about how he suddenly understood the situation, but I wished he'd lay off.

Even if we were in a better situation now, we were still up against Habatake, the punk, three zombie toughs, and two workers. One of those toughs was still petrified. The two that the woman had kicked down were slowly getting up again. Two against seven was better than one against seven, but it still wasn't great.

"I dunno who you are, but you sure are a pain in the ass. Get her, boys! She's in the way!" At the punk's orders, the two toughs went for the woman.

"You two, don't just stand there! Do something!" Habatake shouted at the men in overalls, who started moving almost un-willingly towards us. It looked like he didn't have much of a hold on them.

I stepped in front of the mysterious woman and faced the zombified toughs. Her kick was impressive, but I couldn't just stand back and let her do all my fighting for me.

"Ooh, you're protecting me? Who said chivalry is dead?"

"I've lived without pride for so long. I'd like to get some of it back."

I almost took a step back when one of the toughs pulled out a penknife, but I managed to hold my ground.

How many times have I been threatened with weapons now? Come on, guys...

I always thought of the other world as way more dangerous than this one, but violence definitely existed here, too.

I exchanged a glance with Destiny, who was at my feet and glaring at the toughs. We both nodded, like we knew what the other was thinking.

"It's all or nothing now! You—" I raised my voice, trying to intimidate the enemy.

The sudden arrival of a car cut me off. It drove off the road and hurtled across the plaza in a streak of white, right toward us.

"Hey, Senpai! I'm here to rescue you! Aren't you happy to see my pretty face?"

A tanned, blonde girl stuck her head out of the driver's side window. Despite her juvenile choice in makeup, she seemed to be an adult.

The car skidded sideways before coming to a stop right beside us, with only a few inches between me and the bumper.

Talk about cutting it close.

"Nice timing! Come on, Yoshio-kun, Carol-chan!" The woman opened the rear door and hurried us in.

The phrase "the enemy of my enemy is my friend" flashed through my brain. I hoped it was true.

"Get in, Carol!"

"Okay!"

Destiny and I jumped in after Carol, and the second we were inside, the car sped off. Snow blew up around us as we narrowly dodged past Habatake and the punk. They were getting over their shock, but it was too late. They just yelled after us from the sideview mirror.

"We're getting the hell outta here!" said the driver.

"I won't say anything about your speeding just this once, since we need to shake them off." The woman spoke animatedly in the front seat as the car sped onto the main road. I turned around to see a white shape behind us, tiny but getting bigger. It was Habatake's minivan.

"They're coming after us!"

"Oh shit, they are! They're serious, huh?" The driver twisted her body to see out the back window.

The woman in the suit yanked her back into the driver's seat. "Keep your eyes on the road, for goodness' sake!"

I glanced at the speedometer. We were doing more than sixty miles per hour, which meant the van was going even faster than that.

"They're being reckless, considering these roads in the winter."

"D'you think they might be locals, Senpai?"

The women didn't seem concerned about the approaching van. They were an unlikely pair, one in a sober suit and the other dressed casually but fashionably. I had a ton of questions for them, but that could wait until we were out of this mess.

"I'm gonna move this to the highway. Don't want any civilians getting in an accident 'cause of us."

"Good thinking. The highway around here is always empty."

I didn't know the geography of this place, so I was no help. I just focused on keeping Carol occupied. She had her face pressed against the window, captivated by the view.

She was beaming. "Yoshio! The outside is going by so fast!"

Guess I didn't need to worry about her. I thought she'd be scared, but she seemed to be enjoying herself. I leaned over to buckle up her seat belt.

Our other passenger was splayed over the headrest, a serious gaze fixed on the approaching van. Destiny and I narrowed our eyes and focused on the scene. The punk was driving with Habatake in the passenger seat. I couldn't tell if the rest of the guys were in there, too.

"We haven't introduced ourselves yet, right? Yoshio-kun?"

I turned at the sound of my name.

"I'm Sewatari Seri," said the woman in the suit. "I'm on the side of the major gods. I play a god who governs fortune."

She played a god of fortune? Sounded like she might be related to the God of Fate.

"I'll go next," said the girl in makeup. "What's up, I'm on the major gods' side, too. I work with Senpai, and I play the God of Na—"

Sewatari-san coughed suddenly, cutting her off.

Was she about to say something she shouldn't? Something against the rules?

"I'm a hot girl who likes to chill! My name's Nattyan! Nice to meetcha!"

I didn't know if I would call her hot. And since she was driving, she had to be at least eighteen—more a woman than a girl. I didn't say any of that out loud, of course.

"I'm Carol! This is Yoshio! And this is Destiny!"

I was about to introduce myself when Carol did it for me. Destiny waved its tail amicably from Carol's arms as she held it up.

"You really are adorable, Carol-chan. Would you like to be my daughter?"

"You love little girls like her huh, Senpai? Kinda creepy."

"No, it isn't! There's nothing more precious than the innocence of a little girl!"

Sewatari-san's response was so passionate that I resolved to keep Carol away from her. Just to be safe.

Still, this conversation told me one thing: Carol could understand them. Otherwise, she wouldn't have known to make an introduction after they made theirs. So they weren't lying about playing the game.

"I'd love to explain properly, but we should really do something about our predicament first. Don't they know that clingy men are unattractive?" Sewatari-san looked behind us in disgust.

"I dunno," Nattyan said. "I kinda like it when a man knows what he wants."

I glanced behind us. The minivan was even closer than before. As we were talking, we'd sped out of town and onto a long, straight road that cut through wide fields of snow. It was impossible to tell whether the fields were farmland or simply empty wilderness.

I'd seen long roads like this stretching out toward the horizon on TV before, but the actual sight was so much more impressive that I was at a loss. It wasn't just me; Carol had her face glued to the window again, captivated by our snowy surroundings. It was like our car was racing through a world made entirely of white. A fairy tale.

"It's beautiful, right? Even though there's nothing here. It'd be great if we could slow down, and you could really take the time to—"

Sewatari-san's words were drowned out by the sound of a horn behind us. The van was so close now that I could clearly see the faces of the men in the front seats.

"They're not gonna try an' ram us, right? You've still gotta pay this car off!"

"I've only had it for two years," Sewatari-san said. "I don't think they'll be that reckless. They're not allowed to harm another player directly. Hence all the underhanded methods."

Ramming into us had to be against the rules. Did that mean we were safe so long as we kept driving?

"We can't let 'em keep following us like this."

"Nope. We need to shake them off, but I'm not sure where to start."

The rules worked both ways, unfortunately. We couldn't harm them directly either. But there was *someone* who could.

Destiny was still staring out the back. Noticing my gaze, it turned and looked at me with its big, round eyes. Destiny's powers didn't count as miracles, so they were the only thing that could get us out of this mess. I ran through our options in my head, trying to come up with the best one.

"Um, Nattyan-san? Do you think you could slow down a little?"

"Just Nattyan's fine. Sure, I could slow down, but they'll catch us!"

"That's why I'm asking."

It sounded like an absurd request, but I bowed my head as deeply as I could, hoping I seemed like I knew what I was doing.

"Hey! You got guts, you're kind, *and* you're humble! I like that! Funny, 'cause you look super plain on the outside."

Was she trying to praise me or insult me?

"Yes! Yoshio-kun gets this really cool glint in his eye when he's made up his mind about something." Sewatari-san sounded almost proud, like she already knew me, but I couldn't remember ever meeting her.

"Okay! Whatever you say, Yoshiocchi! How slow should I go?"

"Well, the satnav says there's a big curve coming up. Do you think you could drop to twenty miles per hour just before we reach it?"

"Easy peasy! I do that kinda stuff all the time in games!"

That wasn't particularly encouraging, but I had no choice but to trust her. Now I just needed to make sure Destiny and I were on the same page.

THE NPCs IN THIS VILLAGE SIM GAME MUST BE REAL! ↵

chapter 08 A Battle and the Truth

THE ROAD STRETCHED on and on in a single line. We were approaching the curve, and the oncoming lane looked clear. That meant nobody would get caught up in this if it all went wrong. No buildings lined the road, only trees. This place was perfect for this maneuver.

Habatake's van was so close now that I could read their expressions, but they were maintaining their distance, clearly not keen on actually colliding with us.

"Nattyan-san! Now!"

"I told you just Nattyan is fine!"

I felt my body rocket forward as she slammed on the brakes. Only my seat belt kept me in place. Behind us, panic flared on the faces of Habatake and the punk. They were forced to stop suddenly, sending the van into a skid.

Once they'd slowed enough, I held Destiny up, careful to make sure our followers could see it clearly.

"The front tire."

Destiny glared at one of the front tires and turned the rubber to stone in an instant. The van had braked suddenly on an icy road, and now one of its tires was a rock. It skidded sideways, sliding out of view. Unable to turn the corner, it was flung toward one of the snowy fields, landing on its side in a snowbank.

"You just can't be so rough on the steering wheel on an icy road like this," Nattyan sighed, glancing at her rearview mirror.

I could have had Destiny turn their tire to stone at any time, but it would have been too dangerous when they were going over sixty mph. At the very best they would've been heavily injured, dead at worst. They were incredibly troublesome, but actively murdering them would be going too far. Yamamoto-san had tried to kill me, but I didn't sense that the punk was prepared to do that.

"They won't be back on the road for a while now. Nice one, Yoshio."

"Oh, it's all thanks to Nattyan-sa—Nattyan." A mild glare reminded me to drop the honorific halfway.

Now we could pull ahead and buy ourselves some time. As the tension drained from my body, I slumped back against the seat and let out a deep sigh.

"Nice work, both of you. Now we can talk properly." Sewatari-san turned in the passenger seat and smiled at me. "Allow us to introduce ourselves again. I'm Sewatari Seri. I play the God of Fortune."

"Name's Nattyan. I play a good god, too, but I'm not gonna tell you which one just yet. It'll make things more fun. I work at the same company as Senpai here."

Sewatari-san was the woman in the suit with the straight bangs. The tanned one with the interesting fashion sense was Nattyan. Despite their introductions, I could still barely believe they worked at the same company. Sewatari-san was dressed like your standard, serious office lady, while Nattyan barely looked like she could hold down a job at all. Maybe she just liked to dress flashy on her days off and she dressed more conservatively at work.

"We'll introduce ourselves again too, then."

"Don't worry about that. You're Suenaga Yoshio-kun, you're Carol-chan, and your peculiar lizard is Destiny-chan. Can I call it Deedee for short?"

Most people would be surprised at Destiny's thorny skin and huge size, but Sewatari-san took it in stride as she stroked the basilisk's head.

"Hey, no fair, Senpai! I wanna pet it, too!"

"You're driving. Pet later."

They made an unlikely pair, but their rapport was undeniable. Just listening to them calmed me down. I sat up straight and took a deep breath.

"Sewatari-san, I have a lot of questions for you."

In fact, I had nothing *but* questions, considering what just happened. The fact that they were players didn't explain how they showed up with such perfect timing. And what did they stand to gain by saving us?

"Right. I guess you're confused. It's as good a time as any, since it looks like Carol-chan is asleep."

I followed Sewatari-san's gentle gaze to find Carol snoozing next to me. We'd played a lot in the snow and then went through a car chase. She must've been so exhausted, both physically and mentally. Now she could finally rest. I laid her down against my thigh and gave her a gentle pat.

"You're good with kids," Sewatari-san remarked thoughtfully.

I shot her back a wry smile. "I used to take care of my younger sister a lot."

"Okay, then. Where shall I start? I'm guessing your biggest question is how we know who you are and why we came to rescue you."

She was right. I wanted to know that badly. I stilled the hand that was soothing Carol and waited for her explanation.

"I feel like it would be simpler just to start from the beginning." Her tone turned serious as she started to explain. "You and I both play *The Village of Fate*, Yoshio-kun. Don't you think that's strange?"

I wasn't expecting her to throw me a question right away, especially not one like that.

"Pardon me, but I don't really understand how it's strange."

"There's no need to be so formal. Not with either of us. And you can just call me Sewatari or Seri without an honorific. Let me put it another way. You play the God of Fate, and the game is called *The Village of Fate*. To you, that makes sense. But there are other players playing *The Village of Fate*, all of whom control different gods. Don't you think it's strange that the word 'fate' is used in the title in that case?"

"Well, at first I thought every player controlled a God of Fate, but now that you mention it, that is kinda weird."

The God of Fate watched over the Village of Fate. That always made sense to me. But now I knew there were other players who played gods under the God of Water or the God of Fire...

"You get it, right? You might think they picked the name *The Village of Fate* because it sounds cool, but there's actually a deeper meaning to it. The God of Fate is a minor god—a god ruled by a major god."

"Right, I know that." My villagers had mentioned it before.

"Good, that saves time. The God of Fate is the highest-ranking god among all the minor gods."

"Highest-ranking?"

"Minor gods have ranks. Ranks 1, 2, 3, 4, and 5. The lower ranks serve the higher ranks. It's like a company. The major gods are CEOs, and then the rank 1 minor gods are the managers, then come the department heads, section heads, subsection heads, and then the regular employees. Does that make it easier to understand?"

"Yeah, I think I get it." I didn't realize there was a hierarchy. I thought all minor gods were equal.

"Your God of Fate is a rank 1 god, and my God of Fortune is rank 2."

I could see Nattyan glancing at Sewatari constantly as she spoke to me from the passenger seat. Nattyan was grinning as though something amused her.

"I know there are lots of major gods. However, if you don't mind my asking...um, which one rules over the God of Fate?"

Sewatari frowned at me as I almost slipped into formal speech again, just like Nattyan did before. They were practically strangers to me, so to be honest, speaking to them casually was nerve-racking, especially since they were women. But if that was what they wanted, I had to try.

"The major gods are the God of Light, the God of Moonlight," I ticked them off on my fingers, "the God of Fire, the God of Water, the God of Plants, the God of Lightning, and the God of Earth, right? Which is the God of Fate's manager—uh, ruler?"

"The God of Moonlight. The moon is said to have a strong influence on life and destiny, so that's probably why."

I knew the moon played a big role in fortune-telling from Sayuki. She liked fortune-telling.

"I see. How do you know that, Sewatari-san?" I asked.

"Impatient men are unattractive! Don't interrupt me. And don't use -san."

Sayuki and Seika had told me off for this kinda thing in the past. I was supposed to leave all questions until the end of the lecture, apparently.

"When you level up in this game, you can do more stuff and get access to more perks. There are more miracles you can perform in real life, and the restrictions around them get more lax as your level goes up. When you get to level 5..." She paused and gave me a meaningful smile. "You can chat with the god you play directly. There's a catch, though. You can't post on the forums anymore once you get to level 5. You can still browse them, though."

So that was why there weren't any level 5 players on the forums. It wasn't that level 5 didn't exist, it was just that they couldn't post.

"At level 2, you can only see the forums restricted to other players of the God of Moonlight. The games for players under other major gods have different titles." Sewatari turned to Nattyan. "I think the players under the God of Fire play *Villagers of Burning Passion*, right?"

"That title's so cringey. Though I guess it fits for the God of Fire," Nattyan said, frowning.

"If you don't m—um, but I saw some players on the forum who looked like they were under the God of Water." No matter how much I told myself it was okay, it was exhausting to be casual with virtual strangers.

"They must be level 3 or over. Once you reach level 3, you can use boards assigned to other gods. But they're not allowed to tell people level 2 or under about that, so if they try, the post will be censored."

That was probably the kind of stuff they spoke about in the thread for players level 3 or over.

"By the way, players aren't supposed to talk to each other in real life, so think of this as an exception. As you've seen, there are certain corrupted god players who don't bother to follow that rule."

So corrupted gods had different rules, or their rules were laxer. In which case, the minor god players were at a disadvantage.

"What level are you, Sewatari? I've been wondering since we met."

I was fairly sure I already knew from our conversation, but I wanted to check with her.

Her eyes softened, and she grinned like she'd been waiting for me to ask. "What level do you think I am?"

"Level 5?"

"Exactly! Kinda boring that you got it on the first guess. I wanted to see you gasp when I told you that you were wrong, actually, I'm level 5!"

"Yeah," Nattyan pouted. "Why didn't you play along?"

Why was I getting criticized for giving the right answer?

"Apologies. Have you been playing for long?"

"Apologies?! You're being too formal *again*! Anyway, about two years."

I didn't know how long that was in the grand scheme of things, but it was longer than I'd been playing.

"Do you know when the game was first released? I got it when it was still in alpha, so I guess it's been in testing this whole time?"

Sewatari paused thoughtfully. "Going by the rumors on the forums, it's around ten years old at this point. There's no real evidence to back that up, though."

Ten years ago. Coincidentally, that was the same time I became a shut-in. Ten years was a long time to be running an online game. It was also an absurdly long alpha test period, but the fact that a game like this existed at all was enough to show me that anything was possible. A long testing phase was maybe the least mysterious things about *The Village of Fate*.

"Okay, now for why we came to rescue you. I spoke to the

God of Fortune, and he asked me to come rescue you, the God of Fate's player. Nattyan and I live in Hokkaido, which is probably why we were picked."

"I see. Thanks so much for rescuing me, really." I bowed my head deeply and noticed Carol copying my behavior. She must've woken up at some point. Even Destiny was nodding in her arms.

"That was some amazing teamwork, though," Sewatari said. "I'm kind of jealous. You know, I found it hard to believe when the God of Fortune said there was an accident and a girl from the other world was sent here with a book, but she's so pretty I don't think I mind her being here."

"Make sure you keep Carol-chan away from Senpai, okay, Yoshiocchi?"

I *had* noticed a passion in Sewatari's eyes as she stared at Carol, but until now I thought it was just my imagination.

"I'll be careful," I promised.

"Hey, I just like cute things! What's wrong with that?"

"You take it too far, Senpai. It's creepy."

The two of them began to quarrel. While Sewatari criticized Nattyan's lax dress sense, Nattyan accused her of being a lolicon.

"What are they talking about, Yoshio?" Carol asked.

Apparently, their conversation wasn't being translated this time, likely because it wasn't child appropriate. I was glad for it.

"Um..."

"We were just talking about how cute you are, Carol-chan!"

"Thank you, Oneechan!" Carol giggled bashfully, her cheeks reddening.

"Did you understand what she said then, Carol?" I asked.

"I did now, yeah! But I didn't understand what they were saying before that."

Just like me, it sounded like Sewatari and Nattyan were able to switch between Japanese and the language in the game world. It must have been something all players could do.

"Question," Sewatari said. "Would you mind if Carol-chan stayed in this world so I could adopt her as my sister?"

"Yes, I'd mind."

"'Course he'd mind! Forget the rules, you're a menace to society. Y'know what, I think I'm gonna call the cops right now."

I hoped Sewatari was joking, but she looked a hundred percent serious.

"Look at that pure smile of hers! It makes me wanna give her three extra-large helpings of dessert!"

"Carol, make sure you stay away from that woman when the two of us aren't around, okay?" I warned her.

"You're being unreasonable! It's not a creepy thing! I just like little girls! I hate the smartass boys around her age, though."

From her tone, it sounded like she hated boys more than she loved girls. I wondered just what sort of trauma led to this situation.

I hoped someone would change the subject, since this one could only get worse.

"Oh, there's something else I wanted to ask," Sewatari said. "I know you plan to send Carol-chan back to her world, but what about the book?"

"Well, yeah. I wanna send the book back, too."

That made sense, right? The holy book originally belonged to my villagers, so why shouldn't it go back?

"You're not greedy in the least, huh? You understand you can use that book to get a bird's eye view of anywhere you've ever been? You can even see into buildings, which I'm sure you know by now. There are a ton of possibilities with this thing."

I'd had the same thoughts myself. Undoubtedly, it was the most powerful navigational device in the world. Its true value was far beyond my imagination. Forget the ten million yen the corrupted gods were asking for; there were probably people who would pay well into the hundred millions for something like this.

"I know that. But this belongs to my villagers. It's not mine to keep. Besides, if they don't have this, I can't send prophecies or save them if they get into trouble. I wouldn't even be able to watch over them." Their safety was worth more than any amount of money ever could be. "This book and my villagers are priceless. They saved me when I was at my lowest. They're just as important to me as my biological family."

I stroked Carol's head softly as I spoke. I had no proof that my villagers were still alive, just faith. They were alive, and right now they were working hard to rebuild the village. I needed to return Carol and the book to them as soon as possible.

"That's really great. There are tons of players, even on the major gods' side, who act like their villagers are just video game characters. You're not one of them, Yoshio-kun. I knew there was a reason I believed in you."

Sewatari's praise made me happy, but what did she mean she "believed in me"? It was a weird thing to say to someone you just met. Unless...I was finally becoming popular with women? Wait, wait. According to the Internet, it was super pathetic to mix up a girl being nice or complimentary to you with genuine interest. Though I guess I already knew I was pathetic...

Carol peered up at me. "Why is your face going all funny, Yoshio?"

Oh great. I didn't realize I was that easy to read.

"Now that that's out of the way, let's get something to eat! You hungry, Carol-chan?"

"Yeah! I'm real hungry!" Carol chirped.

"Same!" Nattyan agreed. "I could really go for some bubble tea."

Both their hands shot up in the air. It was nice of Nattyan to show solidarity, but I wished she'd focus on driving.

I looked outside. I'd been so focused on our conversation that I hadn't noticed it getting dark.

"Since you're in Hokkaido, let's grab some Genghis Khan! You know, that grilled mutton dish? I know a good place. We'll go there!"

Genghis Khan was a famous dish. I'd always wanted to try it.

My main priority here was to meet the developers, but we were still a long way away from their building. No point in starving ourselves just to get there quicker. I also wanted Carol to eat all the delicious stuff she could. I wanted her to remember this, the country of the gods (well, Japan), as a fun place to be.

I felt someone watching me. I turned to find Destiny glaring.

Don't worry, I want you to eat delicious food, too.

I asked Nattyan to speed up a little, if only to stop Carol and Destiny from tugging on each of my sleeves to tell me they were starving.

part 11

HOLES AND
OPEN SEAMS ↵

THE NPCs IN THIS VILLAGE SIM GAME MUST BE REAL! ↵

chapter 01 A Pure Heart and My Conflicted Emotions

WE ENDED UP at a hotel. Our destination was still a fair distance away, so we had no choice. Hokkaido was a large prefecture.

Realizing there was a blizzard incoming, we chose the closest place we could. These conditions were too dangerous to travel in.

Instantly, we ran into a problem. The room we booked was large, but it was intended for a family of four. There were only two double beds between me, Carol, Sewatari, Nattyan, and Destiny.

"Maybe we should've booked two rooms," I said, pushing a chair into the corner of the room and sitting down.

The four of them were sprawled out across the beds, chatting away, Destiny included. They all turned to stare at me.

"You're still going on about that? We agreed it's safer not to split up. Cheaper, too," said Sewatari.

"It's fun to be with everyone!" Carol said.

"Don't tell me you're thinkin' impure thoughts, Yoshiocchi?"

The girls were ganging up on me, dismissing my discomfort. At least Carol wouldn't understand what Nattyan was getting at.

Destiny! Don't just shrug! Why do you look so disappointed in me? Listen, it's not like I'm scared or anything!

I knew full well that there might be corrupted god players coming after us at this very moment. We couldn't be too cautious. Sewatari didn't need to point out the safety issue to me. It wouldn't be easy to chase us down in this blizzard, but we didn't know what powerful miracles they had at their disposal. They might have the ability to control weather, like I did, or some other method to get through the storm.

I was just concerned about a man sharing a room with two women. Not that I planned to do anything weird—I did have *some* level of self-restraint. I was honestly more worried about Sewatari, who was hugging Carol with a weird smile on her face.

"You just want to stay in the same room as Carol, don't you?" I asked.

"Yep!" she responded with an angelic smile.

I would pull Carol away if she looked uncomfortable, but she was smiling, too. Besides, Sewatari wouldn't try anything with Nattyan watching, would she?

"Shall we go take a bath? They have a huge public one here!"

"A huge bath? Yay! Let's go! Come on, Seri! Nattyan!"

"I'll wash you. Okay, Carol-chan? Senpai's not allowed."

"Why not?!"

The three of them gathered a change of clothes and left for the bath. I accompanied them halfway, before making my way to the men's bath.

I ducked under the cloth marking the male baths and walked

into the empty changing room. Either it was a little early in the evening for bathing or this place didn't have many bookings.

"The girls are probably having fun without me." Alone, I spoke aloud out of habit.

I unzipped my bag with my change of clothes, and Destiny poked its head out of the gap. I'd thought about leaving it and the book in our room, but that didn't seem safe. Besides, Destiny could protect me if something happened.

"Wait in the locker for me, okay? I won't lock it. If something happens, make lots of noise to warn me." I scratched its chin as I spoke.

Destiny stared back with its large eyes, then nodded slowly. I felt much safer with my guard lizard around.

I closed the locker and opened the glass screen to the bath. The steam hit me all at once, enveloping my body. The showers and the bath itself were so huge, I felt self-conscious having them all to myself. I rinsed off before heading into the water.

"The heat really does melt away exhaustion, huh?" My body and mind were so tired that it felt even better than it normally would. I could've stayed for ages, but I didn't want to leave Destiny hanging around in that locker for too long. "It can't hurt to take a little time, though."

I tried to space out, but my brain refused to let me, spinning in circles. Thoughts of Habatake and the punk. Thoughts of Sewatari and Nattyan.

I knew Habatake and his group were bad news, and I was pretty sure Sewatari and Nattyan were the good guys. It was possible they'd end up betraying me, but I doubted it. What would be in it for them? They could have easily jumped in and taken Carol and the book outside the station without pretending to defend me. No, they were definitely my allies. Sewatari made me feel...safe, for some reason.

Despite that, I was keeping my guard up. I'd used the book to watch the two women earlier when they'd left me and Carol, but they didn't do anything suspicious. I wouldn't be so paranoid if it were just me at risk, but this involved Carol, Destiny, and even the other villagers. I couldn't leave room for mistakes.

I sank down into the water until it was up to my chin and stared at the ceiling. "Maybe if I were smarter, I could come up with some kinda plan."

Before I got my hands on *The Village of Fate*, I'd never used brainpower on anything more intricate than beating a video game. I'd squandered my days without bothering to accrue knowledge or connect with reality. I must have done more thinking in these past couple of months than the rest of the decade combined.

"Thinking sure is tiring, huh?" I asked the golden lizard that was swimming around in the bath in front of me, its tail waving through the—"Wait, what the heck are you doing here?!"

It was supposed to be in the locker!

Flustered, I glanced around, but there was no one else here. God, imagine if one of the other guests saw a huge lizard in the public baths. I jumped out of the water, grabbed a bucket, and tossed Destiny inside.

"Why did you come out here? I thought I told you to stay in the locker!" I glared down at it. Destiny blinked up at me and poked its tongue out innocently.

"Nope, you're not getting out of this by acting like a regular lizard!" I sighed. "Okay, I'm sorry. I guess you wanted to come too, huh?"

I couldn't stay mad when it looked at me like that. I mean, I did leave it in a locker while I went to enjoy a nice warm bath all by myself.

"All right. You can hang out with me, but we gotta leave as soon as someone else comes in, okay?" I stroked Destiny's head gently, its eyes narrowing in pleasure. There was no way it couldn't understand what I was saying.

I decided we'd only bathe for a few more minutes. I didn't want to leave the girls waiting for me. Once we were done, I put Destiny back into the bucket. The changing room was still empty, and when I checked our locker, I found that it was frozen shut.

"Oh, that was smart," I said to Destiny. "Good work."

Destiny had ensured the holy book and the rest of our stuff would be safe. I dried the both of us off quickly before putting it back into my bag. It would be uncomfortably humid in there since Destiny just got out of the bath, but this was the only real option.

We left the baths and sat down on a bench to wait for the girls. They must have still been bathing. With nothing else to do, I pulled out my phone and clicked on the *Village of Fate* app. It opened on the area around the baths from a bird's eye view.

"Seeing into buildings like this shouldn't be possible with our current technology."

Same with the game's characters. They were supposed to be powered by a high-performance A.I., but I found that hard to believe. I mean, I'd had doubts from the beginning, but now there was no other explanation. Still, that meant the game was linked to another world, and...well, that didn't seem likely either.

As I fiddled with the app, I realized that this phone could look into buildings, and at the moment, it was showing me right outside the bathhouse. If I zoomed in...I could see into the baths themselves, right?

I needed to know Carol was safe, after all.

"Kidding. I would never do something so sleazy."

"What's sleazy?" a voice whispered in my ear.

"Gah!" I leapt to my feet.

There stood the girls, their cheeks flushed.

How long have they been there?!

"Here." Sewatari passed me a cold bottled drink.

I took it gratefully; I was parched after the bath. I drank, trying to wash away my indecent thoughts.

All three of them were in the *yukata* provided by the hotel. The outfit suited Sewatari particularly well. Her beauty was enhanced by the traditional clothing. Nattyan looked like...a high schooler going to a festival. All she needed was cotton candy in one hand and some dried squid in the other. Carol simply looked like a tourist, but the way her blonde hair clashed with the yukata just made her cuter.

Apparently the three of them were hitting it off.

"You looked kind of anxious there." said Sewatari. "Don't be. There's not much point worrying about the game anymore. You need to speak to the developers directly. It won't be long now."

"Yup!" Nattyan agreed. "No point in stressin' at the moment."

"Yeah, take it easy."

They were right, and I nodded, despite that not being at all what I was anxious about. They didn't need to know that.

"You're right," I said. "I'll stop obsessing over it. It's more important to focus on getting there safely."

"That's the spirit! Now let's go grab some dessert!"

"Yeah!" Carol threw a triumphant fist in the air, Nattyan joining in. Despite only knowing each other for half a day, they were totally comfortable together. I wouldn't be surprised if they were close in age. Mentally, at least.

I watched Carol grin, happily letting Nattyan and Sewatari hold her by the hands. I had the sudden urge to reach out and haul her back. Carol always kept it together really well, but she was still a child. She had to miss her mom, which was making her take to any female presence very quickly. I understood that, but I still felt a little left out.

"I wonder if we'll finish up this journey soon."

Provided nothing went wrong, we were due to meet the developers tomorrow.

This might be the last evening I spend with Carol.

Loneliness gripped my heart. For her sake, I couldn't let it show.

I finished my bottled tea, stood up, and went to join them.

When I woke up at the hotel, there was a woman sleeping beside me.

Just kidding. I woke up with Destiny. It was snoozing comfortably in my arms but not offering much warmth. Destiny usually slept with Carol, but Nattyan and Sewatari kept her company last night. I sat up to make sure they were all accounted for. They were, thankfully, and still fast asleep. Sewatari and Nattyan had worn their *yukata* to bed, and I caught seductive glimpses of their chests and legs. As much as I would've liked to keep looking, I forced myself to avert my gaze.

It felt weird to let them keep sleeping, so I grabbed my phone and switched on the alarm. They woke with a start. I waited out in the hall while they got changed, then went in to change myself, before we all headed to reception to check out.

The sky was clear today. According to the weather forecast, we'd have perfect driving conditions all day. I hoped it was right.

We left the hotel with the expectation that we'd reach our destination before noon, but as I looked out over the landscape, anxiety overcame me. We'd seen nothing but trees for a while now. The road we drove along wasn't even paved, and it was a wonder how our car even made it this far. The thick foliage blocked out the sunlight, turning the world gloomy, despite the weather. The road was so bumpy that I kept bashing my head against the car ceiling.

"Are you sure this is the way?" I asked.

"Of course! This is quicker than the highway."

"Yup. I mean, Senpai's got no sense of direction, but we'll be fine as long as we follow the satnav. Modern technology, am I right?"

Nattyan's reassurance had the opposite of its intended effect. Today, Sewatari was driving, and while *she* looked confident, I wasn't. I peered at the satnav. This mountain road we were on wasn't even marked. Why were neither of them worried? Still, they were the locals, not me, so I had to trust them. I didn't even have a driver's license.

Maybe I'll try to get one once I'm back home...

I clung to my seat belt and looked out the window. The car was rocking so badly it felt like we would run off the road at any moment. Oh, did I mention there was a steep drop to the left of the path? It was steep enough that we'd be lucky to make it out alive.

"Ah, whoops. Nearly skidded a bit there!"

"Man, this is intense!"

I was *definitely* going to get my license if I made it home safely. I added it to my list of ways to get my life together.

"There are so many trees here! It's just like the village!" Carol said excitedly. Her face was plastered to the window as she watched the abundant nature passing by.

I hadn't made the connection before, but she was right. The village *was* surrounded by trees just like this.

I wonder how my villagers are doing...

I checked the app. My Fate Points were still increasing, which I decided to take as indication that my villagers were alive. I needed to see them with my own eyes before that became anything more than hopeful speculation, though. I was avoiding talking about the village as much as I could, to avoid upsetting Carol. Sadness clouded her eyes as she looked out the window. It was clear what was on her mind.

"We'll be meeting with the gods soon, Carol. They'll be able to help you out."

"Yeah! I know everyone's safe!"

"That's right. They're safe and sound." I injected as much certainty into my voice as I could. They were fine. They had to be.

"We'll be outta the mountains soon!" Nattyan announced. "Won't be long after that."

Carol and I straightened our backs. A gap opened between the trees on the road ahead, bright sunlight streaming through.

"Past there, we'll be out in the open," Sewatari said.

Relieved that we were finally leaving these terrifying roads behind, I stared out through the windshield at the brightness ahead. I instinctively squeezed my eyelids shut, and when I parted them again, I saw a railway line. We were driving along a road parallel to the tracks as they curved to the right. Instead of the wide fields typical of Hokkaido, this area was dominated by several large factories.

"That railway runs along the industrial estate," Sewatari explained. "A lot of major companies have their production lines here, so it's a pretty busy area even this far from any big towns."

Nattyan nodded. "Yeah, there's a residential area not far from the factories."

I spotted a small train station up ahead with a traffic circle in front of it and some shops and eateries on a strip nearby. I also saw a few chain stores, but most of them looked like indepen-dent local places. There might've even been more stores here than where I lived out in the countryside.

"Must be convenient, having all these restaurants and shops around," I said.

"Yeah! You only gotta drive a few minutes to find most things."

Right, that—wait. How would Nattyan know that?

"Ow!" I inhaled sharply as the car came to a sudden stop, and I slammed my head against the driver's seat in front of me. I looked up to complain, only to find that the two of them had undone their seat belts and were looking back at me expectantly.

"We're here, Yoshio-kun."

"This is the company that develops *The Village of Fate*: Isekai Connection," said Nattyan.

I followed their gazes. A four-story mixed-occupancy build-ing stood next to us. I recognized it from the satellite image I'd seen when I looked up the address. It was even shabbier in real life than it had looked online. The outer walls were a drab gray, and the building looked decades old. This might not look like the dwelling-place of gods, but what else could the developers be?

"*This* is where they made the game?"

I climbed out after Nattyan and Sewatari. The building be-side Isekai Connection housed a small boutique and café, drawn from the same old-fashioned design. Pedestrians roamed the streets.

Unable to believe the company behind such an impossible game was just out in the open, I checked the directory outside the building. The first floor housed a travel agency. The second, third, and fourth floors all belonged to Isekai Connection. Now that I was finally here, my nervousness grew.

If you compared my current experiences to a video game, everything that had happened up until now was just the prologue. This was where the real game began. Time to speak with the developers and find a way to send Carol home.

"You're looking a little stiff," Sewatari remarked.

"I'm just getting nervous thinking about what's ahead."

"Oh, about that. We should probably apologize." Sewatari scratched her head awkwardly and averted her gaze. "The truth is—"

"You guys work here, right? Either as developers or something else."

Her eyes grew round, and she stared at me. She clearly wasn't expecting me to say that. Nattyan, who was playing with Carol nearby, overheard and looked over in surprise.

"You...knew?"

"It was obvious. I mean, you kept throwing hints my way, didn't you?"

From all the conversation we'd had in the car, it had been easy to work out. They were way too familiar with this area, talking like locals. Anyone could work that out.

"Well, yes, we did. We thought it would be easier on you if you figured it out instead of us just telling you out of the blue."

I should be grateful for that. It was like she said. Since I'd worked it out already, I could take the revelation in stride.

"Wait, we did?!" Nattyan looked shocked. Apparently, she hadn't been in on Sewatari's plan.

Carol and Destiny looked like they couldn't care less, peering through the large window of the travel agency on the first floor. They noticed me looking, and I beckoned them back toward us.

Sewatari waited until we were all grouped together, then smiled. "Welcome, player Suenaga Yoshio. Welcome, other-worldly villager Carol. And welcome, basilisk Destiny. I am one of the game's developers. I am the God of Fate."

THE NPCs IN THIS VILLAGE SIM GAME MUST BE REAL! ↵

chapter 02 A Company of Gods and My History as a NEET

SHE WAS THE God of Fate? I knew she worked for the company, but I never guessed that Sewatari...*san* was the real God of Fate—the god *I* played as. I couldn't drop the honorific now that I knew who she was, even in my mind. Maybe I shouldn't even be thinking of her as Sewatari-san but as the God of Fate.

She was who I'd spoken to on the phone before, I was suddenly sure of it. Wait, how had I not noticed before? She hadn't been using a voice changer or anything.

"You're wondering about my voice, right? Well, I am a god. Blocking your awareness of something like that is pretty minor."

"C'mon, it wasn't *your* power, though. It was one of our coworkers." Nattyan...san winked mischievously.

"Hey! I'm trying to sound impressive and godlike." Sewatari-san—the God of Fate—poked her right back.

I didn't even say anything about the phone call. Had she read my mind? I decided to test her.

"You're thinking that I spoke really informally on the phone, right? Well, I didn't want to give myself away. That's all it was."

Oh my God, she really *could* read my mind. She responded to my silent question perfectly.

"There are limits to my ability, though. I can't just read your mind wherever I want. Our power is strongest when we're in this area, which is how I'm doing it now. Sort of unfair, though, isn't it? Me being the only one reading minds. Hold on a second." Sewatari-san pulled out her phone and tapped the screen a few times. "Okay, that should do it. I borrowed the book's power to block my mind reading. It'd be bad if everyone on the second floor found out about my ability, too."

According to the directory, the second floor was owned by Isekai Connection. Didn't that mean they were her coworkers? Other gods?

If Sewatari-san was a god, then Nattyan-san had to be one as well. I couldn't be informal with them like I was before.

"Yoshio, what did Seri just say?" Carol asked.

Sewatari-san was making sure Carol couldn't understand her, huh? I shot her a glance, and she scratched at her head awkwardly.

"If Carol-chan finds out I'm a god, she won't look at me in the same way."

Right. In the other world, gods were highly revered, and no one seemed to doubt their existence. Not like me, who hadn't believed in gods until very recently.

"We were saying that the two of us help the gods with their work here and that we're sorry for hiding it."

"You help the gods?! Wow! All I can do is help the people I live with." Carol looked up at Sewatari-san, her eyes shining with respect.

Sewatari-san replied a little bashfully, "Shall we carry on talking indoors? It's cold out here. There's probably a free meeting room somewhere."

"I'll go reserve one and get it unlocked." Nattyan-san raced away up the stairs without waiting for the God of Fate to respond.

The God of Fate let out a small sigh. "Let's go, then."

"Yes, Lord," I said.

"Stop that. We're heathens in this world, really, so just treat us like regular humans. Don't bother with honorifics either."

"Okay, Sewatari...san."

I couldn't help but add the "san" even after she told me to stop. She frowned, and even that small expression seemed heavy with power.

We walked in through the glass door Nattyan-san left open behind her. The building was so much warmer compared to outside. The stairs were right in front of us, with an elevator to our right. On the left was the door to the travel agency.

"Our department's on the third floor. You don't mind using the stairs, do you? I can explain a little more on the way up."

Sewatari-san took the lead. I followed her, leading Carol by the hand. Destiny clung to my back and rested its head on my shoulder.

"That travel agency on the first floor's got nothing to do with us, so we don't talk about the games with them, even if we're friendly. Patching up people's memories is annoying."

Yeah, I'd been wondering if there was any connection.

Wait, what did she just say?

"What do you mean by 'patching up memories'?"

"Oh, one of the other gods who works with us can perform a miracle to manipulate memories. It's what we use when someone gets a game over."

That happened to Yamamoto-san right in front of me—he lost all his memories of the game. With everything else going on, I took the whole thing in stride, but it was interesting to know it was miracle-based.

"I know we look ordinary, but we *are* gods. I've got other powers, too, though there are limits."

"Limits?"

She mentioned limits when she spoke about her mind-reading power, too.

"That's right. I'll tell you more about those later. Long story short, we lost a lot of our powers when we came to Japan."

When they came to Japan? The look on her face told me it was a sensitive subject. Besides, she said she'd go into detail later. I could wait until then.

"Right, this is the second floor."

This landing had a door to the main section of the building and an elevator hall, just like the first floor. The main door was big and made of glass, flanked by houseplants. Beyond it were desks with computers, set up in neat lines. It looked like any other office I visited for my cleaning job, a completely ordinary open-plan design. Fifteen or so people were hard at work or talking on phones. Only three of them wore suits; the rest dressed casually. Not what you'd expect from office workers.

"There's no dress code at our company. I usually dress a little more casual than this, but I wanted to look smart for when we came to pick you up, Yoshio-kun. Does it suit me?" Sewatari-san put one leg up on the stair above and struck a pose. With her slender figure and pretty face, she looked like a model right out of a fashion magazine.

"Yes, it suits you incredibly well."

"I told you not to be so formal! I get that you're nervous in front of a god, but just try to be like before, okay?"

"I will do my best."

It was a tough ask. I wasn't brave enough to treat a god like my friend. Even though her appearance hadn't changed, she *felt* different. Divine. I knew she was telling me the truth.

"Don't try and look up my skirt, either. Unless you want to feel my wrath."

I chuckled nervously. "I'll be careful."

Was that a joke? Was I supposed to be smiling, or would she find it rude?

"Ugh, this is why I didn't want you to know we were gods until the very end! I told you, we're heathens here! We're only gods in the other world. You don't have to be so nervous."

She could tell me as many times as she wanted, but I just couldn't turn off my new knowledge. This wasn't an everyday occurrence. How was I even supposed to react to this?

Sewatari-san sighed. "Okay, I'll keep talking. Don't go into the office on the second floor. You can do what you like on the third floor, but the second is completely off limits." Sewatari-san put her hands on her hips as though expecting that to help the message hit home.

I didn't understand. The second floor was owned by Isekai Connection, too, so these were her colleagues, weren't they?

"The second floor is a different department. We don't really get along with them, if I'm being honest. A lot of people on our floor are prejudiced against them, and vice versa, though I'm not one of them. Just, stay away." Despite her light tone, a frown was carved across her brow. It was intimidating enough to make me shiver, her true divine nature shining through.

Carol, Destiny, and I nodded.

"I'm glad you're all so sensible!" Sewatari-san giggled. "And now we're at my department!"

She walked briskly to the door. The third floor looked identical to the second, what with the elevator hall and the decor. The only difference was the type of houseplants.

"Come on in!" Sewatari-san beckoned.

On the other side of that door was an office full of gods, and here I was, a former NEET. I couldn't really go in there, could I?

I stalled, overcome with fear. Carol, meanwhile, charged right on in with Destiny in her arms. I admired her childish innocence and curiosity. I couldn't let her show me up. I puffed out my chest and walked in with long strides. Completely feigned confidence, of course.

"My player's just sent another crazy prophecy! Dammit, can't I just confiscate that book already?"

"Are you sure you wanna be using that many miracles? You'll barely have any points left..."

"My screen's looking weird. Someone call IT!"

"I swear, if those corrupted gods overstep the mark one more time..."

The moment we stepped inside, voices buzzed around us. The spacious room was full of desks, each with three cubicle walls to give its occupant their own space. The ceiling was just over fifteen feet high by my estimation, and there had to be close to a hundred desks, around half of them manned with people...no, *gods*, going about their work.

Their appearances ranged from all over the world. Some were obviously Asian, while others looked Scandinavian.

"Are these all gods of the other world?"

"Yes. We have humans in here sometimes, but today it's just gods."

Their faces, clothes, and speech made them all look completely human, but the inhabitants of the other world were humanlike as well. That made sense then, since a lot of our gods looked human, too.

Despite their appearance, I had to remember their divinity and be careful not to be disrespectful. I braced myself as best I could. The fact that some of them were snacking as they worked or yawning and playing with their phones didn't help, honestly.

"Shall we go to the meeting room, then?"

"Y-yes, ma'am." I followed Sewatari-san stiffly. I kept glancing around, but I couldn't tell this place apart from an ordinary office.

I *did* notice some of the workers giving me a hard stare, though. I couldn't blame them; any human, especially one as unremarkable as me, would seem out of place here.

I tried not to make eye contact. Even with more than a hundred people working, the office felt spacious. It certainly looked much bigger than it had from the outside; so much so that I could barely believe it. From the size of the building, it shouldn't even be a tenth of this size. I couldn't deny what I was seeing, though. Normally I'd be gaping in surprise, but after everything I'd been through, that would just be an overreaction. This office was home to a bunch of gods. Manipulating space was probably nothing to them.

A door to our left flew open, and Nattyan-san's tanned face poked out from behind it. "Oh, hey, you made it. C'mon, in here!"

Her friendly smile reassured me. Even through the knowledge that she was a god from another world, her attitude put me at ease.

"Thanks, Nattyan! This way!" Sewatari-san beckoned us forward.

I quickened my pace and slipped into the room behind her, relieved to be out from under everyone's stares.

The meeting room contained a long table surrounded by folding chairs and bookshelves crammed with files. A large tank swarmed with multicolored tropical fish. A whiteboard hung on the right wall, blank except for a few smudges, like someone had erased something in a hurry. I squinted, wondering if I'd be able to read anything.

"Corrup...tion response. Microtransactions... Lower pri..."

"Stop that. Those are business secrets!" Sewatari-san erased the rest of the board and turned around. She slammed her hand on the whiteboard and grinned. "Time to get into the nitty-gritty detail!"

I sat down on one of the chairs. A hot drink was placed in front of me, and I looked up to find a woman with black hair down to her waist. Well, I assumed she was a woman because she was wearing a blue dress, but her hair completely obscured her face.

"Thank you," I said.

She held the tray to her chest and gave me a quick nod. I hadn't even noticed her come in; I didn't remember hearing the door open. When I looked up again from my drink, she was gone.

"Huh?"

I thought she'd left silently again, but then I noticed her sitting alone in the corner. She reminded me of a ghost, with the way she looked and acted. Maybe that was rude to think. Anyway, she seemed to be here to take part in the meeting.

She held up a small basket of snacks and beckoned to Carol and Destiny. They approached hesitantly, entranced by the promise of candy. If she kept them entertained, I could focus on what Sewatari-san was saying. I bowed my head, and she quickly waved away my thanks. I couldn't see her face, but I'd say she was embarrassed. Neither Sewatari-san nor Nattyan-san reacted, so I decided to leave it alone.

"First, I want to apologize for lying to you about our identities. I'm sorry."

"Yeah, sorry."

The two of them bowed their heads. I leapt to my feet, unable to deal with this.

"P-please don't apologize! I-I don't mind that you lied!"

This was way too much to deal with. What were a pair of *gods* doing apologizing to a NEET?!

"We'll stop apologizing if you stop speaking to us so politely!" Sewatari-san glanced up at me, still bent over.

I didn't realize this was a negotiation. "But I'm just trying to be respectful!"

"I thought Japanese people weren't really religious? That's what we hear in the divine business circles."

There are divine business circles?

She was right, though. There definitely *were* Japanese people who celebrated Christmas or went to visit a shrine on New Year's Day, but we still had a high percentage of atheists and were viewed as a secular country when compared to others. But that didn't mean any reasonable person would be brave enough to act with indifference when faced with a real god. But there was really no point in holding my ground if they didn't want me to.

"O-okay, I will... I'll try to be more casual."

"Great! We'll keep going then!" Sewatari and Nattyan straightened up again. Although Sewatari said she couldn't read my thoughts anymore, I took care not to add honorifics to their names in my mind. "First up, you should know that we never expected Carol-chan to end up in this world either. The system wasn't supposed to let humans or other live offerings through."

"That's right. Humans shouldn't be able to go through the portal."

Living things couldn't be sent? And what did they mean by "portal"? They were going too fast for me. I had to ask.

"Can I ask a question?"

"Go ahead, Yoshio-kun." Sewatari, who was now wearing a black-framed pair of glasses that I hadn't even noticed her put on, thrust a pointer at me. I didn't know where that came from either. She was probably trying to project confidence, but she just looked like she was cosplaying a teacher.

"You said living things couldn't be sent as offerings, but what about Destiny?"

"Ah, right. Since it was still an egg, the system probably recognized it as food. That was also our bad."

It thought it was food? How exactly did this system work? "What did you mean about portals?"

"Oh, yes, the portal! To explain that, I think we need to go back to how us gods arrived in this world and began developing the game."

Apparently, I'd asked something pertinent. I straightened up, ready to listen to every single word.

"You should know that the world we come from exists on a slightly higher plane than Earth. Imagine that our world and Earth are two different fish tanks. Our world's tank is located higher than Earth's. Geographically, I mean." Sewatari took her drink and walked over to the tank, where the tropical fish inhabitants were floating around leisurely. She crouched down in front of it and held her mug out slightly below it. "Long ago in our world—the game world—the corrupted gods faced off against the major gods. It was a fierce battle that ended up opening a fissure in the world. An invisible crack that covered everything. Think of it as a small hole in the side of this fish tank."

Sewatari tapped her pointer on the lower part of the tank. If there *were* a hole there, all the water would come streaming out.

"Us gods tried desperately to plug that hole—or portal—but repairing it proved far more difficult than we expected. It was only a small hole, so it had no effect on the powerful major or corrupted gods, but the weaker minor gods started getting sucked through it and falling down into the other fish tank." Sewatari waved the pointer, miming water flowing into her cup.

"So you minor gods fell down into the cup—in other words, Earth?"

"Exactly! You got it."

That made sense. Well, it did if I momentarily forgot everything I knew to be true about the world.

"When you say portal, you don't mean something physical, right? It's more something...spiritual?"

"I think the major gods said it was, like, some kinda barrier between worlds. Something invisible that transcends time and dimensions, uh..." Nattyan trailed off.

"Yes, that's right." Sewatari nodded.

A barrier? I think I get it.

"Anyway, our divine power began to leak out of that hole bit by bit. It was just like water, flowing downward, and since our world is above yours, that's where it went. That divine power flowed down into Earth."

"Wait, so some invisible mysterious power...like your aura or something, started pouring into Earth?"

"Yes. Yes, that's it. 'Aura' is a good word to describe it."

Really? It was just the first word that came into my head.

"Us minor gods are made up of this intangible divine aura, so we just started sliding out of the portal down to Earth. Like this." Nattyan put her arms up and wiggled her body in demonstration.

"We've been trying to get back ever since, but it's hard to swim up against a constant waterfall of divine aura. Even worse, we lost most of our powers when we fell to Earth." Both Sewatari and Nattyan's shoulders drooped, and they sighed. I couldn't tell if it was a genuine display of disappointment or if they were exaggerating to get the message across to a human like me. "It was all we could do to keep physical forms like this, and there was no way we'd be strong enough to return to our world. All the minor gods who fell here ended up coming together to survive."

These gods suddenly found themselves lost in an unfamiliar world. As uncharitable as it was to think about, it had probably been pretty funny.

"We were in total panic mode. We used the last of our power to fix the memory of the guy who owned the land where the aura was falling, taking it over along with the structure built on top of it. Then we started the game company right where you're standing."

"Why games?"

"I thought you'd ask that. Us minor gods need a constant supply of divine aura, or we can't survive. We can be away from it for a few days, but we can't use our powers when it isn't close by."

If they could use their powers, we probably would've had an easier time escaping from those corrupted god players.

"So we were stuck in Hokkaido, where the aura was pouring into. We needed to find something we could do without leaving this office space, and it just so happened that there was a game development company already here in this building. I guess you'd call that fate, huh?"

Was that a joke? I wasn't sure if I should laugh or not. And what had happened to the people who had worked here before? Part of me didn't want to know.

"Divine aura is generated by people's faith in gods. Without that, we'd simply disappear. We created our game both to secure followers and to make ourselves the money we needed to survive in this world."

Fair enough.

Still, I wanted time to process all of this absurdity. I rotated it in my mind, trying to make sense of it, but all that did was generate more questions.

"I guess that's all for now," Sewatari said. "Anything more would just confuse you at this point. We'll explain more later, so it's your turn now, Yoshio-kun. Questions? Concerns?"

"Is it possible to send Carol and Destiny back to their home world?" I asked without hesitation. Carol, Destiny, and the woman in the corner all turned toward me at the mention of their names, candy in hand.

"Right, that's the biggest concern here. I think it *is* possible."

Relief washed over me. I exchanged a glance with Carol. She beamed.

Sewatari said, "I know that sounds like good news, but I'm afraid there is a 'but' coming."

Carol and I paused mid-high five to look at Sewatari. She bowed with her hands together.

"It's nothing major," she promised. "We just can't send them back immediately. Give us a little time, and it should be possible."

"Really?" I didn't want to be caught off guard by another "but."

"Like I said, the divine aura is flowing down from our world like a waterfall. It's easy to drop something into the pool below. It just flows down with the water. But trying to bring something up from the pool to the top of the waterfall again is basically impossible." Sewatari gestured to the fish tank and her mug again to explain. "The offerings were easy to bring to this world, since they followed the flow of divine aura. Trying to send things back, though... I mean, if we were able to do that, we wouldn't be stuck in this world ourselves."

Of course. Why would they stay in another world if they didn't have to? If it were so easy to go back, they wouldn't have bothered setting up a whole game company just to survive.

"And even if we could fight back against the flow of aura and make it to the top, the portal is too small for us minor gods to get through. It used to be bigger, but it looks like the major gods patched it up to stop too much aura from getting out."

"It's way too tight for us to get through." Nattyan demonstrated by making a ring with her fist and poking her finger through. She didn't seem to realize that gesture could be wildly misinterpreted.

"Wouldn't that mean sending Carol and Destiny back is impossible?" I asked.

"The divine aura affects us gods much more than it does humans and monsters. How should I put it..." Sewatari turned to Nattyan for input.

Nattyan pointed to herself as if to confirm Sewatari wanted her to explain, then began rocking her head back and forth in thought. "Uh, let's see...well, we're made up of aura, so for us it'd be like swimming against a muddy, flowing stream. Since humans and monsters don't really have any aura, for them it'd be like swimming through a still pool."

"Yes! That's it! Good job!"

Nattyan grinned bashfully at Sewatari's praise.

"In other words, it's easier for humans and monsters to fight the current than it is for gods. The portal is a perfectly fine size for you. We just need to make a few adjustments, which will take some time. Not much, though!"

"Okay. Please...send them home!" I bowed my head down so hard it nearly slammed against the desk.

"Please!" Carol chimed in.

I just had to trust them, and wait, and be satisfied that they were doing their best.

"Leave it to us! Oh, and I wanted to ask you something. While we're fixing up the portal, d'you want to do some work for us?"

"Uh, excuse me?"

THE NPCs IN THIS VILLAGE SIM GAME MUST BE REAL! ↵

chapter 03 — A Company of Gods and My Work

"**G**OOD MORNING!"

"Good morning!" Carol echoed.

"Morning, guys," one of the gods yawned.

We paused our cleaning as the gods made their way up the stairs to the third floor and their jobs. We greeted them cheerfully. Carol, who was wearing a huge smile and her own pair of coveralls, gave an even-more-enthusiastic greeting than I did. The gods couldn't help but smile at her as they passed.

I'd been surprised they managed to get *me* coveralls, let alone ones small enough for her. She looked more like she was cosplaying than working, but she was so adorable that it hardly mattered.

I'd been assigned the task of cleaner at Isekai Connection's building. It had been Sewatari's idea—I would stay and work here until Carol was able to return to the other world. I'd been worried she was going to ask me to help develop the game, but this was perfect. I'd used up more than half my savings to get us to Hokkaido. At this rate, I wouldn't have anything to spend on *The Village of Fate* once I got back home.

They asked me to clean the bathrooms, the elevator hall, the stairs, and the main hallway. Apart from that, I did odd jobs, like taking out the garbage. I'd planned to work alone, but Carol insisted on helping me and wouldn't take no for an answer. As for Destiny, it was curled up in front of the heater in the third-floor office. Just like any old lizard, it disliked the cold. Hokkaido was way rougher on it than where we came from. Any motivation it might have had to work was immediately sapped by the air temperature. I was worried it would be a bother, but it seemed wildly popular with the staff—or gods—and was having a wonderful time relaxing and eating candy.

"Yoshio, should I wipe down the stairs?" asked Carol.

"Yeah, good idea. I'll use the vacuum cleaner—uh, this thing here—to suck up the dirt, so could you use that mop to clean up behind me?"

"Okay!"

I put a sign at the bottom of the stairs that read "cleaning in progress," and turned on the vacuum. You were generally supposed to start cleaning at the highest floor and make your way down, but the fourth floor and the stairs up to it were off limits. The elevator had a fourth floor button, but nothing happened when I pressed it. When I mentioned it to Sewatari, she said it was top secret. I was curious, but I also wasn't brave enough to try and poke around in divine affairs, so I left it alone. The fourth-floor stairs were cordoned off with those ropes that acted like shrine talismans, and it was so dim you couldn't make out the landing, even in daylight. The effect was frightening, like the darkness was waiting to swallow up anything that dared approach it. Looking at it made me shiver.

I turned back to Carol, and we began to clean. When we were done with the third-floor stairs, we moved to the elevator hall on the second floor. While the second-floor hallway was also on my list of places to clean, I was warned to keep my guard up. This floor held a deep, dark secret of its own.

"Oh, you the new cleaner who's workin' here all of a sudden?" a voice called from behind us as I waited for Carol to finish with the mop.

I turned to face a shady-looking man with a shaved head, sunglasses, and a striped suit. He had to be over six feet tall, making him even more intimidating. He reminded me of a villain in a TV drama.

"That's me. Nice to meet you."

"Keep up the good work. Make it nice an' clean fer us."

His accent wasn't one I expected to hear up in Hokkaido, but I figured he had to be a god, too—I mean, everyone who worked here was, apart from the travel agents on the first floor. Although he sure seemed to have a lot of free time.

"What'sa matter? Something on my face?"

"Oh, no. I'm not—"

"Your head's all shiny! Why are your glasses colored?" It was, of course, Carol asking the impolite questions, not me. I quickly jumped in to cover her mouth, but it was too late. I felt the man's glare through his sunglasses. Carol took no notice, staring at the god's head in wonder.

"D-don't ask things like that, Carol. I'm very sorry, sir."

"No worries at all. I think she's got potential. Want some candy?" The man gave her an unnerving smile and offered her a sweet from his pocket.

Maybe my initial impression was overblown, but I still felt we should be cautious. I knew who he was. The third-floor workers were minor gods, but everyone on the second floor was allied with the corrupted gods.

I knew a little about the feud between the two groups from my villagers' conversations. A group of gods known as the sacred eight ruled all the others. One day, the strongest among them led a rebellion of minor gods. He didn't like the direction the other seven were taking the world.

The weaker gods each picked a stronger god to ally with, and the battle raged on for over a year, eventually culminating in the defeat of the rebel god, whereupon he was sealed underground. That was the main corrupted god. The only corrupted god, in fact.

When I first heard the story, I was surprised by the lopsided lore. Since there were seven major gods, I expected the other side to balance out, but it really was just one versus seven. The corrupted god had several minor gods in his cadre, but the power differential between minor and major gods was enormous.

In other words, that one corrupted god had to be incredibly powerful.

Despite this man's rough appearance, he seemed kind. I started to doubt my initial assessment.

"You wary 'cause I'm a corrupted god?"

A chill ran down my spine. Could he read my mind? No, Sewatari said she put a stop to that.

"Yer way too easy to read. Anyone'd know you're nervous right now by lookin' at yer face."

Really?

I touched my face curiously, only to look down and find Carol nodding at me. I always thought I was good at keeping a lid on my emotions, but apparently not.

"D'you even know the difference 'tween the corrupted god an' the major gods?"

The difference? Not really. I only knew the story the villagers told, and the pieces I put together in my run-ins with corrupted minor gods. "Only that there was a big war."

"Thought so. Thing is, the war got started 'cause of a difference in values."

"A difference in values?"

That seemed odd. I thought he was going to say something about the corrupted god being displeased with the others.

"That's right," he said quietly. "The major gods favor people n' animals, but they detest monsters. Think they're dirty. But our god says monsters are equal to people. Says all life is equal, an' it's not fair to support one species over another."

I swallowed. If what he said was true, then the corrupted gods were less evil than I thought.

"Same thing happens on Earth, right? They say history's written by the victors. Notice how it's always the good guys who win? Still, if I was human, I'd probably wanna side with the major gods, too. They're the ones favorin' me, see?" the man murmured.

I studied his face. It didn't look like he was lying, but I had no evidence that he was telling the truth either.

"Your face's gone all crinkly, Yoshio." Carol beckoned me. I crouched down so I was at her level. She poked a finger to my brow, rubbing as though trying to smooth out my frown.

"Don't worry. I was just thinking."

It was a waste of time trying to figure something out that was beyond my understanding by its very nature. I decided to ask Sewatari or Nattyan about it later.

"She's adorable, huh? Just lookin' at her calms me down." The shady god smiled at Carol. An almost lazy grin, with none of the solemnity he'd shown moments ago.

"Anyone would think you're creeping on her, Gen."

"Shuddup and get outta me hair."

A woman with a short, rounded hairstyle appeared. If I recalled correctly, the hairstyle was called a "bob." Sayuki's favorite model had the same haircut. This woman had almond-shaped eyes and bright red lips. She wore a suit similar to Sewatari's, a rare choice of dress around here.

"Aren't you supposed to be working, Gen?"

"I'm busy admirin' this little girl, aren't I?" Gen replied.

"You should be careful saying things like that with how you look. Any reasonable person would call the police."

I almost nodded my head to agree but quickly stopped when Gen glared at me.

"You're always so serious, Un-chan. No matter what world we end up in!"

"I've told you time and time again not to call me that." Her low, threatening voice was almost drowned out by the sound of wind.

It blew against my bangs, so hard I had to close my eyes. I pried them open again and froze. Un-chan's foot was pressed against Gen's throat. She must have kicked out in the split second I had my eyes closed.

"Way to overreact! Gods aren't s'posta fight each other, re-member?" Gen wrapped a hand around her ankle, keeping her from choking him.

"We're quarreling, not fighting. I was simply kicking you for getting on my nerves." Un-chan stared at him coolly, not bother-ing to lower her leg.

As a human, I was at a loss to diffuse this situation. All I could do was watch in silence. I put Carol behind me and began to back toward the stairs. Just then, I felt a hand on my shoulder. I turned to find Sewatari frowning past me.

"Un-chan! Gen-chan!" Sewatari stepped forward and flicked both of them on the forehead. "You're embarrassing yourselves in front of the humans!"

Un-chan's face flushed red. "I'm sorry, Senpai. That was im-proper of me." Un-chan's face flushed red. She slowly lowered her leg and smoothed down her skirt. The violence had completely vanished from her demeanor.

"You're only actin' like a goody two shoes now 'cause she

showed up!" Gen growled. Sewatari had called her "Un-chan," and she didn't correct her. In fact, she looked happy about it.

"I know you're a hard worker, Un-chan, but you need to make more of an effort to get along with your coworkers."

"Yes, ma'am. I'm sorry, Gen...even though you're a pedo."

"B-bitch!"

 Not much of an apology, really.

"Glad you two have made up," Sewatari said "By the way, Gen-chan...Yoshio-kun and Carol-chan are my dear friends, so I trust you won't cause them any trouble." She smiled as she spoke, but it didn't reach her eyes.

"Y-yes'm," Gen grumbled, paling. Going by appearances, he shouldn't have been afraid of the slender Sewatari, but she was a god of the highest rank. She most likely outranked him, too. As he slunk away silently, I honestly felt a little bad for the guy.

"Is this your player, Senpai?" Un-chan asked sweetly as she fidgeted. I couldn't believe this was the same god who'd just kicked Gen.

"Yep. You got it."

"Your player..." Un-chan looked at me, and I froze at her icy gaze. For a moment I felt a flare of intense hatred focused on me, before it disappeared. "I ought to introduce myself. I'm the god in charge of fortune. Treat me as a friend, just as you do Senpai. You can call me Un-chan if you like, or whatever you want." She smiled warmly and offered me her hand.

I couldn't forget that death glare. I stretched out my hand cautiously, only for her to grab it and pull me forward.

"Don't get too familiar with Senpai. Understand?" she whispered into my ear.

"Y-yeah..."

Wow, forget calling her Un-chan. More like Un-sama. Was she really the God of Fortune? Speaking of, Sewatari had said she played the God of Fortune when we first met, right?

"I'm glad you two get along. Do you mind keeping an eye on these two, Un-chan? Make sure no one bothers them?"

"Of course, Senpai. Anything for you!" She immediately let go of my hand as though it were filthy and rushed to take Sewatari's.

I can smell yuri...

Un-sama *definitely* didn't appear to like me being around Sewatari. It seemed like she would do anything for the God of Fate.

"If you would excuse me, I must be getting back to work." Un-sama retreated to the second-floor office, glancing over her shoulder ruefully several times along the way.

Wait...the second-floor office? I was sure she worked for the major gods. After all, she was on good terms with Sewatari and hostile towards that one corrupted god.

"Sorry you had to see that, especially from gods. Like I said before, you need to be careful of the workers on the second floor. No matter how nice they seem, they're still our enemies."

Does that include Un-sama? I wanted to know, but I kept my mouth shut. No point in sticking my nose too far into the affairs of gods. Even if they looked as human as me, or showed me kindness, I had to remember that they were beings from a different dimension altogether.

We managed to work without any further interruptions, and by noon we'd finished cleaning. I packed away the tools and got changed in the cleaner's staff room. Then we headed to the third floor to report in.

Carol and I found Sewatari sitting at a desk by the back window, hard at work. I still couldn't get over how huge the office was. Nattyan had explained that the divine aura twisted the space, which was how it managed to be so big. I just nodded and pretended I understood. I'd tried to count the number of workers in here, but I lost count around twenty and had to start over. I never did make it to the end.

"We're done cleaning."

"Nice work. You can go home for the day then." Sewatari waved her hand at me, eyes glued to her computer screen.

Carol and I bowed our heads and left her to her work. We stopped in front of the office door to pick up Destiny, who was curled up under the heater. I stashed it back in my bag.

Outside the building, I breathed out a long plume of white fog. We'd arrived in Hokkaido five days ago, and I still wasn't used to the cold, though seeing snow every day made it lose its novelty. The white-blanketed scenery seemed perfectly normal now.

"Let's have a snowball fight later, Yoshio!" Carol was still enamored with the snow, racing around excitedly. I supposed she didn't have much time left to enjoy it. Sewatari had said it should only be four or five days before Carol could return to her world. We'd arrived at Isekai Connection three days ago, so that was tomorrow at the earliest. This was Carol's final night in the snow. I could put up with the cold.

"All right, let's drop our stuff off at the hotel, then we can snowball fight."

"Yay!"

My remaining time with Carol was limited. I decided I would play with her as much as I could, until I ran out of energy or she got bored.

THE NPCs IN THIS VILLAGE SIM GAME MUST BE REAL! ↵

chapter 04 Their Journey and My Protective Gaze

"I'M REALLY SORRY."

"Hey, no worries. We're not really in demand this early in the year. January tends to be slow. I was actually feeling bad that I wouldn't be able to offer *you* much work."

I was on the phone in the hotel room apologizing to my boss back home. He'd known I was in Hokkaido, but nothing more than that. Sewatari ended up contacting him to ask whether I could officially take on a cleaning job at Isekai Connection.

"Y'know, Yoshio, sometimes I think you're a little too honest. You didn't have to get me involved. You could've just done the work and taken all the money for yourself."

"I couldn't do that. I only know how to do this kind of work because of you and your company."

"Well, I'm happy you feel that way. But since you're technically still working for my company out there, you don't need to worry about us back home. Enjoy as much of Hokkaido as you can. Think of it as a business trip. I'll give you a bonus, too—just make sure you bring us some souvenirs!"

"Thank you." I bowed my thanks, even though he couldn't see me.

The truth was, Sewatari only contacted my place of work at my insistence. I wanted to do something to pay back my boss for everything he'd done for me, and I needed some way to clear the guilt I felt for going off to Hokkaido instead of returning to work. It was good motivation to work hard out here, too, since my performance would reflect on the company.

I was about to hang up the phone when I remembered another question. "How's Yamamoto-san doing?"

After he attacked me on New Year's Eve, Yamamoto-san had lost all his memories of the game. The boss told me he'd come back to work in the new year full of motivation, like he was a whole new person. Still, I was worried the memory loss might have side effects.

"He's doing good! No doom and gloom, not since the new year."

I was glad to hear it. My anger at Yamamoto-san had vanished once I learned he was controlled by that punk. Still, he did cause me, my villagers, and Carol a lot of trouble.

"I see. Please tell him and Misaki-san I say hi. Bye, now."

I ended the call and connected my phone to the charger. Just before I'd called the boss, Sewatari had contacted me with news. Carol and Destiny could go home tomorrow.

"Aren't you gonna go to sleep, Yoshio?"

Carol was playing with Destiny on the bed. She patted the duvet as though telling me to get in with her.

This is the last night we'll be able to see each other.

I'd only spent a week with Carol, but our short time together was irreplaceable to me. In Destiny's case, we'd been together for months, and it was like another family member at this point. It was still a little early for bed, but I sat down on it anyway. Destiny was to my right, and Carol lay down on its other side.

"Did you have fun in Japan—in the World of Gods, Carol?"

"Yeah! It was great! Mommy and Daddy are gonna be really jealous of me!" Seeing her gesticulate so enthusiastically as she spoke made my heart well up with emotion. I really had gotten more in touch with my feelings now that I was in my thirties.

"What's wrong, Yoshio? Do you have a tummy ache?" Carol and Destiny peered up at me anxiously. I couldn't help but pull them both in for a hug.

"Let's sleep now. We've got a big day ahead of us tomorrow." If I was better with words, maybe I could've come up with something better to say. But all I could do was show them how I felt through my actions. I sat and watched over them until they were both fast asleep.

I arrived at the building early the next morning. The passing gods greeted me as cheerfully as always. I only ever really spoke with Sewatari, Nattyan, and Un-sama; everyone else I was just on casual terms with. I occasionally nodded at the woman who gave me tea in the meeting room, and sometimes I'd have a quick chat with Gen, the corrupted god. Some of the gods obviously held me in contempt, but most of them behaved perfectly nicely. So much so that if I hadn't known better, I would have no idea they were anything more than human.

I usually detoured to the staff room to change into my coveralls, but today I headed straight for the meeting room in my normal clothes. I said good morning to everyone as I passed; their voices were just a little bit different today. Kinder and warmer. Some of them said nothing but gave me a light pat on the shoulder.

I felt like I'd seen people behaving like this in movies before. I was on the verge of remembering the context as I stepped into the meeting room. Sewatari, Nattyan, and the tea lady were already inside.

"I see you made it, young hero." Sewatari spun around dramatically to greet us, a curtain wrapped around her shoulders like a cloak. The two beside her gave a somewhat forced round of applause.

Why do I suddenly feel like I'm in a cult?

"Hey, at least *try* to look impressed! You're gonna hurt my feelings!"

"S-sorry. I just wasn't expecting this."

"Sending those two back to the other world is, like, a ceremony of grave importance. We wanted to make sure to get that across."

I'd seen better performances at my high school culture festivals, but I didn't tell them that.

"Ahem! Let's not bother with any further formalities." Sewatari tossed aside her curtain-cloak and coughed, her cheeks flushed with embarrassment. "We'll be sending Carol-chan and Destiny-chan back to the other world now. As long as you're ready?"

Carol thrust her hand in the air. "I'm ready!" she declared enthusiastically. Destiny, who was sitting on the table, raised a foreleg and tail in response.

"Glad to hear it! Come on, then! We're going up to the fourth floor."

"The fourth floor?" I echoed. I thought that floor was restricted.

"That's right. That's where the portal is."

"The portal you all came through?"

"That's the one."

So that's why no one's allowed up there—there's a portal connecting Japan to another world!

"Let's get going. It'll be quicker to show you than to explain everything down here."

As we left the meeting room, I felt the gods in the office staring at us, eyes heavy with emotion.

Nattyan put her hands on her hips. "Guys, quit starin'. You're gonna make us nervous."

It was only now that I realized what those stares meant.

"Are they worried about us?" I leaned forward to ask Sewatari, who was at the head of the group.

"Uh, well...wait, let me switch into Japanese," she whispered back into my ear. She must not want Carol to overhear. "It's normal for stuff to get sent from the other world to Japan through the portal, but this is the first time we're sending something back."

They were staring because this was unknown territory. Their gazes were the same as those in movies bidding goodbye to soldiers heading to the battlefield.

"Is there a chance this won't work?"

"Yes, but I'm confident that it's minuscule. We tried sending an object across the portal already, and that worked out fine."

"Have you sent any people across?"

"Well, no. This'll be the first time!" She winked at me cheekily, but she wasn't fooling me.

I'd already prepared myself to say goodbye, but that certainty was giving way to anxiety. Wouldn't it be best to hold off on sending them back if there was any chance of failure? I couldn't face my villagers again if anything happened to Carol. Although I guess there really was no safe way to experiment on humans. Maybe someone else could go through before Carol?

I didn't know what to do, and I was running out of time. Before I knew it, we were in the elevator hall on the fourth floor.

It looked exactly like all the other floors, except where they had a glass door leading to an office, this floor had a huge steel gate, so dark it was almost black. It was at least three meters tall and three meters wide, with doorknobs molded to look like the hilts of swords. A pattern resembling a twisted vortex was carved into the doors. The whole effect was incredibly sinister.

"We're going in."

Nattyan and the tea lady grabbed a door handle each and slowly opened the gates. I could feel the weight through the vibrations in the floor, the sound of scraping, rusted metal filling the air. Behind the doors was pitch-black darkness. No light penetrated from the hall, like there was some kind of barrier keeping it out. I squinted, but I still couldn't see anything in there. Just more darkness.

"Spooky, right?" Sewatari scratched the back of her head awkwardly before raising a hand and snapping her fingers. "Let's make it a little more welcoming." The area beyond the doors lit up.

Flames appeared, flanking a path past the gate. The space was much larger than I imagined, almost freakishly so. It was easily twice the size of the third-floor office. There was no ceiling—only more darkness. Inside were tall candlesticks, and it was their flames that lit the path, far brighter than regular candle flames should have been able to. That light revealed a floor paved with white marble.

Romanesque pillars stood spaced out at regular intervals, bigger than any I'd ever seen before, and far thicker than I was tall. They melted away into the darkness above our heads.

Sewatari and the others didn't hesitate. Carol and I exchanged a glance, nodded, and each took a deep breath. Then, we held hands and followed them. Destiny clung to my back, staring ahead solemnly.

"We're counting on you," I whispered to Destiny. Its tongue flicked out of its mouth. It winked at me encouragingly and twitched its tail.

At least someone was confident.

We walked along the flame-lit path, and it wasn't long until the three gods in front of us stopped.

"This is the portal."

The three of them turned, stepping aside to reveal a large metal pedestal in the center of the path. It looked like a pyramid with the top cut off, pipes of various lengths snaking away from it across the floor. Atop the pedestal was a large circle of...something. A spherical, crystalline vortex. I couldn't tell what color it was, but it wasn't transparent either. Maybe a reddish, blueish black with rainbow hues. My brain refused to identify it, even though I was looking right at it. Squinting didn't help.

I couldn't stop staring into that abyss. It filled me with terror, yet I couldn't help but be pulled towards it. I wanted to avert my gaze but also stare at it forever. Conflicting emotions battled in my mind.

A loud clap snapped me out of my trance. I looked up to see Sewatari with her hands together.

"It's probably a little unhealthy to stare at it for too long," she said cheerily. "It's not native to this world."

I suddenly realized that my nose was inches away from the portal. When did that happen? I took several hurried steps back, trying to swallow through my dry throat.

"All the preparations are complete. If you jump through here, you'll be back where the village was. Be warned; I can't tell you how the village is faring right now. That would be against the rules—it would give you an unfair advantage."

I was aware of that; I'd asked her about it before. That left me in a predicament, however. Suppose they were all dead, the village destroyed. I would be sending Carol back to die alone. I pictured

Carol and Destiny standing there in shock, surrounded by the ruins of the village. That image made my chest ache.

Holding Destiny tightly in her arms, Carol took a step toward the portal. Then another. One last step—a big one—and she would be on top of it. I couldn't help but stretch out a hand toward her tiny, fragile back. I opened my mouth to say something, but all that came out was a ragged breath.

I was pathetic. She was about to undertake a journey into the unknown, and I couldn't even come up with words of comfort.

Carol stopped just in front of the portal, turned around, and beamed at me like she always did. "Thanks, Yoshio! It was super fun!" Carol waved, and Destiny stared at me from her arms. I clenched my outstretched hand into a fist and turned to look at Sewatari next to me.

"The portal *is* safe, right? I mean, for humans?"

"I'm confident in the work we've done. Still, I can't give you a guarantee. We've never sent a human through it. Gods can't use it, and it's not like we could just pick someone up off the street to send them through as a test."

Right. I figured.

"Can people from this world go through?" I asked.

"No reason why not. Actually, it'd probably be easier for them, since the humans in this world aren't affected by divine aura, so—Hey!"

I ran forward before she'd even finished her explanation. As I raced past Carol, our eyes met. Hers were round with surprise. I shot her a thumbs-up.

"Me first."

Smiling wildly, I dove through the portal.

part 12

MY PRECIOUS

FRIENDS ↵

THE NPCs IN THIS VILLAGE SIM GAME MUST BE REAL! ↵

chapter 01 The Other World and My Intrusion

EVERYTHING WENT BLACK. I saw nothing, my vision painted with darkness. If I had a body anymore, I couldn't feel it. The fear of being swallowed up by the dark pulsed through me, but there was no use fighting it now. I was just glad Carol wasn't the guinea pig. This was reckless—even for me—but I'd already wasted the last ten years of my life. Sacrificing myself for someone else wasn't such a bad way to go. The thought that I could help the people I cared for deeply made the end more bearable.

"I wonder if they'll be sad when they hear I'm dead. Mom, Dad, Sayuki...and Seika."

Only a few months ago, I was nothing but a burden to my family. Back then, I figured they'd be happy if I died. What was the point of looking for work? I just squandered my time, anyway. But then I stepped outside. I became...well, not respectable, but I put some effort into my life. I began to believe that a time would come when I could repay my debt to my family and Seika. My life was back on track. Losing that was frustrating.

"I'm sorry, Dad, Mom, Sayuki, Seika."

All I could do was send my desperate apologies into the void.

"Yoshio! Wake up! Wake up!"

Someone was calling my name. A girl's familiar voice. I felt a wet sensation against my cheek. Whose voice was that? And what was this slimy feeling on my face?

"Wake up, wake up, wake up!" The desperation pulled me back to my senses.

I'm...Yoshio. I jumped through that portal into the darkness...

I remembered now. Who I was and what I'd done. My eyelids were as heavy as lead, and prying them open took effort. When I finally managed it, I saw Carol looking down at me, crying, and Destiny licking me with its long, thin tongue.

"Carol. Destiny," I croaked.

Carol flung her arms around my neck. "You're safe! I was so scared! You weren't moving!"

"Oh. I'm sorry." I sat up and patted Carol's head, then Destiny's, who was clinging to my chest and blinking up at me sweetly. I still felt woozy, and I took several deep breaths, filling my lungs. The air was cold, freezing me from the inside out. I could smell plants—lots of them.

We were surrounded by trees, the ground blanketed in short weeds. Frost covered everything, numbing my hands where they rested on the ground. Wherever this was, it wasn't Isekai Connection. We weren't in a building anymore, and the portal was nowhere in sight. We were in the great outdoors. We were—

"Who's there?! W-wait. Carol?!"

A voice called out from behind us, the anger quickly draining away, replaced by surprise. I turned to find a man with a double-handed sword and a chiseled face. Behind him stood a fence made of logs, set with a wooden gate.

A log fence out here in the wilderness. A man wielding a sword, who recognized Carol.

I knew this place. I knew this man.

We made it.

My senses were returning to me now, so I resolved to lose my composure later. I needed to wrap my head around this miracle.

"Carol. You're alive! Get away from that stranger, quick!" Gams's look of relief was quickly replaced by anger, and I found myself facing the tip of his blade. I couldn't blame him for finding me suspicious.

"Gams? What are you shouting—Carol?!" A young woman in religious dress appeared at Gams's side.

Then, a timid-looking man and a red-haired woman raced up, their faces racked with emotion.

"Carol! Carol!"

"Carol! Is that you?!"

They cast their weapons aside. Carol leapt into their arms. "Mommy! Daddy!"

The three of them wailed and wept as they held each other. I knew then that it had all been worth it, just to see them reunited like this. I sighed and tried to suppress my own tears, trembling on the edge of escaping.

Thank God...

I wanted to keep watching Carol and her family and let relief wash over me, but I still had a glimmering blade in my face. "Who are you, and why are your clothes so strange? Why were you with Carol? Fair warning, a wrong answer will be deadly."

Gams had a deep, masculine voice. I would have been afraid, but he wasn't the type to hurt anyone thoughtlessly. I knew him better than that. I knew them all. The gentle girl hiding behind him and watching me warily, the embracing family of three, the bipedal red pandas who just showed up, and the beautiful androgynous elf. I could never forget a single one.

Just looking at them now made the tears flow from my eyes.

"Crying won't get you out of this! Tell me who you are!"

"I'm..." I stopped. What was I supposed to say? I didn't want to pretend I didn't know who *they* were. Not now.

I knew the man with swords in both hands was their toughest fighter, Gams. I knew the pious girl behind him, so fond of her brother, was Chem. I knew the family of three were Carol, Rodice, and Lyra. I knew the one aiming her bow at me from a distance was Murus. I knew the two pointing their spears my way were Kan and Lan.

"You're all safe, I see." I was so happy I couldn't stop crying. I'd wanted to meet them for so long, and now they were here in front of me. I couldn't contain my joy.

"You sure are creepy. Since you're not talking, how's this?" Gams brought his blade so close to my face that it was touching my nose. If I so much as twitched, he would cut it right off.

I knew he wouldn't hesitate to kill me if it meant saving the others' lives. He was just that kind of guy.

Come on, think! What's the point if he mistakes you for a threat and you die here?!

"The truth is, I'm—"

"Don't bully Yoshio, Gams!" Carol threw herself between us and flung her arms out to protect me.

"Carol! That's dangerous!" Gams pulled his sword back swiftly.

Carol pouted and glared at him. "Yoshio's helping the gods! He protected me this whole time!"

Carol was standing up for me against *Gams*, who she adored. My heart swelled with emotion.

Thanks. I'm feeling more confident now.

I put a hand on Carol's shoulder and got to my feet. I held Gams's gaze as I spoke. "It's nice to meet you, chosen ones. My name is Yoshio, and I am a disciple of the God of Fate. I have come here to return Carol to you. She was placed in the Lord's care in the World of Gods some days ago." I didn't dare show how nervous I was. I smiled to assure them I meant no harm. I wasn't used to using my face muscles this much, and I could feel my cheeks twitching. This was the same story I'd used on Carol.

"A disciple of the Lord? And you think we'll believe—"

"It's true, Gams! We played together in the World of Gods! And I had loads of yummy food there!"

Destiny clambered up onto Carol's shoulder and waved its foot and tail in support of her fervent argument.

"I dunno, Carol. And what's that monster on your shoulder?" Gams frowned at the lizard.

"This is my friend, Destiny!"

Gams didn't attempt to pull Destiny off her back, so he probably figured it wasn't dangerous. Destiny looked almost divine with its body bathed in the sunlight. Its golden skin stood out against the trees.

"I understand your suspicions. This is a little sudden, after all. But first, please allow me to return this." I pulled the holy book out of my bag and offered it to Chem.

"The book! You really are a disciple of the Lord!" Chem let out a cry of delight, fell to her knees, and bowed deeply. Gams immediately put away his weapons and knelt to join her. The next second, all the villagers were on their knees. Only Murus stayed standing with her arms folded, her gaze cool.

"Please forgive my ignorance and my rudeness!" Gams cried. "I'll—I will take full responsibility! Just please, spare the other villagers! They've done nothing wrong!"

You're totally overreacting.

"My brother was simply unaware! Please have mercy! I shall offer myself up, so please be kind in your judgment!" Chem begged, driving her forehead down into the ground.

Was this how it felt to be an all-powerful god? This was awful. This wasn't what I wanted when I said I followed the God of Fate.

"Please get up. I am not angry in the slightest, and neither is the Lord. Gams, you have protected the village well. The Lord is pleased with you." I wasn't trying to lie—I really was filled with the utmost gratitude for him. "I am also glad to see everyone is safe." Not particularly divine or poetic, but that was all I could come up with.

I was used to RPing a god from all the prophecies I'd sent, but speaking so politely and calmly on the spot was way harder. Arranging all the words together without a single slip-up was almost too much for me.

"Thank you! Please, we cannot stay out here in the cold. We are still carrying out repairs on our village, but please allow us to welcome you there." Chem said, her eyes sparkling. She was a fervent believer of the God of Fate; my assumed persona was probably what she herself aspired to be. She and the other villagers stood up and beckoned me to follow them.

"Very well, I shall join you. I am eager to see how your village is faring, and I would like to tell you about Carol's experience in the World of Gods."

I followed them, looking around in wonder. I'd seen this view tons of times through my computer screen, but it was a completely different experience up close. The sun filtering through the gaps in the trees. The faces of my villagers. The feeling of the earth beneath my feet. The thick smell of vegetation and nature.

This really is a whole other world.

At first glance, the log fence around the village looked the same as it did before it collapsed on the last Day of Corruption, but up close I could see the differences. The logs were newer, and the fence enclosed a larger space. It was incomplete for now, with one section cordoned off with rope instead. A wooden gate was built at the fence's center. It had only been a week, and yet my villagers had already gotten this much done. Even if they'd gone without proper rest, they really shouldn't be this far along.

Maybe I was remembering wrong. That day had been a life-or-death situation, after all. Perhaps the damage to the fence hadn't been that bad.

"Welcome to our village. It's not much, but..." Gams pushed open the gate, and Chem beckoned me inside.

The area beyond the fence was unrecognizable. The space was several times larger than before, scattered with hut-like structures. They weren't made of wood, closer to tents made of slightly grimy cloth. They had pencil-shaped peaks, and they looked just like yurts—Mongolian portable homes.

"What are these tents?"

"We received these from a merchant. They are dwellings made from cloth and easy to set up. All you need to do is drape some canvas over a post."

A merchant? Must be Dordold. He does most of his trading after the Day of Corruption.

The tents were large enough to house a family each, and there were maybe ten or so.

"You have many more than you need, don't you?"

"Yes, well... Come out, everyone! It's safe!" Chem called, and several faces I didn't recognize peered out of the tents.

Who are these guys? No, really! Who are they?!

There were ten or so humans and five beautiful, long-eared elves, both male and female. And there might be more people inside the tents. On the other side of the fenced-in area were the remnants of a landslide. That was where the cave used to be.

How did all this happen?

The enclosure contained a well and some farming plots. Up by the rocky walls stood a wooden fence and some log huts. This was completely different from what I'd seen through my PC screen.

"Please, come this way." Chem held open the entrance to the one tent that was dyed in bright colors—the rest were in hues of brown and gray—and stepped aside for me.

They were treating me like a guest of honor, even though I was just a normal human like them. It made me feel a little guilty. I stepped inside the tent, noting the thick wooden post at its center that reached all the way up to the ceiling. Beside it was a sunken hearth and a wooden God of Fate statue beside an altar.

I wonder if this is their church.

The floor was covered by a rug, so I automatically went to take my shoes off. There wasn't anywhere to put them, though, and up close I could see shoe prints on the rug itself. It must have been okay to wear shoes indoors here, just like it was abroad.

This tent was way bigger on the inside than it looked. A whole family could live in here quite comfortably. Gams, Chem, Rodice, Lyra, Carol, and Destiny all followed me inside. Murus, Lan, and Kan stayed by the entrance to keep watch.

I sat down on a thick cushion, and immediately all of them (except Murus) fell to one knee and bowed their heads low. I only now realized that Murus hadn't said a word since I got here. She simply kept her distance and observed me. Suspicion crowded her gaze, and maybe a touch of loneliness.

I recalled that Murus's village had also been assigned a god—another player like me. Her home had been destroyed when that god abandoned it, but this village was still graced with its god's protection. Faced with a token of this god's love (me), this couldn't be easy for her.

Everyone stared at me silently, like they were expecting a speech.

"There is no need to be so formal. Right, Carol?"

"Yeah!"

Having Carol on my side would definitely make things less awkward. She scampered up to me the moment I caught her eye, hopping into my lap.

"C-Carol! What are you doing?! Get up at once!" Rodice cried.

"We're so sorry! We promise we'll scold her later!" Lyra joined in with her panicking husband. She beckoned to Carol desperately, but Carol just looked up at me without moving.

"It's all right. We spent a lot of time together in the World of Gods, didn't we, Carol?" I said.

"Yeah, we did, Yoshio!" We smiled at each other.

The other villagers looked at us doubtfully, but at least they relaxed a bit.

"Please sit comfortably. I may be a disciple of the Lord, but underneath I am still as human as you are. We are all equals here."

Really, I was as human as they were both underneath *and* on the surface.

"Please, could you tell me what happened after you sent Carol to the World of Gods? The Lord relies on the holy book to see into this world, but He lost that power when the book was sent to Him."

"I see. Please forgive us for doing something so—"

"There is nothing to apologize for." I stopped Chem before she could lower her head again. I was used to apologizing myself, not the other way around. I couldn't handle much more of this.

"A-anyway, I'll explain what happened." Chem was stiff with nerves. I wanted to tell her to relax again, but I was afraid that would just stress her out more. "We were ready to lose our lives after sending Carol away, and so we were about to leave the room we were sheltering in, before Kan and Lan stopped us." She glanced over at the pandas by the entrance, who nodded.

"The room where we were hiding had boarded up walls. The two of them told us about an escape route hidden back there."

I thought back to that day, remembering Kan and Lan huddled at the back of the cave. I'd assumed they'd given into despair. Thinking about it now, it made sense. They'd lived in that cave before the villagers arrived and knew its secrets. The hidden storerooms, and now an escape path. I was a little annoyed they hadn't mentioned it sooner.

"We removed the boards and found that hidden passageway. We lit up the explosives left in the cave and escaped before they went off. The monsters were all killed in the resulting landslide, as far as we can tell."

The villagers escaped while the monsters died. That was good. Still...

I know this is petty of me, but I really wish I'd gotten to see the explosion!

I couldn't believe I missed the cave blowing up and taking all the monsters along with it. I bet it was spectacular. Of course, it was more important that my villagers survived. They'd done great.

"Our entire village was destroyed. We were at a complete loss, but then Dordold arrived. He loaned us the materials we needed to restore our home, as well as food to tide us over. These tents used to belong to nomads, so he let us have them for a very good price."

Nomads? That explains why they remind me of Mongolian yurts.

"He also brought some migrants with him, as we requested previously."

That explained the new faces.

"Some of them lived with us in our old village, and some are survivors from Murus's town. We have all been working hard to restore things here, and the results so far are what you see now."

The people Dordold brought with him already knew my villagers, then. That was perfect; the merchant did a great job. And he showed up at exactly the right time. I hoped I'd get the chance to thank him personally.

"I get it—I mean, I understand what happened. You've clearly all been working tirelessly. I am sure the Lord is most pleased with your efforts."

I almost slipped back into casual speech there.

Get it together! Remember you're supposed to be a disciple of the God of Fate!

Chem raised a timid hand, gaze still on the floor. "Might I ask you a question, Yoshio?"

"Anything."

I wished she would stop being so formal, but of everyone here, she was the most devoted to the God of Fate. I doubted I could get her to chill out.

"Why did you come to this village with Carol, sir? Did the Lord give you some sort of mission to fulfill?"

Ah! I was so happy to see my villagers safe and Carol reunited with her family that I totally forgot!

I jumped through the portal without a second thought and without even asking the gods for their permission. They were probably pissed. I only did it to make sure Carol would be safe, but it would still count as an act of defiance, right? If I really did provoke the wrath of the gods, I'd probably be punished. Guilt prickled in my chest. What had I done?

"O-oh, please forgive me. Perhaps that was rude to ask," Chem said, noticing I was staring at the floor in silence.

"No, not at all." I tried to keep my expression calm, even as a panicked storm raged through me. "The Lord asked me to check on the condition of the villages and to aid in your repairs." That was the first excuse that came to mind, so I said it without thinking.

"Oh, I see! That means you shall be staying with us for a while, rather than returning to the World of Gods?"

"Y-yes, as long as it's not an inconvenience..."

Oh, yeah. That was a question.

How was I supposed to get back to Japan?

THE NPCs IN THIS VILLAGE SIM GAME MUST BE REAL! ↵

chapter 02 My Trip to the Other World

I'D MANAGED TO CONVINCE them that I meant no harm, but my real problems were just beginning. I didn't want to get in the way of the villagers' work, and I reckoned Carol would want to spend some time with her parents alone, so we all dispersed after that. Carol could tell everyone about her short trip to my world. Her parents would probably rather hear it from her than me.

"Man, my shoulders are stiff."

I'd spent so much time speaking formally and trying to keep a serene smile on my face. I didn't realize acting could use up so much energy. I glanced around to make sure I really was alone before collapsing backward and stretching out on the rug. To think they'd left me in this huge tent all by myself.

I zoned out and stared at the ceiling. It sure was cold. Even with the rug, the chill crept up through the ground. I sat back up and crossed my legs. Suddenly, I felt something crawling on top of them. Destiny was curled up on my lap.

Guess I wasn't alone in here after all.

I stroked its cool, scraggy back and set my thoughts into motion.

"I'm actually in another world, aren't I?"

Calling this unexpected was an understatement. When I began *The Village of Fate*, I bought myself some *isekai* novels and manga as reference, but I wasn't expecting them to end up as how-to guides. Commonly, those protagonists had a superpower or cheat they could use in the new world to give them an advantage. Did I have an ability like that? I held out my hand and tried to imbue it with power.

"Guuooorgh! Aaaargh! Nnnnngh! Haaaaaah!"

Nothing. I was just some weirdo holding out his hand and grunting. Thinking about it now, most of those protagonists gained their powers from a god or similar creature who entrusted them with a task. I came here without even getting the gods' permission. Of course they weren't going to bless me with power.

More pressing than that—how was I going to get back to Japan? I already had a good idea—well, it was my *only* idea.

Couldn't I...be sent as an offering like Carol was? Sewatari-san said that sending things from this world to Japan was easy. So...no reason to panic. Since I was here already, I might as well spend a little time getting to know the place. Besides, I was sure the gods would chew me out when I got home, and I wanted to put that off as long as I could. Maybe I could let them cool down a little. Kind of a naive hope, but still.

"If my phone works here, I can call them up and apologize." I took my phone from my pocket and tried turning it on.

It powered up, but there was no signal. Not expecting anything, I went to my contacts and tried calling "Developer – Sewatari."

"Wait. It's ringing?!"

That didn't make any sense! I was in a totally different world! The tone rang three times, and before I could decide whether to hang up or not, she answered.

"Yoshio-kun! Oh, thank goodness you got through!" Sewatari-san's voice came out of the phone.

Not just her voice. Her anxious face filled the screen. Wait, this wasn't even a video call!

I leaned the phone against the pole in the center of the tent, knelt on the rug, and slammed my forehead down onto it. "I'm really sorry for doing something so stupid!" I apologized as sincerely as I could, right from the depths of my heart.

"Hey, why did you apologize that fast! I had an incredible lecture prepared!" She sounded way less angry than I'd been expecting. I carefully inched my face from the floor.

Wait. She isn't mad at all?

"Look, there's a lot of stuff I should say to you right now, but I know you did that for Carol-chan's sake, right? I get that. I am a god, after all!" She winked, and in that moment, she really did look godlike.

"Hey, don'tcha get carried away! You gotta realize how much the other guys were tellin' Senpai off." Nattyan-san's face appeared, blocking out Sewatari-san's. Her tanned skin made it difficult to tell, but she seemed to have dark circles under her eyes. Her hair, usually in perfect shape, was disheveled. "It was a huge pain in the ass to alter the portal to let electronic waves go through. I'm exhausted."

"I'm so, so sorry!" I aimed my forehead at the carpet again. Even when Sewatari-san's reassurance that it was fine, I still knew I caused them a lot of trouble.

"Hey, come on now. We were just wondering if you had any questions. Honestly, it was good you went in first. Made it safe to send Carol-chan and Deedee through. Thank you, Yoshio-kun." Sewatari-san smiled gently, and I found myself enraptured. She'd spent so much time getting drunk in Hokkaido and whining about her job that I'd been harboring doubts she was actually a god. Now I just felt bad for thinking anything otherwise.

"I seriously apologize."

"Good. Why don't we move on to something a bit more constructive, then? Are you planning to live in the other world permanently, Yoshio-kun?"

I couldn't answer immediately. In fact, I was sure I misheard her. "Sorry, what?"

"You can stay in that world as the God of Fate's disciple if you like. I mean, that sort of thing is popular in recent novels and anime, right?"

That was true, but those were all fantasy stories. This was real life.

"U-um, are you being serious?" I asked.

"A hundred percent. I thought it was a dream of every Japanese person to be transported to another world? And everyone respects you there. You'll be treated like a king. You could even have a harem. I've given you an app to use miracles from your smartphone."

If the villagers saw me performing miracles right in front of them, they'd probably respect me even more. Enough to follow my every command. It was tempting compared to the pitiful existence I'd be leaving behind, but did I really want to throw my whole life away?

"I—"

"You don't have to answer right away. I want you to stick around there for a while now anyway. Have fun, okay? Just think of it as a little vacation."

"Do you *want* me to stay forever?"

"No, just...it's the second floor. They found out we sent someone from Japan to the old world, and it's causing a little friction. We're trying to fix up the portal so that nothing else can be sent through from this side. I know there are some corrupted gods after you, too, so just sit tight. I'll try and convince them not to go after you directly."

If she was this concerned for my safety, what else could I do?

"Okay. Please let me know when things have calmed down, and I'll try to enjoy myself here until then."

"Thank you for not arguing. I'll try to smooth things over as quick as I can. Before the next Day of Corruption, at the very least."

I nearly forgotten about that. I was in the Village of Fate itself, meaning that I'd be facing a Day of Corruption personally if I was still here at the end of the month. And real monsters. My sunny thoughts of worship instantly dried. My villagers went through this on a regular basis, but I really didn't want to be here for any large-scale attacks.

"I'll be in touch, okay?"

"W-wait, I—oh, she hung up."

She was a kindhearted pers—god, but I wished she was better at listening. At least I knew I had a way back now. All I needed to do was wait and make sure I kept up a convincing act in front of the villagers.

"Which won't exactly be *easy*."

The thought of forcing myself to keep up this formal disciple schtick weighed me down, but I didn't have a choice. If my villagers started getting suspicious about me, the God of Fate's disciple, it could damage their faith in the god herself. If I wanted to keep playing the game when I got back home, I had to keep up the act.

"So, what now?"

Ruminating with no end in sight was just a waste of time, so I decided to see how the village was doing. Then I could figure out my next move. I stood up, Destiny clinging onto my chest and poking its head out of my coat. I knew it hated the cold, but it probably wanted to see what was going on, too.

As soon as I left the tent, I immediately felt the villagers' eyes on me from all directions. When I looked back, they immediately averted their gazes and scattered like baby spiders.

Is this what being famous feels like?

I doubted they got many divine disciples showing up from the World of Gods. I'd be staring too in their position. I tried to ignore them, while still remembering that I was always at risk of being watched. If I was outside the tent, I had to be careful. I stretched, then made my way confidently to where the cave used to be.

"There really isn't anything left, huh?"

The old mine was completely destroyed. I'd seen it from afar, but I couldn't help sighing with regret. This place had been vital to my villagers' survival back when Gams was hurt.

I put my hands together. "Thank you for protecting them all this time." I wished I could see the space they'd lived in, but it was gone. After an explosion like that, anything we unearthed would just be dust.

Could there still be some useful stuff in there?

A couple of pickaxes and handcarts sat nearby; clearly my villagers had the same thought. I roamed the area, coming across a space surrounded with wooden boards. This was new.

"What's this? These boards are just a little taller than me..."

They stood close to the former cave, so I followed them until I reached a log cabin. I couldn't tell anything about it from out here, except that it was large. The door was shut, and I didn't want to trespass. I could come back later.

I strode over to the log fence that surrounded the village, and, walking along it, I came upon the villagers at their work. The men were busy lengthening and strengthening the fence. The elves were helping Kan and Lan shave down pieces of wood. Elves were good at woodworking; they lived in harmony with nature. Murus, while a skilled physician and marksman, wasn't so good at crafts.

She was overseeing things from a distance. Just like humans, elves had their individual strengths and weaknesses.

I continued my walk, coming upon the watchtowers. They used to only have one, built from logs. Now there were four, taller and made of tough wooden boards. With the village's recent population increase, the watchtowers could now be manned at all times.

The explosion had left the village with nothing, but it had been restored into something even better. A higher population created strength, and doubtless the village's development would continue in leaps and bounds.

I returned to the makeshift church tent, my home for the time being. I sat down in front of the sunken fire pit and stared at the God of Fate's statue through the dancing flames. The old statue had been roughly carved, difficult to tell if it was supposed to be masculine or feminine. This one had been sculpted by a far more skillful hand. I imagined Kan and Lan made this when the old one was destroyed in the explosion.

"What's a disciple of the God of Fate supposed to do all day?" I didn't come to this world for a fun vacation. I really just wanted to spend more time with the villagers after so many hours of watching them through the computer. But my story meant I was representing their god, and I didn't want to ruin their perception of her. The fact that I knew her personally now made that feeling so much stronger. Maybe I should just ask them if they needed help with anything.

I acted the moment that thought popped into my mind.

I'd learned that was the way out of being a NEET—act right away. I left the tent again and searched for a villager who didn't look too busy.

"This...is...pretty...tough..." I gasped as I swung my pickaxe outside the former cave.

Earlier, I'd left the tent and found Chem.

"Please don't be absurd! I couldn't ask the Lord's disciple to lift a single finger!"

I'd been expected her to say something like that. I was prepared with my counterargument.

"The Lord asked me to help the village, and if I don't, He will scold me when I go back. Please allow me to help. You will be doing me a service."

Chem couldn't argue when I brought her god's name up. She gave me a summary of jobs that needed doing, and I decided to go for one of the more physically demanding tasks. Between my workouts and cleaning job, I expected it to be no problem, but it was tougher than I anticipated. Swinging a pickaxe used a different set of muscles, and I could feel the strain of every swing in my arms and waist.

I was mining, currently. With the cave collapsed, it might be possible to ring some ore from the old mineshaft, and Dordold had promised to buy any we could find—a new source of income. Even after its total destruction, the cave that had once sheltered my villagers were still aiding them. It was hard to imagine where they would be without it.

Mining was a secondary task. The villagers only focused on it during breaks in their other restoration efforts, and they barely had enough people for those. That was why I volunteered to help. Out here alone I didn't have to worry about constant observation. I could drop the act and relax a little.

I wiped my sweat away with a towel from my bag, let out a deep sigh, and rubbed my shoulders. Sewatari-san had given my bag to Carol before she followed me through the portal—a very literal godsend. It was full of useful stuff. I checked my phone. It wasn't even midday yet; I'd been working for about two hours. I'd been charging my phone with a solar-powered charger I'd miraculously thought to pack. I'd won it in a contest a long time ago, but since I never went outside, it spent its whole life at the back of my closet.

With it, Sewatari-san could contact me whenever she needed to, without any worry of my phone running out of juice. And I could perform miracles. I'd tested the app out by changing the weather. It worked exactly as designed. I could rely on the miracles if I needed them.

Taking a break, I sorted through the photos I'd taken since I arrived here. I wanted as many as possible, but if I kept up this pace I'd run out of storage space any time now. I felt like I'd never get tired of just snapping the vistas around the village, and the villagers themselves.

Last night I'd had the chance to speak with my original

villagers in the tent. I showed them the pictures I'd taken of Carol in my world.

"That's what the World of Gods is like?! It's so bright! And there are so many people!"

"What are these strange tall buildings?"

"Oh, look at Carol's smile! She looks like she's having so much fun!"

My villagers were glued to the screen, amazed at what they were seeing.

"This is called a shrine, and we went to a festival! This fluffy food was so yummy!" Carol boasted. Rodice and Lyra couldn't stop smiling at her.

Gams's expression didn't change, he just stared silently at the phone. Chem gasped in astonishment, her jealousy at Carol spending time in the World of Gods evident in her gaze. She was so religious that I couldn't blame her. No wonder she longed to go herself.

Every time the photo on the screen changed, Kan and Lan would sit ramrod straight and throw their arms in the air. It caught them off guard every time. Murus tried to pretend she wasn't interested, but I noticed she never took her eyes off the phone. Personally, I figured it was a shame she didn't come over for a closer look.

I'd only shown them the photos on a whim, but we ended up going through them until my phone died. We'd have to go through the rest sometime.

Speaking of photos, I asked Gams and the others to take

me out hunting. I wanted to see a monster up close at least once while I was here. I carried a borrowed spear just in case, but I still had no idea what I was doing and promised to hang back and watch. I thought I could lend them a hand if they needed it. But things didn't turn out how I expected.

Two black wolves appeared. I was already familiar with them from my time playing the game. Gams, Kan, and Lan dropped into fighting stances, Murus readied her bow, and I...backed away. Real monsters? Were terrifying. Being chased by a big dog was scary enough, these were actually terrifying creatures of legend. I was so scared I could barely think.

They were each as big as a full-grown human, saliva dribbling from between long, pointed fangs, and the ripple of muscles bunching visibly under their jet-black pelts. They let out low, threatening growls. Anyone would be scared when faced with monsters like these. A cold sweat broke out all over my body, and my legs trembled. My throat felt impossibly dry. I had no urge to fight, only to run. I only managed to remain standing by propping myself up with my spear.

I stood back and watched as the villagers defeated the beasts with ease. One of the wolves had its head cut clean off, and another recoiled in a spurt of blood as an arrow penetrated its eye. The scent of the trees around us mingled with rusted iron, making my nose sting. The cloying stink and flying gore made nausea rise in my stomach, and I just managed to hold it back. I couldn't remember what the villagers said to me afterward, but when we returned to the village, I collapsed to the floor of my tent. I knew then that I wasn't fit to fight monsters in this world like an *isekai* protagonist. I was better suited to slow-paced work, so that's what I would do.

"I'll put as much effort as possible into mining." I put my phone away and faced the sediment in front of me again. I wanted to extract every piece of ore I could.

As I dug, I felt someone watching me. I turned and locked eyes with a pair of villagers peering out at me from behind one of the tents. One was a woman around Lyra's age, and the other was a little girl. I nodded to them, and they responded with deep bows before scampering away.

"It's always the same thing."

The villagers were clearly interested in me, but they never approached. I'd tried closing the gap several times, but they responded so formally that it was hard to keep up a conversation. Chem's behavior stuck out most of all. She always stared at me with such great respect. I was used to it at this point, but I still hadn't managed to have a proper conversation with her.

"Good morning." I tried a greeting.

"Y-Yoshio! H-how do you do? Th-thanks be to the Lord for another beautiful day!"

"Well, it's raining a little. Hopefully it clears up soon." I was so nervous trying to keep up my formal speech that I barely knew what I was saying.

When I tried talking to Gams, he replied with: "Yes," "I know," or "Got it," no matter what I said, conversation over. Rodice and Lyra constantly apologized for their daughter imposing on me.

Kan and Lan barely spoke at the best of times, so my interactions with them weren't much better than the ones I had with Gams. Whenever I bumped into Murus, she would nod at me before making herself scarce. I hadn't spoken to her at all yet. It was obvious she was avoiding me.

"What's wrong, Yoshio? You look sad! You gotta smile!" Carol hopped out in front of me and pushed the corners of my lips up with her fingers. She was still wearing her teddy backpack from Japan, Destiny's head poking out from the zipper. She'd started wearing her clothes from this world again, but she never took that backpack off.

"You're a good girl, Carol."

Carol was the only person in the village who spoke to me without hesitation. She complained that her parents and Chem scolded her for being so familiar with me, but I fervently hoped she wouldn't stop.

"Are you worrying about something, Yoshio?"

"Yeah. I want to get to know everyone in the village better, but they're keeping me at arm's length."

"Everyone says it's rude to speak to you because you're God's disciple. I don't think it's rude, though, because you're Yoshio!"

See, I didn't blame them for this behavior, and I didn't mind it from the new arrivals, but I'd known my original villagers for so long now that their distance kind of hurt. I'd watched them for months through the game, but of course, they didn't know that. This was a one-sided relationship that I probably should have foreseen.

"If God said they had to be nice to you, then I think they would be nice!"

I chuckled. "Yeah, that...might work."

I never thought of that!

Chem had the holy book again. There was nothing stopping me from sending a prophecy with my phone.

I decided to give it a try. I was sick of being ignored!

THE NPCs IN THIS VILLAGE SIM GAME MUST BE REAL! ↵

chapter 03 God's Message and My Hope of Friendship

NOW THAT I'D DECIDED to send a prophecy, I needed to figure out how to word it. Would persuading them to be more friendly with me be the right approach? This felt like cheating—putting words into their god's mouth—but I decided not to think too hard about it. I pulled out my phone and typed out a draft message.

"My dear followers. Thank you for taking care of my disciple. I would ask that you treat him kindly as one of your own. That is my will."

Tonally, maybe a little off. I didn't know if the God of Fate would make such a shallow request—if shallow was even the right word. But I guess I *had* asked for love advice before.

Was it right for a god to try to cozy up with his followers? Maybe I should put more majesty into the request and make it sound more like a duty.

At this rate, I'd just end up thinking myself into knots.

"Yoshio, you look weird."

"Oh! Sorry." I'd almost forgotten Carol was with me. I should get back to work and ponder the prophecy while I dug.

"I gotta go back to work, Carol. What are you up to?"

"I'm gonna help Mommy! Then I'm gonna make Gams spend time with me!"

No mention of Rodice. I felt bad for him. Carol had spent most of her first day back with her parents, but by day two she was all about Gams again. I was pretty jealous of Gams, not to mention Rodice. I'd only spent a week with Carol, but she was the most special of all my villagers to me. There was nothing unseemly about my feelings. I saw her like a daughter of my own.

"Oh, does God have any messages for us? Everyone's worried because there are no new prophecies in the book."

Wait, was Carol on to me?

"Everyone's really excited to get another one, too, 'cause it's been ages!"

Of course, what was I thinking? Her question was entirely innocent. My villagers had been missing their holy book for a week. That meant no prophecies and no miracles. On top of losing everything, they could no longer feel the presence of their god. No wonder they were anxious.

I couldn't send a prophecy for selfish reasons. If I wanted my relationship with the villagers to improve, I had to put in the work myself. Having made up my mind, I changed the approach to my next prophecy. I'd express my relief that they were all safe and tell them to make good use of the disciple the God of Fate sent.

"Could you let Chem know there'll be a prophecy soon? The Lord told me earlier that He was going to send one," I said.

"Oh! You can talk to God with that glowing block! Right! I'll go tell her!" Carol waved as she raced away. I waved back and then got down to business.

"My dear followers, I am immeasurably pleased to see you all safe and to witness your brilliant triumph over adversary. Be assured that I will afford my protection to all the village's new arrivals. My disciple will remain with you for a time. Please put him to work as you would any other member of the village; he has no need of special treatment. That will help him feel more at ease."

This was my first prophecy in a while and I was a little rusty, but I knew my villagers would kindly overlook any sloppy word choice.

I had to get to work on my own relationship with the villagers. I could only just remember the new names and family compositions; I had a long road ahead of me. I should start with my original five, plus Kan and Lan. Murus was openly avoiding me, so I'd leave her alone for now. She'd come and find me when she felt ready to.

"Guess I'll start with the pandas."

And I *didn't* just choose them to steal a chance to touch their fluffy fur or because just looking at them improved my mood. More because that while they believed in the God of Fate, their faith wasn't particularly passionate. They were generally reserved as well, so getting to know them shouldn't take too much conversation.

I stepped out of my tent and immediately felt the stares. I smiled at the villagers, doing my best not to let my mouth twitch. They bowed as one before scattering in every direction. I was left all alone, my only company the cold wind whipping leaves past my feet. My heart felt empty. Being special and respected wasn't all it was cracked up to be.

Kan and Lan had built their new hut where their previous home and workshop stood before the explosion. The exact same spot. Outside the hut was a stone kiln, built for simple iron smithing.

As I approached, I heard wood being stripped inside. They must have been working.

"Hello? It's Yoshio. Do you have time to speak with me?"

A pause. "Come in."

The door opened to reveal the panda with lighter fur, Lan. Even up close she just looked like a big red bear wearing clothes. These two were hard to read, since even their faces were covered with fur. There was never much inflection in their speech either. Their feelings were still a mystery to me.

Back when I was playing the game, I spent a lot of my downtime watching these two. I had some experience with their body language. Right now, their ears were standing straight up, and they were staring at me. That meant nerves or anxiety. Flat ears meant fear, and raised arms were for intimidation. So far so good.

"I apologize for interrupting your work."

"It's okay."

"No problem."

Kan, who was shaving wood inside the hut, stopped what he was doing and tottered over to me.

Why do they have to be so cute, dammit?!

I fought hard to keep a big dumb smile off my face. You couldn't tell by looking at them, but these two were older than Rodice and Lyra. They wouldn't appreciate being cooed over.

Gritting my teeth, I somehow managed to maintain a sober expression. "Did you two carve the God of Fate statue in the tent?"

"Yes."

"We did."

Silence. I'd been expecting this conversation to take some work, but this was ridiculous.

I asked them more about their work and other matters, but they only responded with, "Yes," "No," "That's right," and "That's wrong." Even the virtual assistant on my smartphone was a better interlocutor than this.

Luckily, I was prepared. I opened my bag and rummaged until I found what I was looking for.

"What is that?"

"Show us."

It was the first time they'd shown interest in anything since I got here. They stared unblinkingly at the objects I took out. "These are carpenter's tool from the World of Gods. This is a Japanese plane, and this is an ink line."

These were two traditional Japanese carpentry tools. I bought them secondhand online. At Sewatari-san's insistence that both people and objects could pass through the portal, I'd picked up some souvenirs for my villagers. These were two of them.

"This is the ink line. You lay out the string like this, and when you ping it, it leaves a black line behind. The line is perfectly straight. I thought you could use it for your woodwork."

I demonstrated on one of the pieces of scrap wood in the corner of the room. They both gasped in astonishment.

"This is a Japanese plane. You can use it to shave down a surface and make it perfectly even." I demonstrated with the same piece of wood, and they gasped again. Their round little paws were squirming with excitement, and their eyes were sparkling, eager to try the tools out for themselves. "I'd like to give these to you as gifts to mark us getting to know each other. Will you accept them?"

I held the plane and the ink line out toward them. The pandas looked at each other, nodded in unison, straightened up, and held out their paws to me.

"We accept."

"We'll take them."

I felt my heart clench again at their mannerisms. I kept as straight a face as I could, somehow managing to pass them the tools without breaking into a huge smile. After that, their attention slid off me to focus solely on their woodworking. They were facing away, but I could sense their delight. Not wanting to get in their way, I turned to go.

Before I could leave, their voices called out from behind me. "Thank you."

"These are great."

That was all I needed to hear. I lifted my hand in a wave and left Kan and Lan's little house behind.

"Who next... Wait, I've got an open invitation, right?"

Rodice and his family had already requested I come over so they could thank me properly. Carol was excited to have a meal together. Still, I didn't want to just show up out of the blue and demand they cook me something. I needed to give them advance warning. "I should've asked Carol before when she was with me."

There was no helping it now. I searched the village for her—not too difficult since, though it was bigger than before, it still wasn't huge. I found Carol straight away, carrying firewood.

"Hey, Carol."

"Yoshio!" She ran up to me, beaming. I immediately felt my own spirits lift.

"Are you helping out?"

"Yeah! Mommy told me to bring this firewood for her!" Carol was wobbling under the weight of the wood. Clearly, she had grabbed as much as she could possibly handle.

"Could you tell your mommy and daddy that I'd like to come and see them?"

"Okay! But what about the firewood?"

"I'll take it for you, so don't worry about it."

"Okay!" Carol handed me the firewood and sprinted away.

I wish I had her energy...

I thought about immediately racing after her but decided against it. They would probably want to prepare for the disciple's visit. Spruce the place up a little, but also prepare themselves mentally.

I walked as slowly as I could. The village was small enough that a normal pace would bring me to their door in less than a minute, but I managed to drag it out to three. I put down the firewood beside the entrance and dusted my hands.

"Hello? It's Yoshio."

The curtain across the door immediately moved aside. They must have been waiting for me.

"Welcome, Yoshio! I'm afraid it isn't much, but please come on in!" Rodice's face was pale with nerves, painted-on smile clearly forced.

I stepped inside without hesitation.

Carol stood in front of a low, round table with cushions arranged around it. "This is your seat, Yoshio!" she announced, patting the cushion next to where she was sitting. I joined her.

"Mind your manners, Carol," Rodice warned, wiping the nervous sweat from his brow.

Lyra appeared, bringing out a tea set with unsteady steps. Her steadfast reliability seemed to have vanished in my presence.

"Please do not be so nervous. I'd like it if you could treat me in the same way Carol does."

"B-but, sir! We couldn't possibly speak so casually to a disciple of the Lord!"

"My husband is right! It's unacceptable!" Lyra cried, holding a plate up to her face.

Rodice usually spoke in a formal tone, but it was weird hearing Lyra talk like that. I almost asked her who she was, and what she had done with the real Lyra.

"I am a human, too. I am speaking in a manner which befits a disciple of the Lord, but I did not speak this way with Carol. Did I?"

"Yeah! Now you sound weird!"

I laughed. "Sorry. Sometimes grown-ups gotta change how they speak around each other." Carol was so easy to talk to; she was the only person in the village who didn't seem afraid of me. Lyra and Rodice stared at me speaking so plainly to their daughter. "You see? Please don't feel you have to be overly polite."

"See?! You guys didn't believe me!" Carol said, puffing out her chest. Apparently, her parents hadn't believed I could be chill.

"I understand, but we are still in your debt, sir. Thank you so much for taking care of our daughter." Rodice and Lyra bowed their heads.

"It was nothing. I enjoyed the time I spent with her a great deal. So much that I find myself wanting to thank you." I wasn't just being polite; I truly meant it. I never once felt like Carol was a burden, even if she definitely ran me ragged. "Ah, I know. Would you two like to see the pictures we took in the World of Gods together again?"

"Yes, please!" They spoke in perfect unison.

I'd already shown them these photos at the welcome feast, but we had to go through them quickly just because of how many people were there. Lyra and Rodice probably wanted to take a proper look. I pulled up the images on my phone and went through them, one by one.

"These are from the festival, aren't they? We saw them the other day."

"You can buy loads of yummy food at these stalls!"

"That does look nice! Everything's so pretty, too."

"Yeah! The World of Gods is really colorful and bright!"

As we went through them, Carol and I explained the origin of each photo. Her parents nodded along with interest, their faces alight. We'd looked at about ten, when a hungry growl echoed through the tent. Carol's face flushed as she put her hands bashfully on her belly. Apparently seeing all the food in the photos made her hungry. We were so deep in conversation that lunchtime was long gone.

"Hungry, are we?" Lyra laughed. "I'll make some lunch. Would you like some as well, Yoshio? I must warn you, it won't be too fancy."

"Yes, please, if you're offering. Would you mind letting me make something small, too? I only need a corner of the kitchen."

"I-I couldn't—"

"Yoshio's gonna cook?! What are you gonna make, Yoshio?!" Carol interrupted her mother's objection.

I took something out of my bag to show Carol. She immediately threw her hands into the air and started bouncing with excitement, just like she always did when she was at her happiest. "That's my favorite! Mommy, Daddy, I promise it's real good food from the World of Gods!"

"From the World of Gods?!" Rodice and Lyra exclaimed.

"All I need is some hot water," I said.

"That's all?"

I slipped past the confused Lyra and got started. Which just meant taking the lid off halfway, emptying in the powdered soup packet, and pouring in water. Lyra boiled some vegetables and sautéed some meat. There was rice, too, and I completed the meal by giving everyone a container of instant noodles.

"There are three flavors, so have a taste and pick the one you like best." There was soy sauce, pork, and curry. "Will you show your parents how to eat them, Carol?"

"Okay! Watch this!" Carol proudly took one of the cups, removed its lid, and began to stir up the contents with a fork.

Her parents took a cup each and followed her example. They had a taste, their eyes narrowed in a mixture of curiosity and anxiety. Their expressions cleared simultaneously.

"Th-this is delicious!"

"I've never tasted anything like this before!"

"See?! Try some of mine!"

The three of them swapped the cups around to try the other flavors. I watched the happy family and sampled some of Lyra's cooking. It was flavored only with salt and pepper, but it was good. Dordold sold spices, but they were highly valuable in this world, which meant Lyra brought out her best for me. I savored the taste, grateful to her for using such precious ingredients.

Thanks to Carol's presence, I made good progress with Rodice's family. Next in line was Chem. She would be easier to get close to than Gams. Chem respected me a lot and would never dream of talking back to me or disagreeing. While Gams wasn't as devout as his sister, his faith in the God of Fate was still strong. He was silent at the best of times, but even more so when I was around. I guess I made him nervous.

Chem was usually in the church at this time of day, but that church was currently my quarters. Lyra said she might be doing laundry instead.

The villagers used to do their laundry at a spring inside the cave, but that had blown up along with everything else. I was worried they'd been going all the way to the river, but Lyra gave me directions and I followed them to that area surrounded by boards I'd come across earlier. The wooden hut's door was open this time, and I went right in. Beyond the door were several shelves to the left and right, with another two doors between them. I knew what sort of place this was immediately.

"A bathhouse?"

The shelves had to be shoe racks, and the blue and red doors were meant for men and women respectively. The Japanese-style design of the place might have been influenced by the game's players, since it was built recently.

There were four pairs of shoes on the shelves by the women's entrance, meaning Chem wasn't here alone. Lyra said this place was used for laundry during the day, so I could just go right on in through the women's entrance. But that was just too awkward. I walked up to the door and cleared my throat.

"Hello?"

"Yoshio?"

A voice came from behind me. Shocked, I spun around. There was Gams, frowning at me.

"What are you doing here?" I asked.

Wait. Don't tell me he's here to perv on the girls. He always looks so serious...

"I came to get Chem. We're going hunting and patrolling."

That made sense. Though Chem wasn't a fighter, she could use healing magic, dealing with any minor injuries in an instant.

"I see."

"Why are you here?" Gams said.

"I'm...going around the village. I wanted to talk with everyone. I was just with Rodice's family."

"Oh. Well, I'll hunt alone then." Gams turned to leave, but I put a hand on his shoulder to stop him.

"If you are going to fight monsters, you ought to be prepared for anything. I can speak with Chem another time." The village's safety was more important than me making friends.

"I see. Goodbye." Gams opened the door to the women's entrance and stepped in without hesitation. I followed him, resolving to be as bold as he was.

The inside was large, with an open-air bath and washing area paved with stone. The bath was big enough to hold maybe ten people, with stone spouts sitting at one end, one for hot and one for cold. Chem was doing laundry, along with Murus. I hadn't realized she would be here.

"You have hot water here, too?"

"Yes," Gams said. "The explosion opened up a hot spring be-side the original cold spring. We can draw from both sources now." It was rare to hear Gams say so much in a single breath. Still, they should have mentioned they had a bath! They keep bringing me buckets of hot water; it was starting to make me feel guilty. What I wouldn't give to kick back in a luxurious hot spring!

"Oh, Gams. And—Yoshio?!" Chem, who had been washing with her back to us, quickly sprang to her feet and bowed deeply. Murus just glanced at me before continuing her work.

She really doesn't like me, huh?

"You nearly done with the laundry? I want to go out."

"Yes, I've just finished. Will you be coming with us, Yoshio?"

I wasn't expecting that question and found myself nodding automatically. She must have thought that was why I was here, even though last time I just made a fool of myself. Still, I wanted to try again.

"Do you mind?" I asked. "I'll try not to get in the way."

I had to expose myself to the monsters at least a little, to try to lessen my initial panic response. I couldn't afford to lose it in an emergency. I didn't need to be able to fight them—just not end up paralyzed with fear when someone needed me.

Chem and Gams exchanged a doubtful glance.

"It's fine if he just stays out of the way and watches, isn't it?" I wasn't expecting Murus of all people to stick up for me. She didn't look thrilled, but I was grateful for her support nonetheless.

"If I get in the way, you can send me back at any time."

"Well, if you insist. Gams?"

"Okay."

I thanked them, and we agreed to meet at the village gates in five minutes. I quickly returned to my tent to sort through my bag. Just as I was about to set off, I caught sight of Destiny, curled up in the bed and watching me accusingly.

"Wanna come with?"

It nodded its head eagerly. I opened my bag, and it immediately dove inside. I still had a couple of disposable hand warmers in there.

"Your job is to guard me, okay? I'm sorry for relying on you so much, but you'll protect me, won't you?"

Destiny winked.

I'm glad I have such a reliable lizard.

I arrived at the gates to find the three from the bathhouse waiting for me, along with Kan and Lan.

"Kan and Lan wanted to come, too," said Chem.

"Thanks for the tools."

"We'll guard you."

They offered me their fluffy paws. I accepted their handshakes without hesitation.

They're so fluffy! And their paw pads! Hnngh!

"You made friends?" Chem said.

"I had a chance to speak with them earlier."

Though it was the gifts that won them over, rather than my conversational skills. Either way, I was grateful for their protection. With Destiny along as well, I shouldn't be getting in the way of any battles.

I nodded as we passed the new villagers keeping watch at the gate. They stiffened and bowed at perfect ninety-degree angles. By now I was used to it. I just smiled and waved.

This was only the second time I'd stepped outside the village; I hadn't been back since that run-in with those wolves. I readied myself, determined not to act so shamefully this time around. Out in the wilds, it was dangerous to let your guard down for even a second. This was a world swarming with ferocious monsters.

Before they'd found the cave, my villagers had slept in the open forest. It must have been terrifying. So much about a place couldn't be conveyed through a screen. I needed to drink in as much as possible while I could, before I went back to playing the game normally.

We walked through the forest in silence. Gams took the lead, followed by Murus, Chem, me, and then Kan and Lan bringing up the rear. The formation would protect us from rear or pincer attacks.

I'd seen the area around the village enough times to know we were headed into the northeast section of the forest. Directly to the north was the "Forbidden Forest." The villagers typically avoided that area, but it seemed they'd already hunted all the monsters close in.

"We've taken to going this way just recently, so we can cut down the monster numbers before the Day of Corruption," Chem explained.

That made sense after the close encounter with destruction last time.

The monsters surrounding the village weren't necessarily

those summoned by other players. Many of them had been living here for a long, long time, and they rampaged on the Day of Corruption just as much as any player-controlled horde. Whittling down their numbers made sense.

We continued northeast, keeping our guard up. I took out my phone to give me a bird's eye view of the area, which was when I noticed it. Movement in the southeast. I zoomed in.

"Gams. We've got green goblins coming from that way." I pointed. Gams frowned doubtfully, but he put a hand to his forehead and squinted into the distance. Murus stared out attentively. She didn't bother to hide the fact that she didn't believe me.

Yup. She really does hate me.

"It does look like there's something."

"I hear footsteps."

Their frowns were replaced by looks of surprise. Chem clasped her hands, looking at me with admiration. I felt more guilt than happiness. Really, it was the game that spotted them, not me.

I took a few steps back to keep out of the way. Lan stayed to guard me, and Chem stepped away as well. Kan stood beside Gams, the two of them readying their weapons. They glared through the many large trees and obstacles that blocked their vision. Gams hid behind a tree to the right while Kan took one on the left. Murus crouched and whispered something. The weeds there began to grow, concealing her.

"That's a spell..." It wasn't even flashy magic, but I couldn't contain my excitement at seeing it for the first time. Just another reminder that I really wasn't on Earth.

Lan, Chem, and I hid ourselves and looked on, staying quiet until we heard soft footsteps that grew slowly louder. Gams nodded at Kan as the green goblins appeared between the trees.

I managed to remain calm this time. I'd seen a green goblin before, even if it was an illusion. Who knew that encounter on the train would come in handy?

The goblins walked right past Kan and Gams, and a moment later, two of them had weapons in their backs. The third goblin turned at its allies' groans, but it didn't have time to scream before it fell lifelessly to the forest floor, a single arrow protruding from its skull.

The attack was perfectly smooth, a completely different experience from watching it through a screen. My skin prickled with nerves, and realizing I'd stopped breathing at one point, I took a huge breath. I was a little surprised at myself for managing to keep cool at the sight of three humanoid creatures dying in front of me. Perhaps all the stuff I'd been through had made me mentally tougher. That would be nice.

Still, the smells of the forest mingled with the stench of blood *wasn't* something I thought I could get used to. I approached Gams, trying not to look at the dead goblins. "That was impressive."

"Three goblins are nothing." Gams's tone was indifferent rather than boastful as he dealt with the remains. They piled up the bodies, doused them with oil, and incinerated them, taking all necessary precautions to make sure the fire didn't spread. They'd done it loads of times in the game—burning the remains so other monsters weren't attracted by the smell of blood.

"We'll keep going, if that's all right," said Gams.

"Of course."

He was offering me the chance to go back to the village, but I was fine. This was going way better than my first attempt.

We explored the forest for another hour or so without further incident. We were about to head back to the village, when a scream echoed through the trees.

"Help!"

It sounded like a woman. I turned to ask Gams what we should do, but he was already moving, dashing off in the direction of the voice, Murus close behind. They didn't hesitate for a second. Staying behind was dangerous, so the rest of us hurried to follow. The screams came intermittently. Whoever it was still clung to life, but probably not for long. I ran as fast as I could, but Murus and Gams were pulling ahead. Even Chem had to regulate her pace to let me catch up. The inhabitants of this world were impressively fit.

Gams and Murus were just specks in the distance when they suddenly veered to the left toward the sound of clashing metal.

A swordfight?

"Don't worry about guarding me, Lan! Please go and help them out!"

Lan glanced at Chem. Chem nodded. Lan dropped to all fours and raced away at an incredible speed. By the time I caught up with everyone, gasping for breath, it was all over. Bodies scattered the ground. A couple of black wolves, a person in leather armor, two horses, and a broken cart. The cart was fancier than the one in the village, painted white and heavy with ornamentation.

Our fighters were unharmed. I had time for a split second of relief—before my breath was snatched away again by the stranger at the scene. She had golden hair that brushed her shoulders and sleek, straight-cut bangs. Her features were beautifully crafted and perfectly symmetrical. Her lips were red, eyes lightly painted. This was the first time I'd seen someone wearing makeup in this world. The woman was just a little shorter than Chem and wore an elegant dress, giving her an upper-class air. Beside my villagers, she stood out.

Gams offered her his hand, and she stood up.

"Oh."

I gasped out loud. Chem and Murus were beautiful themselves, but this woman was out of this world. It wasn't just her face but the way she held herself. She just oozed feminine charm. Chem gave her a terrifying scowl, staring at where the woman held her brother's hand.

Oh God. Chem and Carol were definitely *not* going to take well to a gorgeous, refined woman in their midst.

I feel a bloodbath coming on.

chapter 04 · My Final Decision

I WAS POSITIVE the woman's arrival would cause a huge fight over Gams, but in the end, she left a couple of days later with a group of hunters. They'd been searching for her, apparently. I'd been worried about Gams's safety for nothing, it seemed.

The woman's name was Salem, and she was the daughter of a noble household. She'd been attacked by bandits while on the road near the Forbidden Forest and fled into the woods to avoid capture. The soldier guarding her was secretly in league with the thieves, but just when they were closing in on her, monsters attacked. The bandits fled, and Salem thought she was done for, until Gams showed up to save her. Charmed by his skills, she tried to hire him as a guard during her time at the village, but he turned her down.

When it was time for her to leave, she took his hand, seeming reluctant to be parted—and earning her a pair of nasty glares from Chem and Carol.

Any other game would probably have some event to let her join the village, but she left after only two days, which was probably safest for all concerned.

"Sounds like a lot has happened since I've been away!"

We were in my tent, and Carol was explaining the events of the past few days to a plump man. He was the well-spoken merchant with a meek smile: Dordold.

Not more than twenty minutes earlier, Dordold had been on his knees bowing down to me a mere instant after I introduced myself.

"The God of Fate's disciple! My name is Dordold! I'm a lowly merchant!"

Out of all the reactions I'd gotten, his might've been the most overblown.

"Please raise your head. I am a mere servant. Please treat me as you would any other villager. The Lord has told me that He is grateful to you for the help you provide His beloved people."

"O-oh no! Such praise is wasted on me!"

I took Dordold's hand and knelt down on one knee. "The God of Fate grants you His protection."

Large tears welled up in Dordold's eyes, dripping to the ground. I came up with the words on the spot, but they seemed to do the trick. Dordold dropped his extreme formality and spoke to me without reservation. Being a merchant, he was more flexible and comfortable with change than my villagers.

"How long will you be staying in the village, Yoshio?" Dordold asked. Chem and Rodice, who were with us, looked at me with interest.

"I intend to leave before the Day of Corruption."

Although Sewatari-san hadn't contacted me yet, which made me nervous.

"I see," Chem murmured, looking at the floor. Rodice didn't say anything, but he looked a little downcast as well. They must've been thinking back to the tragedy of the last Day of Corruption. Maybe they'd been hoping I would be around to help, given my connection to the God of Fate.

"Please do not worry. The Lord is always watching over you. Though I may be gone, His protection will stay. I shall ask the Lord personally to ensure it." I gave them an encouraging smile, hoping to clear the heavy atmosphere. Their expressions softened a bit.

Well, that put their minds at ease. Now all I had to worry about was my own.

Dordold and the others took their leave. Alone in my tent, I let out a heavy sigh. According to my phone, it was January 25th— just six days until the Day of Corruption.

"I wish they'd get in touch already..."

My phone rang, like it could hear me. I jumped nearly a foot in the air, but quickly composed myself and checked the screen. "It's Sewatari-san!"

I answered the call and switched on my video.

"Whew, sorry for the delay, but we've got everything in order now! You can come back whenever you want. Even right this second, really."

"Thank you." I'd been anxiously awaiting her call, and yet I could feel my heart sinking.

"You don't seem happy."

"Sorry. Could I ask a favor?"

"Just ask! No need to be so formal!"

I took a few deep breaths to compose myself. My request was reckless but also necessary. I wouldn't be able to face myself in the mirror, otherwise.

"Could I stay here until after the Day of Corruption?"

"Wait, are you serious? Do you even know what you're asking?"

"Of course." I knew the dangers as well as anyone.

"If you die there, that's it. You won't just get a game over screen and appear back in Japan."

"I know."

"Well, you seem to have already made up your mind. Can I ask why?"

"I can't run and leave my villagers to face the danger by themselves. Just sit safe in my room and give them orders from there. That would be pathetic."

My *whole life* up until this point was pathetic, so what was a couple more cowardly decisions in the grand scheme of things? But it didn't matter why I was doing it, whether it was to prove something to myself, or what. But I wasn't a NEET or a shut-in here. I was the God of Fate! Or her representative, at least.

"I see," said Sewatari-san. "Well, I did say that you could live there forever if you wanted to. Show everyone your miracles, tell them you're a disciple of God. Form a harem. I'll even throw in an upgrade of your choice."

"Stop trying to tempt me. I'm not going to do that."

Sewatari-san laughed. "You sure are a singular kind of man, Yoshio-kun. Well, maybe half a singular man. You'll get there. You've grown a ton since you started playing. It's like you're a different person."

"You've been watching me?"

"Well, I mean...*you've* been watching the villagers go about their lives this whole time, too. I'm a god. I can do that."

"What about my, uh, private time?"

She paused. "No comment."

I did not love that moment of hesitation, but I didn't push.

"If you've made up your mind, I won't stand in your way," she said. "And as reward for your bravery, I'll give you a gift and some advice. Both the players you fought in Hokkaido are planning to target your village on the Day of Corruption. Watch out for that."

That bland salaryman Habatake and that punk, huh?

If they attacked together, we'd have to rally.

"I'll give you the gift on the day of. Uh...I guess I'll say something godlike before I go." She cleared her throat. "I have heard your request. When the Day of Corruption draws to a close, you shall return to your homeland of Japan." Sewatari-san spoke in a majestic tone. She actually did sound pretty godlike.

"Thank you so much for entertaining my selfish request."

"Eh, this is the good kind of selfishness, so I approve. I was right to choose you as a player."

"By the way," I said. "I've been wondering this for a while. Is there criteria for choosing players?"

"Kind of, but it's a trade secret. I might be able to let you in on it if you level up high enough. Just make sure you survive the next attack, okay?"

"I'll do my best. Oh, I've got one more question. It's about the corrupted gods..."

When the call ended, I felt weak, all the tension draining from my body. I'd really had to brace myself to ask something so unreasonable of a god, no matter how nice she was.

"Now I can't run away. I've just got to stay and face this." I said the words aloud for motivation. The only way out was through. I'd survive the danger along with my villagers, and we'd come out the other side victorious. My love for my villagers would only grow...and maybe even my love for myself.

I was going to leave my negative thinking and the useless parts of me behind in this world. I would return to Japan as someone with a truer soul. Dying here wasn't an option!

Determination flaring in my chest, I started tapping at my phone. I was going to utilize every bit of know-how to rise to this challenge.

The Day of Corruption was tomorrow. I didn't do any mining today, instead going to meet with Kan and Lan in their workshop. This village's survival depended entirely on the weapons and tools they crafted. I offered them support and shared some ideas. Currently, they were working on making new arrows—hundreds of them. The new elven villagers were archers, just like Murus, so you could never have too many.

The village men were repairing and reinforcing the log fence, running busily around town. They'd finished the fence two days ago, but they were checking every last log for weak points, quickly switching out any parts that seemed faulty.

The women and children were working to prepare as much food as they could in advance of tomorrow. Lyra and Chem were in charge of the cooking.

The village's defenses were stronger than ever, and some of the new villagers were fighters, rendering our offensive forces much more powerful. Most of all, I was grateful for the elves. As proficient archers, they could climb the watchtowers and snipe enemies from afar. We'd have a leg up right off the bat.

Dordold sold us weapons and armor at a good price—we didn't lack anything. We had eight close-range fighters including Gams, Kan, and Lan. Six elves took care of long-distance attacks including Murus. That was three times as many offensive hands as before. I'd also saved up my FP for miracles or summoning the golem. I'd barely used any of it since the start of the year, so I had plenty in reserve without spending any new money. But I still asked Sewatari-san to convert my earnings at Isekai Connection to points.

The evening came on, and Gams and his patrol returned. I was in charge of dinner for today, aware that this might be my last chance to eat with everyone. I cooked using Chinese spices I brought from the other world in a red can and a Japanese-style broth. A multinational dish.

Everyone finished their plates with relish.

Looks like Mom taught me well.

After dinner I went to relax in the baths, Destiny coming along with me like it was the most natural thing in the world.

Finally, everyone gathered in the center of town.

"The Day of Corruption starts at midnight! Let's get through it together!" Rodice declared, earning him a cheer from the crowd.

The village had no formal chief, but Rodice appeared to fill that role naturally. I'd declare him the formal leader in a prophecy at some point.

"I won't talk for long because everyone needs rest. Yoshio? Have you any words for us?"

I straightened my back. I thought he might ask me to say something; I already had my speech prepared.

"There is just one thing I want to say. Let us get through this together. Know that the Lord is watching over you always. May He bless this village and its people!" I tried to keep my tone bright. Not much, but it was the best I could do.

The villagers gave thanks to the God of Fate with tear-choked voices. I touched each of their heads as they bowed in fervent prayer, speaking their names in turn. When I was finished, I smiled and told them to raise their heads.

The moment I was back in the tent, I dropped to my knees and slammed my head into my blanket.

That was sooooo cringey! Did I really do that?! Me? GAAAAARGH! I know I'm trying to get into my role, but that was way too much! AAAARGH!

I floundered around in my blanket, unable to take the embarrassment.

Look, I did my best, okay?!

Maybe I should count it as impressive that I could manage to do something so cringeworthy just to encourage my villagers. I probably couldn't have done it if this weren't my last evening with them. After some more squirming and reassuring myself, I finally calmed down.

"I did everything I needed to. Now I just gotta wait until tomorrow...which is less than three hours from now, according to my phone."

I lay down and pulled the covers over myself, but I was way too alert to sleep. I sat back up again, casting my gaze around the tent. This was my last night here. I'd only slept here for about a month, but it was still strange to know this was it. I looked at the wooden pole in the center and the rough-hewn wooden cabinet propping up my bag.

Since I'd arrived, I'd worn the same clothes as the villagers. My clothes from Hokkaido remained folded up in my bag. I'd only kept my coat—my villagers seemed to use it to pick me out of a crowd. Besides, it was cold outside.

Destiny was curled up in a basket beside my bed, sleeping comfortably. Apart from that, the tent contained the wooden God of Fate statue, the fine one carved by Kan and Lan. The statue held two swords to wield whenever I activated the golem. Controlling it was a little fiddly on my phone—the D-pad and buttons appeared, and you had to use them spread out across the touchscreen. I'd practiced every night, though, so I wasn't worried about messing up.

My villagers always went to bed early—I was the only one still up. I'd spent so much of my life without a proper routine, and I still found sleeping at night difficult. My body was tired, but my mind was wide awake.

If I was going to get through the Day of Corruption with my villagers, I had to be prepared for the worst-case scenario. Realistically, this might be my only chance to ever speak to my family again.

"I thought I was totally prepared for this..."

It was the eleventh hour, but I felt frozen. Sitting there doing nothing wouldn't solve anything, though. I reached for my phone, which suddenly flickered to life and started playing my mom's ringtone.

"Hello? You're not causing those villagers any trouble now?" Mom asked. Wow, more concerned for strangers than for me. Classic.

"I'm not! I'm helping them out! How are you guys doing?"

"Fine, though Dad and Sayuki miss you."

"No, we don't! Quit lying to him!" I heard Sayuki yell through the phone. She must've been right next to Mom.

"I'm glad you're doing fine," I said. "Um, this is just a hypothetical question, I guess, but what if I didn't come back?"

"Why, are you looking for work out there?" Mom asked. "That's fine, as long as you're happy. We'll miss you of course, but as your parents, we need to encourage you to stand on your own two feet. I'm sure your dad feels the same way."

It was probably better that she misunderstood me. And I was glad to know how she really felt.

"You're not coming back?" Sayuki's voice came through the phone. She must've snatched it from Mom. She sounded annoyed.

"Sayuki? Nah, it was just a 'what-if.'"

"Do whatever you want, but at least come back to see us before you stay there permanently. You gotta prepare for the move and stuff. And...I wanna apologize to you." Sayuki fell silent.

"It's me." Dad came on the line. "You're not ill, are you?" He was blunt as ever, but I could detect his concern.

"I'm fine. Couldn't be better."

"Good. I don't know what's worrying you, but remember that the failure of following a path chosen for you stings more than the failure of a decision you made yourself. It's important to value other people's opinions, but you always have the final say."

Good advice, really.

"I get it. I'll remember that. Thanks, Dad."

"No problem. It's your life, so live it how you want. You've grown so much, I'm sure you'll make the right choice. Whatever you do, we're your family, and we'll support you the best we can. Make sure you look after your health, okay?"

The line went silent.

That phone call helped me make up my mind, but I still needed a final push. Instead of switching my phone off, I scrolled through my contacts to make another call.

"Hello?"

"Yoshi! Hokkaido's not too cold, is it? Are you sleeping properly in those temperatures? What about Carol-chan? Did she get to see her parents again?"

I couldn't help but smile at her questions.

You were worried about me, huh?

"I'm fine. Carol's with her parents. She's always racing around and making me play with her."

"Oh, that's a relief." Seika laughed. "So what's up? Something bothering you?"

"Not really…"

"You can't fool me! You don't just call me out of nowhere."

I didn't realize I was such a bad liar. No wonder Sayuki and Seika always saw right through me.

"To tell you the truth, the villagers asked if I wanted to live here. They could find me work, so…"

"Oh. What do you wanna do, Yoshi?"

"I dunno. It's a rare opportunity, but then I might not be able to come home." Especially if I died—but I couldn't tell her that.

"I think you should do whatever you want." She accepted it more quickly than I thought she would. I guess I was stupid to think she'd be begging me not to go.

"That's the best way to pick, huh?" I said.

"Yeah. And wherever you go, I'll come see you."

"Huh?"

"I'll come see you, whether it's in Hokkaido or somewhere else. I'm not gonna let you get away again."

I'm not just hearing things, right?

My face felt like it had burst into flames, my body tingling all over from some emotion caught between excitement and embarrassment.

"I didn't know you were the type to chase..."

"I wasn't. All this time I've been holding myself back because I didn't want to hurt you, but I'm not gonna do that anymore. When we started talking again after all those years, I decided I wasn't gonna let you go this time. I waited ten years for you, so you better believe I'm serious!"

I didn't know she could be this assertive. I wondered what look she had on her face right now. Did she feel as awkward as me? Was she blushing?

"Say something, please? I just spilled my guts out."

"S-sorry, um. Y'know. Me too."

"That's all I needed to hear. I don't wanna make you say anything else. Put thought into your words first. Don't promise me anything on the spur of the moment."

When we reunited after so many years, I thought she hadn't changed since we were students. But I'd been wrong. She'd grown out of her meekness. She was incredible.

"Okay. I'll think, and...I'll tell you someday." Just as soon as I had some confidence in myself.

"I can't wait."

"I don't get what you like about me, though. I've been a waste of oxygen for a decade. You should've given up on me." I genuinely wanted to know why she hadn't. If I were Seika, there'd be no way I could fall for a guy like me. I read online that women had higher standards than men and cared more about money than anything else.

"Why would I give up on you? You spend too much time online. I'm not some made-up statistic with the personality of a cardboard box. I'm your childhood friend Seika, who's known you for more than thirty years. I'm...a woman who knows all your good points and bad points."

Okay, that had been a dumb thing to ask, even for me. If a wonderful woman like her was attracted to me, then I had to stop putting myself down.

"Thanks, Seika. I know what to do now."

"Whatever you decide, I'll come to support you, okay? Sleep well."

"Good night."

The line went dead, and I heaved a breath. Now that I knew what my family and Seika had to say, I wouldn't falter. Something tugged on my clothes, and I looked down to find Destiny looking up at me with big, kind eyes.

"Destiny. This is the last night we'll be together. Wanna sleep with me?" I playfully lifted up the covers. It glanced up at me, shook its head as though it were too much of a bother, and curled back up again. Rejection. Well, that was fine. It would probably sleep better by itself, and we had a busy day ahead tomorrow. We both needed rest.

I lay down and closed my eyes. Even if I couldn't fall asleep, I'd get a little rest. And after a while, I felt a weight on my body. I cracked my eyes open to see Destiny lying facedown on my chest.

"Good night."

Its weight on me was comforting. Reassured, I soon slipped into a satisfying sleep.

THE NPCs IN THIS VILLAGE SIM GAME MUST BE REAL! ↵

chapter 05 The Third Day of Corruption and My Challenge

THE ALARM ON MY PHONE rang three times before I stopped it. I checked the time, and, sure enough, it was midnight. The Day of Corruption was here. I'd only slept for three hours, but my head felt strangely clear.

The last two times the attack hadn't begun until after sunrise, but anything past midnight was fair game. I knew who I was dealing with this time; I couldn't underestimate them. Habatake and the punk were ruthless people. It was safe to assume they had a fair amount of knowledge about my village. I wouldn't be surprised if they attacked at night to take us off guard.

I changed out of my village clothes and back into the ones from my world.

"These fit way better." This was my last day acting as the God of Fate's disciple. I wanted to look presentable.

I covered the statue in the tent with a large cloth. We couldn't risk it getting damaged—it was our trump card.

I did some light stretches before stepping out into the night to wander the village. Kan and Lan were up on the watchtower.

They were both nocturnal, with good night vision and thick fur to protect them from the cold. The best choice for night watch by far.

Two of the young newcomers patrolled by the gate. I recognized their faces and stepped up to greet them.

"Pretty dedicated, doing night patrol," I said.

"Sir! What are you doing out so late?"

"Just out on a walk. I'm a little too anxious to sleep, given what day it is." I scratched my head awkwardly.

I was trying to put on a clumsy act to make myself more approachable. I'd gotten that advice from a website about how to bond with your subordinates, back when I was researching how to be more godlike. "Don't work too hard, okay?"

"Thank you! We won't!" They bowed and carried on their patrol, following the line of the fence back toward the center of the village.

My phone would notify me when the Day of Corruption actually started. I probably didn't need to be so cautious, but being here in the flesh was way more nerve-racking than just waiting in front of my computer. The air was tense with the village's anxiety, and it made my body stiffen. I kept reaching for my phone for a distraction, but I couldn't risk draining the battery. I looked up at the night sky.

Stars, stars, and more stars filled the darkness. I'd never seen so many stars before in my life, and I didn't know enough about astrology to tell whether they were different from Earth's. Their sheer beauty was undeniable. This would be the last time I saw them, so I burned them into my memory.

The sun rose, and still no sign of attack. A sleepy Destiny crawled out of my tent with a towel on its head, climbing my legs and slipping into my coat. I didn't mind—the warmth of the hand warmer was pleasant against my chest.

The villagers were waking up and coming out of their tents, too. Everyone got together to eat, the food strictly portioned out. The women hurried to prepare everything as quickly as possible.

I wasn't hungry, but I had to eat. I made my way to the kitchen, when a siren sounded from my phone. The surrounding villagers stared as I checked.

"The Day of Corruption is here!"

The letters flashed in red, bleeding across the screen.

"Everyone, the Lord has let me know that the monsters are about to attack!" I called.

Gams immediately dropped his bread to his plate. "Take your positions!"

"Enemies in the east!"

"Lots of them!" Kan and Lan called from the watchtower.

"Women and children gather together and take shelter!"

"There's no need to rush! Just remember the drill!" Lyra and Rodice collected those who couldn't fight and led them to the safety of a tent.

"Don't worry! Gams is *really* strong!" Carol was reassuring some of the other children, leading them by the hand.

I knew I could count on my original villagers, but I was determined not to let them show me up. I climbed up an empty watchtower to look over the fence, immediately spotting a pack of black wolves careening through the grass. I counted more than twenty.

That seemed like a lot, but...

"Ready your bows! Shoot!"

Arrows rained down from the watchtowers at Murus's command. The elven archers had perfect accuracy, every arrow hitting its target. I knew they were good archers, but I'd never imagined they were *this* good. Their skills rivaled even Murus's. Every last wolf was dead before they even reached the fence.

"Incredible..."

They'd used a lot of arrows for their attack, but we had plenty more saved up. Just last month, this many black wolves would've meant serious trouble, but now they were nothing. I felt hope rising in my chest.

Another attack came thirty minutes later. It contained only a few more black wolves than last time, and the whole pack went down in another shower of arrows. Gams and his fighters didn't even need to do anything. Fingers crossed that the whole day went like this.

Thirty minutes, one hour, an hour and a half, two hours...

The afternoon came with no further attacks. This was a similar pattern from the last Day of Corruption. Back then, Yamamoto-san prevented me from helping my villagers, but this time my enemies couldn't lay a finger on me. I was a world away.

"Are they saving up their forces for one big final attack?"

I doubted that the two persistent and calculating corrupted god players I met in Hokkaido would go for a straightforward frontal attack. I pulled out my phone and checked the village and surrounding area from above. If I couldn't fight, I could at least do reconnaissance.

There were no monsters near the fence, but when I looked deeper into the forest, I saw something wriggling between the trees. Zooming in, I saw countless creatures. Not just black wolves—there were green goblins and a one-eyed red goblin. And *yellow* goblins, which I'd never seen before.

"Murus!" I called up to the closest watchtower. "There's monsters hiding in the forest!"

Murus put her hand to her forehead and squinted out into the distance. Her suspicious frown turned to surprise, and she started ringing the bell that hung from the tower's ceiling as loudly as she could. "Enemies! They're closing in! Everyone take your emergency positions!"

The villagers burst into action, no longer idling about. Elves climbed the watchtowers, and Gams and the close-ranged fighters took up their station in front of the village gate. The villagers who couldn't fight returned to the designated shelter tent. The elves readied their bows, and Gams handed out spears. He crouched and looked out one of the spyholes in the fence.

The message, "The Day of Corruption's final wave!" flashed up on my phone.

I turned away from the village gate and rushed back to my tent. Two villagers stood by the entrance, glancing around warily as they started to go inside.

"Are you here to ask for my help, perhaps?"

One of the villagers jumped and spun around. The other didn't react right away but then slowly looked at me.

I recognized their faces. They were two new male members of the village, built similarly to me, with average looks.

"Sir...that's right! We came to warn you of the large waves of monsters coming." His voice was so hoarse I could barely understand him.

"Thank you for going to the trouble. But I'm afraid I don't quite understand. I was the one who raised the alarm in the first place. Didn't you hear me?" I asked, deliberately making things awkward.

"Is that right? We're sorry, we didn't hear—"

"Why are you holding lit torches? It's the middle of the afternoon. And what's in that leather bag? It couldn't be oil, could it?" I narrowed my eyes at them.

The speaker glanced at the other man, then drew his sword. "How long have you known?"

Every time I spoke to these two in the village, they seemed like pleasant young men. That pleasantness was gone, replaced by hostile glares. The hoarseness in the speaker's voice disappeared, and now it sounded oddly high-pitched and feminine. The other unsheathed his sword as well. He remained silent.

"I've known from the start."

More accurately, it was since a certain person left the village. Ever since then, I'd kept a close eye on this particular villager.

I had my reasons for being suspicious. My first tip-off was a few days ago, when I asked Sewatari-san a question just before hanging up the phone.

298

"Can the corrupted gods only control monsters? Or do they have human followers, too?"

Sewatari-san told me that they did have some human followers, although not very many. Her answer got me thinking. So it *would* be possible for a corrupted god to send infiltrators to my village. It was the most basic of plans; sending spies and saboteurs into an enemy's base was a very common strategy in stories.

So the question became, if the corrupted gods were sending spies into my village, what would their mission be?

Assassinating key village leaders was obvious, but Gams was a strong fighter. They weren't likely to get very far. So if not that, what else could they do? If it were me, I'd destroy the God of Fate statue so we couldn't use the golem. And I would do it with fire. It would destroy our trump card and cause panic when it spread.

"What did you do to the real villagers, by the way? And what's wrong with the guy next to you?" I asked, though I already knew the answer. The worst-case scenario. I asked anyway, just in case.

The speaker had clearly taken someone's place. The guy next to him was likely an innocent victim being controlled by a miracle. Everyone knew everyone else by name in this village. Any spy would be recognized instantly. The enemy's infiltration options were limited.

"You sure know a lot." The spy's tone was cheerful. The outline of the villager in front of me seemed to warp, disappearing to be replaced by a woman in a black robe.

"Nice to see you, Salem."

Salem smirked at me. I never expected her to be a follower of a corrupted god.

"You knew, did you?"

"It was simple logic," I lied. I needed her to believe I was smarter than I was. It wasn't logic at all, just knowledge of the game and previous experiences I'd had in Hokkaido.

I knew about illusion magic because I'd seen Habatake use the same trick. The game app had a feature where I could tap any villager on the map and learn their name and some basic biographical information. When I tapped on her, it showed me nothing, just like it had with Murus before she officially joined the village. That started happening the day Salem left. She probably only pretended to leave before taking on the disguise and sneaking back in.

The villager beside her had his info show up as normal. He must have been being controlled by the punk's miracle, either asleep or drugged.

"Do you mind surrendering yourselves? I don't want this to drag on too long."

I had more pressing matters right now. I heard villagers bellowing behind me, their voices mixed with the cries of monsters and crashes of battle. The full-scale fight had begun. I needed to get the golem out there as soon as possible.

"I am a follower of the God of Charms. I can't back down, even if I wanted to. Apologies, but I'm going to have to end your life here. The Lord told me that your body is just like any other human's, despite your title of disciple." She pulled a twisted dagger from the sleeve of her robe. "You're a little late, I'm afraid. We've already spread the oil all over the tent. There's just one thing left to do." Before I could stop her, Salem tossed the lit torch behind her. It fell toward the tent and set it alight. The flames spread across the cloth in an instant, whooshing up in a giant pillar of fire.

"There, you've lost your lifeline. Now we just need to deal with you." Salem's lips twisted into a smile, and she and the other villager slowly approached me.

I ignored them and pulled out my phone instead.

"Huh? What do you think you can do with that tiny—gah!"

A slash sounded through the air, and the two fell to the ground facedown. Behind them stood the God of Fate statue, its gallant figure backed by flames. This wasn't the time to admire it, but man, it looked pretty majestic.

Even though the statue stepped out of those raging flames, it showed no damage. That was no coincidence.

"You can come out now." The hero of the show poked its head out of my coat pocket. I patted it on the head. "Thanks, Destiny. You saved me again."

Destiny had used its powers to turn the wooden statue to stone. That meant it wouldn't burn and was much harder to break. That was why I didn't panic. I wasn't much help when it came to physical labor or fighting, but I did have plenty of time to think. My previous experience with my enemies allowed me to come up with a counter plan. But this was no time to get cocky.

I used the golem to break down the tent, then activated the weather miracle to summon a downpour and put out the flames. Since this tent was usually the village's church, it was built a distance from their homes, and the fire didn't spread.

I could've used a breather, but the real fight was only just beginning.

"This time's gonna be different!"

All that remained was getting rid of the monsters, and I wasn't going to let anyone else get in my way. I was going to save this village with my own two hands!

chapter
06   The Village and Me

I RAN, CONTROLLING the God of Fate statue with my phone as I went. I headed for the village gate, from where I could hear yells and the sounds of destruction. I kept track of the statue through my phone—it made it there before me.

The gate and log fence were broken. Gams was struggling to fight off the monsters swarming through. He stabbed the spear in his right hand into a black wolf while beheading an approaching green goblin with the sword in his left. His hands full, he kicked a second wolf that was leaping at his face, then finished it off when he pulled the spear from its companion. Kan, Lan, and the other villagers stood behind him in a line, keeping the monsters at bay as best they could.

They fought hard, but the stream of monsters was never ending. The arrows raining down from the watchtower prevented foes from getting into the village itself, but at this rate, it was only a matter of time. Chem was behind the fighters healing any who were injured, but they weren't in any state to go back into battle.

I crouched beside a house with a view of the battlefield and focused on controlling the golem. The villagers didn't need me cheering them on from the sidelines. They needed the power of a god!

"Leave it to me, guys!" I tapped the screen and sent the golem right into the swarm of enemies.

"Stand your ground! If we let them through, it's over!" Gams, his body covered in injuries, stood firm, encouraging his allies as he continued to swing his sword. Then, the God of Fate statue jumped in front of him, a sword in each hand. It bisected a black wolf and green goblin on either side, from their heads down to their abdomens.

"It's the God of Fate!" Gams called out with uncharacteristic delight. Color began to return to the faces of the other villagers, even beneath their bruises. None of the new arrivals had ever seen the statue move, but they must have heard about it. Everyone watched, their eyes sparkling with hope.

As their god, it was my job to answer that hope.

Thanks for holding them off so far, everyone.

The statue couldn't speak, so I made it raise one of its swords high in a display of gratitude. Then I sent it through the hole in the fence. There were monsters out there as far as the eye could see. Black wolves, green goblins, boarnabies, yellow goblins, a one-eyed red goblin...so many monsters of all kinds. Even something that looked like a lion with wings and a humanoid golem made out of rock.

I left smaller monsters like the goblins and wolves to Gams

and the others, focusing on the large and unfamiliar creatures. The first one I spotted was the one-eyed red goblin, and I sent the statue straight for it. I didn't slow down even as green goblins crowded in—the statue cut right through the necks and midsections of any monster that came close.

The statue reached the one-eyed red goblin in an instant, leaving a trail of gore behind it. The goblin tried to ready its weapon, unprepared for the golem's arrival, but it was too slow. The statue stuck its sword right into its large, grotesque eyeball, slashing upward and flinging its brains into the air. The statue stood proudly as the villagers cheered.

I remembered being surprised by the superhuman strength of a wooden statue last time I summoned it, but it was even stronger now. Was it because I was level 2 or because Destiny turned it to stone? It didn't matter. Stronger was better.

With the one-eyed red goblin defeated, the other monsters froze in shock. I sent the statue at its next target, the lion-like monster, cutting down everything in its path on the way. The statue swung its sword, but the lion flew up at the last second, dodging. Its power of flight meant danger for the village. I made the statue grab a green goblin corpse at its feet and launch it into the air, hitting the lion before it could dodge again. Both monsters fell to the ground in a tangle. The statue cut off the creature's head before it could get up. It flicked blood from its sword.

I'd dealt with the biggest monsters, but there were still so many left. Killing them all seemed impossible, but it was the only option.

The God of Fate statue slayed beast after beast. Its sword was long gone, so it made use of a discarded goblin club and its bare hands instead. Its stone punches were strong enough to pulverize an enemy's head with a single strike.

The sky was clear when the fight started, but now rain was pouring down. The area outside the village's fence was slightly lower, so puddles formed quickly and made footing treacherous. The statue was fine, though. With its superhuman strength and new body, the water rolled right off its stone skin. It was far tougher than the monsters. At this rate, it was only a matter of time before we claimed victory.

The only problem was that the monsters had begun to avoid engaging me directly, keeping their distance.

"They've started using their heads." I couldn't move the golem too far from the fence or I'd risk monsters slipping past into the village. This wasn't good. "Are they waiting for my FP to run out?"

They were spread out, staying out of my reach. If I went after any one of them, the rest would be free to focus on the village.

"How many microtransactions did all these monsters cost?" I grumbled, anxiety and impatience fraying my temper.

Yamamoto-san had explained to me that summoning and raising monsters cost money. The bill for this many creatures must have been staggering, but I didn't have time to worry about my opponents' wallets. My FP would run out if this stalemate kept up. I had to do something.

There were about fifty enemy monsters left, but none of them were cannon-fodder black wolves or green goblins. If even a handful of these creatures got in, we were toast. My exhausted villagers would be no match for them.

As though confirming my worst fears, I heard an explosion followed by screams from the north part of the village. I checked my phone for the overhead view. Another group of monsters had snuck around and broken down the fence on the other side.

Of course. I was dealing with two corrupted god players. I should've known they would split up and launch a surprise attack! I wanted to slap myself, but I didn't have time. My initial count of fifty enemies was way off. The other group was mostly green goblins, but there were a lot of them. And if I sent my statue to them, the monsters holding at the front gate would be free to come inside.

"Dammit! I'm stuck here doing nothing!"

Gams and the rest rallied to stand against the second group, but their exhaustion and wounds dulled their responses. The elves had used up their arrows and were forced down to the ground to fight hand-to-hand.

If there was a way to win, I couldn't see it.

Are we just supposed to wait around and die now?

Was this it? Was I going to let my village be destroyed again?

"No! It's not over yet! I can't give up! This isn't the time to run away. Fight until the end!"

Think. Think! Is there a miracle I can use?

I was scrolling desperately through the miracles menu when I felt something cool against my burning face. It was Destiny. It pressed its front feet against my cheek and stared up at me from my coat. It then jumped to the ground and raced away towards the northern side of the village.

"Wait! Wait, Destiny!"

It ignored me, and I could only watch as its figure got smaller and smaller.

Destiny was a better fighter than I was, but its petrifying gaze only worked on one target at a time, and it was currently using it on the God of Fate statue. Its poison gas attack couldn't be directed—it could end up injuring our allies. So what was it doing?

"Come back!" I couldn't bear to lose Destiny on top of everything else. "No...come on, don't give up!"

I slapped my cheek to knock the despair out of me and got back to my feet. I let the determination boil up inside me, then bent to pick up a discarded spear. I needed to do *anything* right now. Anything at all was better than lying down and dying.

I ran after Destiny, but my phone began to admit a blinding yellow light. When it died down enough for me to see the screen, I saw a line of text.

"Will you allow it to evolve?"

I immediately remembered what Sewatari-san had said to me on the phone.

"I'll give you the gift on the day of."

Was this her gift?

Who cares? It doesn't matter right now!

Breathing around the splinter of hope in my chest, I tapped the screen. I looked at myself, the statue, and then back at myself.

Nothing happened. Damn. I'd hoped one of us would get some sort of power-up.

"What did it mean by evolve, then—"

"Aaaaah! So bright!"

Cries echoed from the north side of the village—but they were cries of astonishment, not despair. I turned to look and saw an enormous monster, its body glowing with golden light. Its skin was protected by tough, sharp scales, and its six legs were as thick as tree trunks. It had to be at least a dozen feet long, not including its tail. It was kicking green goblins left and right.

"Destiny...san?" It was like something from a disaster movie, and so incredible that I found myself slipping into polite speech.

It was bigger, tougher, and had more legs than before, but under all that it still looked like Destiny. It breathed out purple smoke, leaving the green goblins writhing in pain on the ground. Other goblins flew over my head, whipped into the air by a sweep of its tail. Others still were turned to stone by a single glare— several of them. When goblins tried to flee, it trampled them. Monsters were supposed to lose their sense of self-preservation on the Day of Corruption, but they still ran away from Destiny.

After dispatching a ton of monsters in a very short time, Destiny turned its large, round eyes to me and gave a satisfied nod. I nodded back. It folded up its six legs and crouched down, kicking off powerfully from the ground. It cleared the fence easily, turning on the monsters grouped around the village gate. It mowed them down with its lethally sharp tail, cut off their movements with its six legs, and tore their heads off with its jaws.

Any monsters who dared approach to try and help their allies were met with a face full of poison breath and rendered immobile.

I stared in astonishment. Monsters fell left and right, powerless to fight back.

"You're amazing, Destiny. Wait! I can't just stand here!"

While Destiny distracted the enemy, I brought the God of Fate statue back to the village entrance. I knew what to do now. The statue raised its right arm into the air. Spotting the signal, Gams turned and disappeared inside Kan and Lan's place.

"We got it!"

Gams and Rodice emerged, pulling a metal rod along in a wooden trailer. Chem, Lyra, and Carol pushed from behind. That was all my original villagers, working together.

The statue approached the cart and took the rod in its hand. My villagers fell to their knees and began to pray. At first glance, the rod looked like a long spear—ten feet long, with a sharpened tip. It was heavy, but the statue could spin it above its head with no problem.

The statue returned to the battlefield, new weapon in hand. The scattered enemies had gathered into a single spot. Destiny stared at them, its rain-soaked back to the village. I directed the statue to stand beside it.

The front row of monsters had been immobilized, but the ones crowded behind were unharmed. They used their stone allies in front of them as a shield against Destiny's gaze. A single poison breath could knock them all out, but right now there was a strong wind blowing toward the village. Destiny had to be careful.

Even so, with the statue and Destiny together, we could win.

It's just...

I glanced at the top right of my phone screen. My fate points had been falling noticeably faster ever since Destiny evolved. We had maybe three minutes.

The monsters seemed to be laughing derisively at us, as if they knew.

"Now's our chance!"

The statue leapt onto Destiny's back and thrust the metal rod up to the thundering skies. Destiny realized what was happening and stepped backward, as close to the village fence as it could. It then lowered itself to the ground and kicked off, mud spraying out behind it as it charged toward the monsters. A split second before it crashed into them, it jumped, flying right over the group of enemies, hitting the ground running. But the statue was no longer on Destiny's back. It had jumped off in the air, landing straight in the middle of the crowd. It thrust its spear into the soggy ground.

Monsters rushed the statue, but I ignored them. I just hit a button on my phone and squeezed my eyes shut. A white flash seared the darkness behind my eyelids, and a thunderous roar hammered my eardrums. My villagers squatted down, hands clasped over their ears. It looked like they were shouting, but the thunderbolt drowned out every other sound.

A blinding flash and a deafening roar, then silence. The villagers on the ground got to their feet one after the other, slowly approaching the hole in the fence. I pocketed my phone and followed them.

The God of Fate statue was wet from the rain, standing under the now clear sky, glittering in the sunlight. Countless monsters lay dead on the ground around it, charred and smoking. My villagers raced up to the statue, got down on their knees, and began to praise the God of Fate, ignoring the mess the mud made of their clothes. It looked like a religious painting: the people gathered around a statue raising a metal rod to the sky in a heroic pose of victory.

"We made it..." I was too overcome with exhaustion to feel much emotion. I slumped back against the fence behind me and checked my phone.

"The Day of Corruption is over. No more monsters will appear today."

"It's over. We did it... We really made it this time!" Balling my hands into fists, I looked up at the sky. Anyone who didn't know better would think the timely arrival of rain had been a miracle. And I guess it was—just a miracle I activated with my phone.

I'd begun by using the rain to flood the area around the village, where the monsters were. Kan, Lan, and I had prepared the spear—the lightning rod—in advance. Once the statue had it, I'd just called a thunderstorm, and the lightning killed every monster with a foot in the flooded area.

This was the plan I'd come up with—using the golem and the weather together, the whole battle leading up to that one moment.

"We did it. I'm capable of more than I thought, huh?"

After getting through the day, I felt a little more confident in myself. I stepped forward to congratulate the praying villagers on their efforts. But then I noticed my feet. They were almost transparent, from my toes to my ankles. I could see the ground through them.

"Right..."

My promised time here was up. I only asked to stay until the Day of Corruption was over. And now it was. As much as I wanted to join the celebration, that wasn't possible. The arm I used to reach out to them was invisible to my elbow. I was going back to the real world, where I would be the player and they would just be characters.

It hurt, but this was for the best. I wasn't going to run away from reality anymore. I might just be watching them from afar, but I'd keep them in my hearts. I'd pray for their happiness.

"Take care, you guys. I'll keep working so I can spend as much on you as I need." I kept my eyes on them, waiting to disappear from this world. Movement in my peripheral vision drew my gaze back down. Destiny was hopping up at my feet. "You're back to normal, huh? Yeah, I think that suits you better."

Destiny stopped hopping and looked up at me.

"Thanks for all your help. I had a ton of fun hanging with you, buddy." I crouched down and offered it my disappearing fist. It put up a tiny front foot to meet it. Huge tears rolled from its round eyes.

Hey, crying isn't fair! D'you know how hard I'm trying to hold it in?

I put my vanishing arms around Destiny, even though I couldn't properly hold it.

"Thank you. Thank you so much. Take care of yourself, okay? And don't eat anything weird. Make sure you're nice to everyone, and...and..." I couldn't speak through my tears anymore. Destiny's face was the last thing I saw. I could swear it was smiling as it cried.

I floated toward a white light, through a space where I was the only thing that existed. It was incredibly comfortable, like lying on a featherbed.

"How was the other world, Yoshio-kun?" a voice said suddenly in the darkness, but it didn't shock me in the slightest.

"Sewatari-san—the God of Fate. Thank you. I had a lot of fun." I spoke right from the heart. Their world didn't have the conveniences of Japan, but my time there was still fulfilling.

"Glad to hear it. You know, most people who go to a different world never want to come home. You're a special case, huh?"

"I don't think I would've come home if I went a few months ago," I said. "But things are different now. There's so much I still want to do, and stuff I *need* to do. And I've got people waiting for me."

I couldn't just throw everything away and escape to another world. I wasn't that ungrateful brat. Not anymore, and never again. My fight wasn't in the other world. It was in this one.

There would be days when I wished I'd stayed with my villagers. Even then, I would be proud of the strength it took to make my decision. I'd made the choice to not run away.

"What was it like interacting with your villagers directly?" Sewatari-san asked.

"I can't see them as NPCs anymore. They're living, breathing human beings just like me."

"I'm glad to hear that. You'll keep taking care of them, won't you?"

"Of course I will! Thank you for letting me see them for real."

"I picked you well, Yoshio-kun." Sewatari-san's voice was gentle.

My vision turned black then, but it wasn't scary at all. It was calming. Floating in that darkness, I remembered what Chem once said about the God of Fate.

"It is said that the God of Fate is the god closest to people. It's even said that He secretly visited this world to live among humans. There are stories of Him having children with a human. The God of Fate loves and cares for humans more than any other god. He helps those in need, and He laughs and cries with us. It's like He is almost human Himself."

Coincidence or not, that was the god who chose me. I would never bring shame to Her name, never.

The darkness faded and I was on a bench, somewhere completely different. Gone were the trees and plants. I was surrounded by dreary iron and concrete. There were electronic noticeboards above me, and in front of me a bullet train rushed past. A long line of people waited for the next train.

This was a station waiting room. I checked the name. It was the station closest to my hometown.

"I'm not in Hokkaido anymore?"

At this point, nothing could surprise me. My bag was at my feet, along with several paper bags. They were full of souvenirs.

"That was nice of them."

I checked my phone. It was noon on February 1st. The Day of Corruption had been yesterday. The past month felt like a vivid dream. The world from the game I played really existed, and I'd lived there with my villagers and fought off monsters. I would sound insane if I ever said any of that aloud, but I knew the truth.

I opened the *Village of Fate* app. My villagers were busy repairing the damaged fence. Despite the trials of yesterday, they were already hard at work. I resolved to send them a prophecy later. I didn't want them to worry about me. Even if my days of living with them were over, I could still see them through the game. Our bond would stay strong.

The God of Fate statue was back in its tent, plain wood once again. Beside it was a new altar, and there were villagers taking a break from their work making offerings there. They'd done it the whole time I was away; there was probably a lot of great food waiting for me and my family at home.

Wonder what they're sending today.

I smiled, watching as they lined fruit up on the altar and prayed together. The light flashed as always, but just before the offerings disappeared, something flickered. When the light faded, the altar was empty, and the fruit was scattered across the floor.

"What was that? Hey, quit it!" I snapped at the lizard tugging on my sleeve next to me. "You hungry? You sure eat a lot for something so puny. You—wait."

Destiny blinked up at me. Destiny, who was supposed to be in the other world. It must've kicked all those fruits off the altar and made itself the offering. Strange, hadn't Sewatari-san said they made it so people couldn't go through the portal anymore?

Wait, I gotta stop thinking of it like a person just 'cause it acts like a person!

"You're back, huh? Should've called you Trouble instead of Destiny. Anyway, it's good to have you here, buddy." I offered it a finger, which it grabbed tightly.

The real world might be crazier than the game world. Most likely there would be troubles ahead, maybe even life-threatening ones. And maybe I'd get so overwhelmed that I'd shut myself off from society again. Maybe one day I'd long for the village. But I knew now that having regrets and messing up was just part of life.

My villagers were working as hard as ever on the other side of the screen.

"I gotta follow their example."

I put Destiny into one of the spare paper bags and stood up from the bench. I'd go give my boss some souvenirs and apologize, give my family some souvenirs and apologize, and give Seika some souvenirs and confe—

Looks like I've got my work cut out for me...

This was the path I'd chosen, and nothing was going to stop me from walking it. It didn't matter if I went slowly, paused to think, or messed up. Even if my path was plunged into darkness, as long as I kept going, there was a chance of something beautiful on the other side.

THE NPCs IN THIS VILLAGE SIM GAME MUST BE REAL! ↵

Epilogue

I LET OUT a long, deep sigh. I'd watched the entire thing, and finally it was over. I shoved my keyboard to one side and flopped down on the desk.

"If you're gonna sigh that hard, at least cover your mouth, Senpai." My coworker sitting beside me shook her head disapprovingly. She finished up the rest of her bubble tea and yawned, stretching her jaws wide open. I didn't point out her hypocrisy this time. She was too sweet, and she'd spent the entire night working hard by my side. There was probably some divine punishment in store for me if I dared criticize her now—even though I was divine myself.

"Thanks for all your help."

"No worries. I didn't do it to be nice or anythin'. I thought if Yoshiocchi was grateful to us for helpin' out, it might make him wanna come back."

I noticed a sharp flash in her eye, but I didn't say anything. She tended to look brainless and flighty, just doing whatever she wanted all the time, but she was smart. She knew what she was doing. She analyzed every situation calmly and acted according to advantages and disadvantages. This made her unpopular with some gods—but not with me. She loved her followers more than anyone, and she always looked out for those who were weak or downtrodden.

"Anyway, I'm glad Yoshiocchi made it through. Those guys were super annoying!"

"Yes. It looks like a lot of information was leaked to the corrupted god players. We need to see about cracking down on that."

Two players had targeted Yoshio-kun persistently, representatives of the God of Temptation and the God of Charms. I wouldn't be surprised if they were the ones who leaked Yoshio-kun's information and offered to buy his holy book.

"We could've dealt with them if they started somethin' here," Nattyan lamented.

"I know..."

That's likely why they didn't try. I'd asked Yoshio-kun to work here to lure them out, but they hadn't been stupid enough to take the bait. They just kept an eye on us from afar.

"I'll go down to the second floor and give everyone a good scolding later. Un-chan'll help if I ask."

"Yeah..." Nattyan's response came through gritted teeth.

"Something the matter?"

"Nope. Just that Un-chan hates my guts."

She was right. Un-chan did whatever I said, but she was always cold to Nattyan. I valued them both, though, and I wished they could get along a little better.

"Hopefully Yoshiocchi's villagers can take it easy for a bit now."

"I hope so, too. But I am the Goddess of Fate, you know."

"Fate likes to play tricks, huh? Even on its own player?"

A player was blessed by the god they played, but that wasn't always a good thing. While I had power over his fate to an extent, gods weren't allowed to interfere in a player's life more than necessary. Anything I did now would only draw attention from the other gods, assuming my interference so far hadn't already.

"The rusty wheels of Yoshio-kun's fate are only just starting to turn. I can't help but wonder what's in store for him."

THE NPCs IN THIS VILLAGE SIM GAME MUST BE REAL! ↵

Commentary of

THIS WORLD

This world is perilous, but our devotion will see us through it. This book will show us the way.

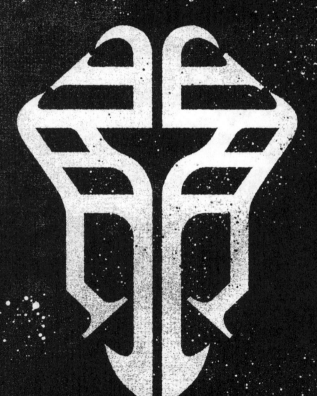

❦ What is Isekai Connection? ❧

> Isekai Connection is the game development company the minor gods set up after fighting between the major and corrupted gods tore a hole in their world and sent them to Earth. The company's building is connected to the portal leading back to their world, so they cannot stray far from it.

Company Profile

COMPANY NAME	Isekai Connection Ltd.
COMPANY ADDRESS	〒0×8-2641 Hokkaido △□ City △△ Town Nishisanjou ○△○□ Building 2nd Floor Email: isekai_connection@mail.com Tel: 090-0×××-×××× Fax: 090-0×××-××××
COMPANY ACTIVITIES	(1) Player Administration (2) Accounting of Microtransactions (3) Miracle-based Assistance (4) Forwarding of Offerings
START DATE	××/××/20××
# OF EMPLOYEES	Over a hundred (exact number unknown) *It fluctuates
DIRECTOR	
FU	

It appears as a small four-story office building that has worn down over time.

The travel agency on the first floor is unaware of the other world and the gods stationed above them. Isekai Connection rents the building's second, third, and fourth floors. The building is equipped with both stairs and an elevator. The employees on the second floor tend to prefer the stairs, while those on the third tend to use the elevator.

Employees working on different floors try not to interact if they can help it.

01.

☙ The Building ❧

The minor gods fell to Japan when a hole was ripped open in our world due to the fighting between the major and cor— rupted gods! I hope they can come back and look after our world again soon!

Company

CHEM'S VOICE

The second and third floors have identical layouts. They each connect to an elevator hall and contain a bathroom, kitchen, and office.

The offices look normal from outside their glass doors, but step inside, and you'll see how impossibly spacious they are. They seem more than ten times the size they should be, but it's hard for humans to judge.

The fourth floor has the same elevator hall as the second and third, but instead of a glass door, there's a huge steel gate. It's so dark that it's almost black and is more than three meters in both length and width. It has a double door with knobs shaped like sword handles. There's a twisted, vortex-like pattern carved into the doors themselves.

The key is special, and it will only open the door if you have permission from the top minor god on either the second or third floor. What lies on the other side of the gate is a secret.

02. ❧ The Company's Employees ❧

There is no dress code, so most employees prefer to come in dressed casually, although maybe ten percent do wear suits. Aside from that, you'll see various outfits. Some revealing, some unrefined, some tracksuits, and even some kimono.

⩔ **Front view**

⩔ **side view**

Sewatari Seri

ISEKAI™ CONNECTION

Nattyan

Kimidori Kusuri

Species: GO...

At ... they ... like ... ... are ... ily ... ... into the real ... ... ortal cre- ... ... ne fi... etween the ... minor gods. They sup- ... e game via their company, ...ai Connection.

Afterword

THIS VOLUME was completely different from the previous one. What did you think?

Until now, it's always been Japan and the game. There were two stories unfolding in parallel worlds, but in this volume they... Actually, there are probably going to be quite a few spoilers in the afterword, so if you're one of those people who like to read the afterword before the story, I'd suggest reading the story first this time.

Okay, the spoilers start now. So far, Yoshio's just been a player of a game, but in this volume he comes into contact with the villagers and gets to experience where he's led them for himself. As I'm sure you know if you've read this far, the main focus of this series is Yoshio's growth. Having passed thirty without working a day in his life, he learns the meaning of hard work and life itself through *The Village of Fate*.

I'm not trying to say that you need to become a corporate drone or live your life how other people want you to. While there's pride and value to be found in work, it can be unpleasant, tough, and sometimes extremely difficult, for some people more than others. I hope my story can make you understand that, if only a little. In case you were curious, I wish I could just win the lottery and spend the rest of my life having fun!

Oh, right, the published version of volume three is actually very different from the web novel. If you're here from the web novel, then I should tell you that in this version, Seika doesn't go to the shrine for New Year's. Yoshio and Carol take the train instead of the ferry. They have more allies, and there are some more changes and additions on top of that. Probably the biggest change is that they spend a few days at the company after arriving there. In the web novel, the company is highly mysterious, but you'll learn much more about it in this version. They spend more time with Sewatari, of course, and ***, so look forward to it! (I'm blanking the name out in case there's anyone who hasn't read the story yet). This change means you'll get to see more of Carol and Destiny, too. I tried to make their cuteness shine through as I wrote, since they're our mascots. They were really cute, right?

I touched on this in the afterword in volume two, but I wrote this story to fit into three volumes. This will be the last volume that gets published like this. I think I did a good job of wrapping everything up, but what do you think?

To be honest with you, this series sold enough to print future volumes. I'm glad people are enjoying the manga, too, and I'm incredibly grateful—also to those who bought the digital version because of the Coronavirus (I know there were a lot of you). It actually sold a lot more than the physical version...

Because of the current circumstances, I wanted to make volume three as good as possible so that people would want to buy it. I actually ended up going back to the beginning and rewriting it. I kept the scenes and lines I liked best from the web novel, so I'd say the printed version is about seventy percent new content. There should be plenty for you to enjoy, even if you've already read the web version. In fact, I think it's even better than the web version—that's what I was aiming for.

If the third volume sells well enough, there's a chance the series could continue, so if you like it, please tell your friends or share your thoughts online. I worked so hard on it, that I even had to ask for an extension on my deadline for the first time ever since becoming an author!

Now, since this probably will be the last volume, I'd like to say my thanks with that in mind.

First, to Namako-sensei. Thank you for your illustrations once again. Sorry for all the new characters and monsters you had to draw! I love the way you drew the monsters and Destiny, though, and I have a great time looking over them. Especially the color pages! They're the best!

Next, to Kazuhiko Morita-sensei. The manga version is great! I'm always looking forward to the next installment, waiting to see how it's drawn, the composition, and how the story is presented in manga form. The impactful fighting scenes and the way you can tell how the characters feel from their expressions are what blow me away most of all. I'm going to work as hard as I can so that your drawings won't outmatch my words!

To my designers, proofreaders, printers, and my editor, N-sama. As always, you've done a lot for me this volume.

Thank you to everyone involved in this volume. The Coronavirus, which no one could have predicted, caused many setbacks, but thanks to everyone's hard work, this volume made it on sale. Thank you so much.

Finally, I want to thank my readers. Whether you're someone who's come in at this third volume, or you've been around longer, thank you for sticking with me.

—HIRUKUMA

The end.

542: Anonymous Information Seeker 15:30:47
   ID : uP7xoZ2QDG
   A corrupted god player came and harassed me in real life.
   Is that not against the rules?

543: Anonymous Player 15:41:05 ID : 8rjkL1GpBf
   Sure they did lol (¯_ツ_¯)

544: Anonymous Player 15:45:54 ID : SJ5QZz0zTi
   (つ` ・ω・) (???????????????

545: Anonymous Player 15:50:11 ID : zZpzbrS4N6
   Nope

546: Anonymous Player 15:54:55 ID : XFl3hA44ms
   Sure this "player" wasn't just in your imagination?

547: Anonymous Player 15:59:18 ID : 55qGn97tWW
   Wait, why do you guys think he's lying? These boards
   don't let you post any false information, right?

548: Anonymous Player 16:04:27 ID : 0S1X9qFtYG
   Oh yeah. Wait, you mean he's telling the truth?